FAERIE MAGIC

The Changeling Chronicles: Book Two

Emma L. Adams

CHAPTER ONE

"It's not that bad," said Isabel, my closest friend, as we prepared to face the music. Or rather, faeries.

"There are fifty piskies trapped in a garden shed," I said. "It's not 'bad'. It's a shitstorm of epic proportions."

The overgrown back garden we stood in practically advertised itself as a haven to faeries, a warren of brambles and rotting trees. The people who lived here had let their pest problem spiral so far out of control, it was lucky they hadn't woken up with all their hair missing.

"Pity the Mage Lord can't appear and displace them all to Antarctica." Isabel might be second in line to the local witch coven, but even she hadn't been able to devise a spell for extracting piskies from a shed.

"Very funny." Vance Colton, Mage Lord and royal pain in the ass, wasn't here—which irritated me more than the oncoming horde of rabid piskies. He'd left on an 'important mission', and to say I was pissed off he'd left without a warning would be an understatement—let alone that he'd been gone a week without so much as a call. Especially as he'd asked me out on a date before he'd left.

"Hey," said Isabel, waving a hand in front of my face. "Now's not a good time to be daydreaming."

I shook off all thoughts of the Mage Lord. We had a horde of piskies to deal with.

Piskie eviction was the lowest of menial jobs, but covering this month's rent payment mattered more than dignity did. Since I no longer worked for Larsen, who ran the local mercenaries, I was forced to rely on independent clients.

For sixteen glorious hours, I'd owned more money than I'd ever owned in my life—and considering I'd nearly died to get it, the spoils were more than welcome. Then the local council had swooped in and taken every last penny to pay for damages on behalf of the Necromancy Guild. And then I'd called Vance, only to be told he'd disappeared of the face of the earth. This after I'd walked away from Larsen, my old boss, thinking a steady job awaited me at the Mage Guild. Someone up there really didn't like me.

So here we were, in the dingiest part of witch territory. Our own house sat at the other end, where it merged with the shifters' lands. This place, on the other hand, lay on the half-faeries' doorstep—which explained the piskies.

Think of the money, I chanted in my head like a mantra, as I helped Isabel set up a protective spell in front of the shed doors to keep them from swarming out all at once. Piskies were the weakest of Faerie's creatures, but it didn't mean they couldn't claw us to pieces when enraged.

I tossed my ponytail over my shoulder and readied my weapons. I always carried at least three daggers, but Irene, my sword, did all the heavy lifting. Iron was fatal to faeries and I hoped waving it around would be sufficiently intimidating to send the piskies into our trap.

The chilly early autumn night wind whipped through my thin jacket, recently cleaned of the most recent spillage of monster guts. I'd hoped to replace my threadbare and bloodstained clothes using the bonus money, but at this rate, I wouldn't even make rent payment this month unless I managed to do the impossible and get those piskies out of the shed.

"Hmm," said Isabel. "I don't think letting them all out at once is a good idea. They'll just swarm somewhere else."

"Yeah. You know your mass sleeping potion…"

"You said it doesn't work on faeries."

"No, it makes them drunk." As I'd found out the hard

way, when Erwin—the piskie who lived in our flat—had fallen asleep in a bucket of the potion when Isabel left some out on the table. We needed to capture the beasts while they were conscious. Not ideal.

Yells and other indiscernible noises rang out from down the road, where the area bordered on half-blood district. *Probably a faerie house party.* I hated the sounds of Faerie—the music alone made me want to curl up into a ball—but luckily the high hedges around their territory muted the noise, along with a million spells designed to keep outsiders away.

Even the half-bloods would call pest control in this situation. Taking a steadying breath, I readied my hands on the lock. Best get this over with. I unlocked the shed door, whipping out my sword as I did so, then jumped behind the protective barrier.

Immediately, the racket coming from half-blood district disappeared under the screams of fifty enraged piskies. They swarmed as one, bouncing off the shield outside the door. Even though the layer of shielding kept them contained, the edges began to smoke.

"Crap," I said. "Guess they must have some magic in them, after all." Small fry like piskies had less magic than brains—and that was saying a lot. But with so many in a single place, they'd whipped up a storm. The inside of the shed became a torrent I didn't want to look into.

"Right," said Isabel, a resigned expression on her face. "It's time for Plan B."

She took out a trapping circle and set it up on the ground. Normally, we'd put sylvan leaves or another kind of bait inside it, but we didn't need to lure the piskies out. They already wanted out, and our only option was to extract them one at a time and get them into the trap.

I shot her a worried glance. Most of the time, I worked alone on jobs like this. Isabel might be tough, but faeries were a species most humans couldn't stand up to. The most dangerous jobs fell to me, from raiding trolls' nests to killing man-eating hydras. Though I didn't work for Larsen anymore, I was well known amongst the other mercenaries as the faerie killer.

I grimaced, reaching over the shield and grabbing for the nearest body. The piskie was surprisingly heavy for an eight-inch-tall twig like creature, and I nearly dropped it when sharp teeth bit into my finger. Wincing, I hauled it over the trap's edge, which snapped into place immediately. One down. Forty-nine to go.

"We should strike 'efficient' off our ad," said Isabel.

"And 'reliable'," I muttered, examining the wound on my finger. Shallow puncture marks. Not poisonous, at least. "Right…"

I dived back in, getting another bite on my arm for my trouble. After ten piskies were safely contained, I stopped, staring at my arms. Blue light spread across them, like when I used faerie magic. Usually the power activated at the last possible moment. Was it because there were so many piskies?

"Ivy? What is it?"

I shook my head. "Nothing. I think they have magic, though. We need to be careful carrying so many of them at once—"

The shed exploded.

One second, the piskies battered against the shield. The next, a blast of dazzling blue light shot up from the shed, and the walls and door burst into a million wood fragments. I threw myself to the ground behind the ward line. The piskies flew upwards in a shrieking horde, as though the line didn't exist.

"Shit!" I yelled, searching for Isabel. She'd been forced to hide behind the trap, which had caught at least a dozen more piskies. Unfortunately, the rest of the swarm tasted freedom and liked it.

The darkening sky disappeared beneath fluttering wings and pointed faces. Piskies didn't fly in formation. They crashed into one another, fighting, clawing, screaming. Sharp teeth dug into my arm and I yelped, swatting the piskie away. I jumped to my feet, waving my sword, trying to drive them towards the trap. Isabel got there first, and the trap expanded to cover half the garden.

Too late—a good third of the piskies had already flown in the opposite direction. I stared after them, unable to believe my eyes. How had the weakest denizens of Faerie blown up a shed and a witch's ward to boot?

Isabel kicked one of the piskies into the trap with surprising anger. Generally, she was as laid back as I was impulsive, a balm to my quick temper. But nothing pissed her off as much as one of her spells not working.

"Guess we have our answer about why Erwin keeps breaking through our wards." I wiped my bloody hand on my jeans. Damn. Who'd have thought they packed so big a magical punch?

"If you say so," said Isabel. "What did that look like to you? All I saw was a big explosion."

"Had to be magic," I said. "A lot of it."

She frowned. "I thought you needed the Sight to see faerie

magic."

"You do." This wasn't right.

"Is that what it always looks like? Blue light?"

I kept forgetting, what with the myriad other problems knocking at my door, that Isabel had far from exhausted her list of questions on the faeries. Since I'd told her my experiences as a captive of Lord Avakis of the Grey Vale, she'd barely been able to restrain her curiosity. I was, after all, the only human any of us knew who was able to see and use faerie magic. Not to mention the only human who'd ever escaped the faerie realm alive. Trust didn't come easily to me, and I suspected it'd be a long time before I grew used to the idea of even my best friend knowing my darkest secrets.

"Blue or green light, depending on whether the magic belongs to Winter or Summer. You've already seen what both can do."

She closed her mouth, forehead puckered in a frown. "I was half unconscious for most of it," she said, referring to the time she'd spent in a necromancer's summoning circle while half-faerie ghosts ran amok outside.

"True." I stared at the sky. The piskies were long gone, though the yowls and screams of their brothers and sisters rang out from the trap. "Damn. Maybe it wasn't faerie magic.

Hang on." I climbed over the splintered remains of the shed door, shattered so thoroughly it had turned into sawdust. Isabel hesitated, then followed. "Might be a trap in here."

I expected to find a trace, at the very least. Isabel was the expert in magical explosive devices—several of which I carried in my pockets. But when she joined me in scanning the ground, her expression told me she was just as clueless as I was about what caused the explosion.

"Nothing," she said. "No spells at all. Are you sure piskies can't combine their magic?"

"Pretty sure I'd know by now," I said. "They swarm, but they can't so much as conjure up a spark. And the light—it didn't look like Summer magic." Piskies came from the Seelie realm of Faerie. The one where people pretended to be nice then stole your money.

"So what was it?"

I shrugged. Angry yells behind us reminded me twenty-odd enraged piskies waited to be escorted back to the clean-up guild at Larsen's place.

I sighed and stood up. "Well. That could have gone better." *Should have brought backup,* I imagined Vance Colton saying, to my intense annoyance. His displacing ability would be damned useful to get rid of those piskies. A cynical part of me whispered that I should have known it was too good to be true. We might have worked on a case together, but I'd been riding the high of being alive when I'd quit my job and put my future in his hands. Too bad my impaired judgement had been stronger than his desire to stick around.

Despite myself, I clicked through to his number on my phone. This was the kind of incident the Mage Lords needed to know about. Whatever history existed between Vance Colton and I was irrelevant. He was head of all the magical practitioners in the entire town—hell, in this area of the country. I couldn't even get a wayward piskie to leave my flat, let alone convince the necromancers not to take away all my money.

Still, his rejection stung—my bank account more than my pride. Vance's sort, descended from rich English aristocrats, were a little out of touch with the cut-throat world the rest of us lived in. I'd hoped to change that when I'd started working with him. Apparently not.

My hand hovered over the call button, and my phone buzzed so suddenly I nearly dropped it.

The number calling me wasn't the Mage Lord's, but my ex-boss. Larsen.

My hand clenched around the phone and I damn near

threw it aside in disgust. The sleazy bastard. No matter how desperate I got, I'd never work for him again. I glared at the phone. Apparently not getting the message, it kept buzzing.

"Why aren't you answering?" asked Isabel.

"Larsen." I spat out his name like a curse.

"Why would he be calling?"

"Because he wants to exploit or blame me for something. Maybe he found out I'm the one doing this job and wants a cut of the profits." I pocketed my phone again. I'd forgotten Erwin the piskie had chewed holes in my pocket, so the phone fell through and clattered on the ground.

"Ivy," said Larsen's voice.

Shit. I picked up the phone, checked for damage, and was about to hang up when he said, "Wait. Listen for a minute."

"Or what?" I glared at the screen, like he could see me through it. "I told you never to speak to me again."

"I have a client who wishes to hire you."

I laughed aloud. "Fuck that. Fuck that, and fuck you, Larsen."

He took my abuse with unusual calmness. "This is urgent," he said. "There's been a murder in half-blood district. The Mage Lords are absent, and every half-faerie in town is calling for blood."

Well, shit.

CHAPTER TWO

Murder in half-blood district. For all their bloodthirsty nature, half-faeries rarely turned on one another, and preferred to settle their disputes without involving humans. They were all, without exception, devoted to their faerie heritage, and had no time for the mortals who shared their blood.

A riot wasn't a nice thing to walk into. A *half-faerie* riot, though—even if I hadn't been walking in the direction of the hedges at the border with half-blood territory, the noise would surely have drawn my attention anyway. The shouts, which I'd assumed came from a house party, grew loud enough to spear my eardrums, while bursts of magic lit up the sky like a fireworks display. Which, presumably, was what everyone else thought it was. Most people were too frightened of the half-bloods to complain to the police about public disturbances.

Faeries. Bringing communities together for twenty years

and counting.

I reached the gap in the hedge where the gate to the half-blood district lay, closed off. Isabel hurried to catch up, clutching a stitch in her side. "You *can't* be thinking of walking in there."

"Someone has to sort them out," I said. "They'll blow up the town at this rate."

On cue, a blast of ice struck against a wall of quivering thorns, just inside the entrance. Bits of plant exploded behind the gate, and the air turned cold then scorching hot. The spells would overstep the boundaries soon. I had my trusty iron blade and a half-dozen daggers, but I didn't have the means to stop a full-blown riot. I looked at Isabel. "Any spells you can think of? Maybe put them all to sleep."

"Probably won't affect them, if it doesn't even work on piskies."

"They're half-human," I reminded her. "It's that or let them kill one another."

"Right." She rummaged in her shoulder bag. "There's no way. I only have a handful of spells on me. No sleeping ones. Just explosives, and I don't think they need any more ammunition."

"Fair point." I cursed to myself. Damn Larsen. What the

hell did he expect me to do, waltz in and sing them a lullaby?

My former boss had almost got me killed through negligence once already. Worse, he was the acting authority if none of the mages were answering calls, so nobody else would be able to help.

Isabel took her phone out. "I'll contact the coven," she said. "Bring backup spells. This isn't ideal, but I can't think of anyone aside from the mages who'd help."

"The necromancers won't want to know," I said. "And throwing shifters into a riot is like throwing a dog into the middle of a street cat fight."

"Tell me about it," said Isabel.

Dammit. This might have started with a murder, but more half-faeries would doubtlessly be killed in the fighting. The blood alone would attract every dark denizen from Faerie hiding in the town's shadows. We'd be chasing death faeries out of the streets for a month. Admittedly, my own rule against spilling faerie blood in this realm had gone out the window lately... *Think, Ivy.* Might my magic be able to calm them? Most likely, no. I didn't dare cross the boundary, not outnumbered like this. I'd only aggravate them further. Or give them a new target.

A blast of cold air slammed into us from behind. Isabel

made a startled noise, while I spun around, sword ready, searching out the new threat. Had the half-faeries brought the fight outside?

The front of the hedge disappeared, swept away in another blast of wind. I bit back a yelp, arms wrapping around myself, bracing my feet to avoid being knocked over. A figure moved past us, driving us aside with the force of the power they—*he*—carried. Clouds drove in, sweeping over the nearby houses. My teeth chattered, legs locking in place as leaves stirred up by the wind whipped against me.

The Mage Lord, tall and imposing, strode past me as if I wasn't there.

"Enough," Lord Vance Colton said, his voice projected by what I assumed was a spell. "If you don't stop, you'll cause irreversible damage to your home and to this realm."

Shocked faces stared through gaps in the hedge, most mid-fight.

"What the hell?" yelled a half-faerie. "It's not your business."

"I am Lord Colton of the West Midlands district Mage Council, and I have authority to have any of you detained for causing a danger to the human and supernatural communities. If you cause any more damage, you'll find yourself at the mercy of every mage in this district."

Whoa. Guess he was prepared to take on Faerie, after all. With the power crackling over his head and slicing up the air, I almost believed he'd be able to face down a Sidhe lord.

Almost.

"Is that clear?" he asked of the ringing silence. I'd been so startled by his sudden appearance, I only now realised the rioting had stopped altogether. *Whoa.*

"Is that clear?" he repeated, moving close to the bars of the gate. The air stirred into a cutting breeze, tearing leaves from the hedge and forcing me to back away, feet braced on the pavement.

"Yes," said the nearest half-faerie, tripping over his own feet in an effort to get away.

I watched, open-mouthed, as the riot dissolved. Vance had stopped the fight like a schoolteacher disciplining an unruly hall of kids.

Which left... us. "Vance," I said. "Is there—"

"Leave them," he said. "Let them sort out their own battles."

He turned heel and vanished—literally. In addition to being able to grab objects out of thin air, the Mage Lord had an interesting relationship with the laws of physics. Like the ability to effectively teleport.

What the hell? Last time I'd spoken to him, he'd promised me a date. Now he'd taken away my job. Again.

"What *was* that?" said Isabel.

I shrugged. The Mage Lord had actually rendered me speechless. Fury surged, and I kicked at the half-faeries' gate. "No clue."

"I thought he was…"

"My friend? My freaking *boss?*" I swore and kicked the gate with my other foot. Now my bruised toes matched. Brilliant.

Isabel stared after the Mage Lord. "I've seen some scary-ass magic, but… damn. I'd rather face down a shifter."

"He's part shifter, technically," I said.

"That explains the temper."

"I know, he's positively cuddly." Actually, Vance was the only person with shifter blood I'd met who'd demonstrated any kind of restraint. Sometimes, anyway.

Okay, so he'd skewered people with invisible swords and came close to accidentally killing me twice. Maybe it was for the best we'd never got a date.

"Come on," said Isabel. "Let's go and fetch those piskies."

"I'd rather walk in there." I jerked my thumb at the gate. "Wonder who died?"

"Probably more than one of them by now, the way they were fighting." Isabel grimaced. "What kind of magic did he use?"

She didn't need to say his name. I turned my back on the half-faeries' place and reluctantly led the way to the house where we'd left those piskies.

"Mage Lord badassery. No clue. He's a displacer, so I suppose he shifted all the air around us to make a dramatic breeze."

"And vanished into thin air," added Isabel. "Is he a stage magician in his spare time?"

I snorted. "He defines 'over-dramatic', but no. As for where he's been the last week, no clue."

"Might have stuck around to help us with this." She indicated the garden up ahead, and the ruins of the shed. How were we meant to explain to the people who'd hired us that the piskies had blown up half their garden? We'd probably get charged for damages on top of not being paid.

I groaned. Time to explain the rules of magic to sceptical humans, again. I doubted Vance would consider the trouble the fight would draw from the other faeries living in this realm. No, some poor freelancer would have to deal with the mess.

Unfortunately, only one person in town specialised in dealing with faerie cases. Yay me.

***

"Paperwork," said Isabel in a singsong voice, depositing a stack inside my bedroom door. I rubbed my eyes and groaned. Unlike me, Isabel was wide awake for someone who frequently pulled all-nighters, dressed in an outfit entirely too bright a shade of green for this hour in the morning.

"Thought you'd let me sleep in," I mumbled, hiding my head under the pillow.

"You need to hand these into clean-up by ten. I would, but I have to be with the coven in an hour."

I groaned again and rolled out of bed. We'd stayed up half the night filling out paperwork to prove the piskies were responsible for the damage to the garden so we'd actually get paid. No money had materialised yet. I didn't blame the garden's owners for being pissed, but it eluded me how a bunch of hyped-up piskies could possibly have blown up a shed.

I wasn't mentally present at all. Bite marks covered my hands and arms because I'd forgotten to use a healing spell after all the excitement. Worse, us coming back smelling of piskie had sent our own resident piskie, Erwin, into a frenzy.

He'd zoomed around breaking things until we'd been forced to trap him in a spell circle.

I shoved on my second-least tattered pair of jeans and a T-shirt that used to be black before the colour washed out, and walked barefoot into the kitchen to scrounge some food. The smell of Isabel's baking cookies somewhat restored my mood. She'd left a tray out on the side, luckily away from the chalk circles covering every other work surface in the flat.

The doorbell rang.

"Oh, for god's sake." I turned heel and went to answer it. *Please not Larsen. Please not Vance.* For once, I wouldn't have minded it being a freaking door to door salesman, if just to avoid being dragged into any more crap.

Like I'd be that lucky. The Mage Lord stood on the doorstep, coat sweeping around him—more due to the autumn wind than his mage special effects.

"Oh," I said. "It's you."

"Don't look so happy to see me," said Vance Colton. "Are you baking?" He walked right past me, and before I could gather my wits, walked over to Isabel. "Those look nice."

"Oh, take one," she said, with a cheery smile. I shot her a glare, which she ignored. Dammit. Compliment Isabel's cooking and you'd pretty much got an open invite for life.

Vance picked up one of the cookies and bit into it. I turned my glare onto him.

"Did you just invite yourself into my house?"

"Technically, your friend invited me in."

"Then I'm uninviting you."

He put on a mock-wounded expression. "Such a cutting tongue. Isabel, can you give me the recipe for these?"

"I—yeah. Sure." Her face flushed like a traffic light.

Great. Not only had he invited himself into my flat, he'd charmed the wits out of my best friend.

"Vance," I said warningly. "Tell me why you're here or I'll have to ask you to leave."

"Really."

I glared at him. "No bullshit. What do you want?"

"Wouldn't you believe I wanted to make a friendly social call?"

Isabel wisely ducked out of sight. I heard her bedroom door close and sighed inwardly. Great. Exactly what I least needed.

"What the actual hell, Vance," I hissed. "It's common courtesy to let people know you're planning to vanish off the face of the earth. Especially when you've just offered them a job."

His smile vanished. "I apologise. I was called to an urgent meeting and forbidden to take my phone with me."

Oh. "Right. Any reason you didn't text me when you came back? Or talked to me yesterday when you weren't pulling your creepy super-powered Mage Lord trick on the half-faeries?"

"I rather think it'd have spoilt the impression."

I crossed my arms. "You think I'd have wrecked your street cred? That's beside the point. You disappeared. Right after we—" Nearly died. As he knew well, the dickhead. He'd also kissed me. Several times.

"You're suggesting I ought to have told the entire town the council of mages were gone?"

"You have my number," I said. "And I had the impression you—" What? Liked me? Wanted me?

One eyebrow rose. "Yes?"

"Intended to finish our conversation," I said, already regretting speaking. "Never mind. I should have figured you'd disappear as soon as you had reason to."

"The leader of the East Midlands mages was murdered," said Vance, stunning me into silence.

"What?"

"Murdered," he repeated, with a flash of anger in his eyes.

"By a half-faerie."

I gaped at him, unable to hide my shock. Half-faeries might be anti-human and pretty much anti-supernatural, too, but even they showed basic respect to the mages. The Mage Lords, most of all.

"Who?"

"That's what we're trying to determine," he said. "It appears to be an isolated act of a madman, but our supernatural alliances are fragile, and this might mean dividing further."

"The half-faeries live behind an impenetrable hedge," I said. "Pretty sure that's as divided as you can get. And one of them was murdered yesterday, actually. By another half-blood."

He raised an eyebrow again. "Really."

"Yes." I didn't say Larsen had told me. Like absolute hell would I admit to the Mage Lord that I'd nearly taken work from Larsen. Even if he'd driven me to it. "Obviously, I haven't been able to poke around, because when we got there, the whole place was about to go up in flames."

"Why were you near half-blood district in the first place?"

I scowled. He always managed to ask the questions I least wanted to hear. "On a job. Might have escaped your attention

I'm short on cash."

He frowned. "You just got paid for our work bringing those children back from Faerie."

He doesn't know? "The necromancers took it." My hands curled into fists. The bastards. Sure, I'd killed one of them, but he'd been possessed by a half-faerie ghost and trying to kill me at the time. The necromancers didn't see it that way.

Vance's icy cold expression could have frozen embers. "I see."

"Don't," I said warningly. "They had reason to. We messed up their territory, and I—you saw me stab one of them when those ghosts took control of their bodies." He'd critically injured another necromancer himself, but even Lord Evander wouldn't dare press charges against the Mage Lord. Instead, he'd waited until I was alone, then pounced. I had no evidence against the testimony of two hundred necromancers and the spirits they summoned.

"Lord Evander and I will have words," he said, putting emphasis on *words* so it sounded more like *I'll hang him up by the neck.* Nobody implied threats quite like the Mage Lord.

"Don't we have a more urgent problem?" I asked. "The necromancers won't do jack shit to help us with the half-faeries."

"Neither will anyone else," he said. "The other supernatural groups hate the half-bloods, and with good reason. The faeries exposed us to the world, in addition to the damage they wreaked."

You didn't get a bad deal, I couldn't help thinking. The Mage Lords were now the most powerful people in the world. Before the invasion, they'd hidden along with witches, shifters, and other supernaturals. Half-faeries, as far as I was aware, hadn't been heard of until the invasion. While most faeries were fighting a war, others decided to seduce humans. I'd put the average age of a half-faerie at nineteen or twenty. What we'd witnessed last night was nothing more than a group of teenagers collectively throwing a tantrum... with deadly magic.

"So what then?" I asked. "Someone clearly needs to *talk* to them, find out who died. Or if anyone knows about this... other death."

His expression darkened at the reference. Had he known this other mage well? Maybe they'd been friends.

Maybe he had an excuse for running off after all. Nobody had handed the Mage Lord a guide to 'not being a dick in social situations'. I'd think twice before trusting him again, but I could count my allies on one hand. I'd rather be on

Vance's side than against him.

"Yes," said Vance. "Someone needs to talk to them. I rather hoped it'd be you."

I froze. Forced a laugh. "What?"

"Half-blood territory is deadly to most humans," said Vance. "As for supernaturals, the half-faeries would attack most of us on sight."

"And you?" I raised an eyebrow. "Pretty sure they wouldn't attack you."

"No, but I doubt they'd confide their deepest secrets, either."

"What the hell do you think I am, the faerie whisperer?"

He arched an eyebrow.

I went on, "You can't be serious. Even if they didn't try to kill me the last time I went in, they're out for blood and begging for a scapegoat. We're not even allowed to take iron weapons into their territory. And unlike some people, I can't bend space and grab a sword whenever I feel like it."

And I'd rather avoid them finding out I had faerie magic. Okay, I'd told Vance and Isabel. And Larsen. But judging by how easily the half-bloods had been fooled by Velkas, the evil faerie lord promising immortality, they'd believe any rumour. The last thing I needed was a reputation amongst them as well as the mercenaries.

"I'm not asking you to go into their territory," said Vance. "Merely meet a representative at their gate. Tell them you're there on behalf of the Mage Lords as a human intermediary."

"What? Everyone thinks I'm a witch."

"You aren't registered."

"Not this crap again." I rolled my eyes. "I thought it didn't matter." *I thought you trusted me.*

That stung. Never mind how he planned to send me running into danger—if not for his being here, I'd probably be off raiding a troll's nest. No—he was acting like a significant portion of the last two weeks never happened.

"It matters to the faeries," said the Mage Lord. "I doubt they'd mind if you were. Witches have no arguments with half-bloods."

"*We* do," I muttered. "Do I get compensation for running risks? You promised me a contract."

"Yes, I did," he said, looking almost insulted. "I'll draw up the contract, but I'll be nearby when you meet with them anyway. Just in case."

"Just in case they decide to skewer me. How thoughtful."

Vance frowned, moving one step closer. "You don't think I've considered your safety?"

"Half-blood territory and *safety* don't fit into the same sentence, Vance," I said. "Yes, I'll do it, but I'd prefer it if you didn't criticise me for taking risks and then send me running into one of the most dangerous places in town."

"Point taken. Anything else you'd like to add?"

"There's only one thing I want from you, Vance."

"Yes?" He lifted an eyebrow again.

Goddammit. "An apology."

"For not telling you where I was?"

"No, for letting the necromancers take away my cash and force me to spend yesterday evicting piskies from a garden shed."

"What?"

I turned away, my face heating up. "What I said. I don't want an argument."

He paused, hands slightly forward like he intended to reach out and touch me but thought better of it.

"I'll see to the necromancers," he said. "For now, I wanted to offer you this assignment. Talk to the half-blood guard. Find out what they know."

"There's a reason I'm not a diplomat," I said. "I'm better at stabbing things than negotiation."

"The Mage Lords aren't welcome in their territory," he

said. "And most are still in Nottingham making arrangements for the election of a new Mage Lord. I came back early to be sure nothing had happened in my absence."

"Did I answer that question?" The words came out snappier than I'd intended. Or maybe I had meant it. Dickhead.

"Ivy—"

"All right, I'll do it," I said.

"Good. Come and see me at the manor at ten."

"Eleven. I have to return a stack of paperwork to clean-up." In response to his questioning look, I added, "Because of the piskies. Don't ask."

Damn him. There'd been no reason whatsoever he couldn't have called me. Sure, his excuses were solid. He hadn't meant to leave my livelihood up in the air, but it had been damned stupid of me to think a kiss or two meant I was safe. I should know better.

"I'll sort this out, then come and find you."

"As you like. I'll be waiting." He turned around, then paused. "I apologise, Ivy, for not telling you."

I blinked, and he'd vanished. Dammit. He just had to get the last word in.

"Whoa," said Isabel. I jumped, not realising she stood

behind me. "What did tall, dark and chiselled want?"

I snorted. "Tall, dark and chiselled?"

She grinned. "Didn't you make out with him before he disappeared?"

"Yes. Unfortunately."

"That bad?" Her expression shifted to say, *no bullshit.*

"No. Good. Too good." I sighed, brushing my hair over my shoulder. "We were supposed to be business partners. No wonder he didn't take me seriously enough to tell me he planned to vanish for a week." Emergency or not, you'd think there'd have been a system in place to deal with people back here who wanted to see him. But the gates to the mages' headquarters had been locked from the inside. "Anyway, he's given me a job in *half-blood* territory. He thinks I'm his lapdog, apparently."

"Reading between the lines, I think he's looking for an excuse to spend time with you."

"He's asking me to walk into half-blood territory again. It's like handing me a Valentine's card with a trip to the gallows printed on it."

"I think you're exaggerating a little."

"I'm the only person who can set foot in the place without dying," I muttered. "And even that's not a guarantee."

Sure, I had my faerie magic, but it didn't mean my survival odds were any higher. I liked my body parts the way they were, thanks.

On the whole, this was not how I'd hoped to start the weekend.

CHAPTER THREE

Two hours, later, after delivering a stack of paperwork to the clean-up guild and managing to avoid Larsen in the process by sneaking in and out through the back door, I rode the bus down to 15 Oak Drive, home of the mages.

Or one mage in particular. It still blew my mind that the huge mansion belonged to a single person. The hedges surrounding the place took up as much room as three regular houses, while the gardens appeared to stretch on for miles. I tried and failed to count the windows as I waited outside the wrought-iron gate, hoping the doorman wouldn't be who I thought it would.

"You," said a lilting voice.

Oh, crap. Typical. Ralph the quarter-faerie glared at me from the shadows, his bright blue eyes narrowed. His too-pretty-to-be-human face wouldn't have looked out of place on the cover of an old-world magazine, if he wasn't scowling like I'd brought a dead rat with me.

"You," I said back. "I have an audience with the Mage Lord." I was tempted to ask if *he* knew what went down in half-blood district, but as far as I knew, Ralph had spurned his faerie heritage. Thinking about it, I didn't know anyone else who had. Most half-faeries worshipped their non-human parents who'd left them here to fend for themselves.

"Does the Mage Lord know you're here, dressed like… that?" He looked me up and down, taking in my tattered jeans and bloodstained coat.

"Yes," I said, through gritted teeth. Generally, Ralph was either trying to stab me or insult me, and I was in the mood for neither. "As I said, I have an invite. Technically, I work here."

"You don't." Ralph moved to bar the way. "We don't let hedge witch scum in here."

Did he *want* me to punch him in the nose? I moved until we stood eye to eye. "If the mages' standards have slipped enough to let the likes of *you* in, then—"

His fist flew at my face. I effortlessly dodged—apparently, he hadn't inherited a faerie's inhuman speed—and grabbed his fist in my hand, twisting hard. He yelped as his wrist threatened to break under the strain. My fighting methods tended towards *hit them until they stop moving* rather than a particular style, but I knew how to bring on the pain.

Ralph's eyes went wide and his free hand dropped to his side. "What the hell—is that *magic?*"

Blue light flared up around my hands, resting above my arms like a freaking halo.

Shit.

"Ivy Lane."

I dropped Ralph's hand like it burned me. He made a faint whimpering sound and scrambled away, but the look he shot me was one of disgust and—fear?

Shit. Shit. He'd seen the faerie magic react to my anger. Apparently, being quarter-blooded meant he still had the Sight.

Vance sighed. "Are you arguing with my doorman again?" The gate lay open behind him, and I gladly scooted inside. I considered telling him I'd exposed my magic to his guard, but decided against it. Ralph didn't scare me, but I really didn't want word about my faerie magic spreading amongst the mages.

"Ivy, if you're going to work here, you need to stop antagonising Ralph."

"He started it," I said. "Seriously. Every time, it's been him who threw the bait."

"Then you shouldn't rise to it."

"Yes, oh wise master," I muttered. My heart beat too fast, and traitorous wisps of blue magic clung to my skin. No wonder even Ralph had seen it. I might as well be wearing a neon shirt that told every faerie in the vicinity I was a human with faerie magic.

On cue, a small figure ran into the hall. Quentin, Vance's brownie assistant. He glared at me, too.

"No, I'm not covered in blood this time," I said. *Quit staring.*

"Give it five minutes," said Vance.

"Ha ha." I rolled my eyes. "What, do you have a faerie lying in wait to ambush me?"

"No, but I do have the contract you requested. Though I wouldn't be surprised if you cut your finger on it."

"Very funny." I looked away, determined not to let him see my reluctant amusement. Now I remembered why I liked the guy. Too bad he'd done enough to piss me off lately I'd be keeping him at arm's length.

Vance led the way into his office. As promised, a straightforward document lay on the desk. I signed beneath Vance's illegible scribble of a signature.

"You could have left a message here," said Vance. "It'd

have reached me eventually."

"Eventually?" I raised an eyebrow. "I stood outside the gate for an hour in the pouring rain, and no one showed up. Was I supposed to sit there all week? I have to pay rent somehow. I hadn't even signed a contract with you at the time. You might have vanished off the face of the earth for all I knew."

"I should have explained the situation before I left."

"Guess we were preoccupied."

I meant with the faeries, and the whole *nearly dying* scenario, but... well. We hadn't done much talking afterwards, either. The gleam in his eyes told me the same thought had crossed his mind, but I refused to acknowledge it.

"Did you require a handbook?" he asked.

"Actually, yes," I said. "You can take the piss out of me all you like, but even Larsen made the regulations clear on the first day."

A shadow fell over his face at the mention of the name. "You took another job from him?"

"No. He told me to look into half-blood territory. You showed up five minutes later, so there was no need to." I glared at him. "Don't you dare judge me. You've never been desperate enough to take any job that comes your way, have you? Larsen might be an asshole, but at least he gave me enough work to keep a roof over my head. That's more than a lot of people in my position can say."

"I did apologise to you. I'll be sure to let you know when I'm leaving town in future."

I looked away. "Okay. Can we get this ill-advised trip into faerie territory over with, then?"

"If you like." Vance put the paper on the desk, and it vanished into thin air. He wasn't even showing off, he seemed to do it on reflex. "I won't be able to come inside with you."

And he wouldn't be able to help me if I exposed my magic again. It was too much to hope to avoid confrontation. Faeries were contentious on a good day.

An awkward silence spread between us as we walked down the hall. I guessed he'd meant he'd walk up to the door to half-blood territory with me. Which meant finding more ways to *not* talk about what had happened before he'd left. I licked my lips, trying not to remember how good he tasted when he kissed me.

"So did all the other mages in this part of town leave?" I asked him.

"Most of them. The council called for a meeting of every mage in the region to discuss the murder." There was a tightness to his voice. "The situation proved difficult to resolve. We all nominated candidates who might take up the new position as the leader of the region's mages. Stability is essential in times like these."

"And nobody knows who might have done it?"

A whisper of cold air brushed against my back, accompanying the threat hanging in the air like an imminent storm.

"There aren't any suspects. Yet. But we know a half-faerie did it. Their blood was found at the scene."

"Faeries never think they need to obey human laws."

"Perhaps not," he said softly, "but I doubt anyone but a powerful Sidhe can outdo a Mage Lord."

Good point. He'd single-handedly scared every single faerie in half-blood district into stopping their fight. How could anyone casually murder someone on the same level?

"How was he killed?" I asked, unable to restrain my curiosity any longer.

Vance said, "He was stabbed. The weapon wasn't found at the scene."

Damn. "Iron? That'd rule out faeries. Half-bloods can't

handle iron even in small amounts."

"We aren't sure yet," he said. "But there's a chance I might get called out of the city again if new developments are made."

"Oh. Okay." It seemed wrong to complain about drawing the short straw job-wise when his colleague had been *murdered.* Another uncomfortable silence descended, and the chilling atmosphere surrounding the Mage Lord followed us down the path and outside the gates to the manor. Ralph glared at me from beside the entrance again, but didn't make any more snide remarks when he saw who accompanied me.

"When will the other mages come back?" I asked Vance, once we were out of earshot. "I'm kind of lost on how this whole hierarchy works. There are... five Mage Lords, right? I only know you and Drake."

"There are five per branch, yes," said Vance. "Only master mages—the highest level—qualify to apply to join the council."

"Master mages. Is that ranked on ability or what?"

"Experience," said Vance. "Most mages are junior level. As for novices, we're running shorter than ever. That's why it's essential to work with the other mage guilds, to ensure we have enough new mages recruited."

"You have to be born with a gift, right?" I asked.

"Without exception," said Vance. "Each new mage is given specialist training from a master with the same gift, or a similar one."

"So you're a master mage. You make the rules?" I turned this information over in my head. Who had trained him? As far as I knew, nobody else had the same space-bending ability Vance did.

"For this district, yes," he said. "That means it's up to me to oversee all use of magic. I meet weekly with the various witch covens, but it's not my job to police what people do in their own homes. And there's never been a clear law when it comes to half-bloods. Mostly because humans can't *see* faerie magic."

Oh, boy. Here we go. "Yes, I can see it, and no, it doesn't mean I can single-handedly police them. I'd rather tag rogue trolls than go on faerie-policing duty. They aren't exactly enamoured with me at the moment."

"There have been injuries, attacks, in my district, due to their magic. I'm sure you understand the dilemma this puts me in."

"Fine," I ground out. "You've got yourself a deal. I'll poke around. But I expect compensation. I've nearly died in their territory enough times. Larsen might not have given me an incentive to risk my neck, but you promised I'd get compensation if one of them bites my foot off."

"I'd hope you'd be able to avoid such a scenario. Like I said, I'll be on call." But if I didn't know better, there was a hint of worry in his tone. Great. Even the Mage Lord was concerned I'd get attacked. I squashed the warmth that rose inside me at the thought. I needed to be on top of my game today if I was going to talk to the half-faeries.

"You'd better be," I said. "Don't make me regret agreeing to work with you again."

"You'll never regret it."

The arrogant ass. Worse, he was probably right.

Half-blood territory was considerably quieter than the last time I'd been here, but I hesitated by the gates, squinting to see if there'd been any new disturbances. By the looks of things, Summer had turned up the heat, and sun beams lit up the grass and flowerbeds inside.

I turned to Vance, but he'd disappeared. *Damn.*

A rustling sounded. I instinctively rested my hand on the hilt of my sword. Irene was strapped to my waist, and I didn't intend to remove her to go into the faeries' territory. I'd made that mistake before. Wisps of faerie magic drifted in the air.

Not from me, but from the whole area. The half-faeries had carved out their territory by putting a big-ass spell over it. I sure as hell hadn't expected to spend the weekend hovering around outside the half-bloods' hedge, hoping a fire imp wouldn't appear and torch my eyebrows off.

"Yes?" said a clipped voice. A six-foot tall, gorgeous elven warrior *melted* out of the hedge. I stared a moment. He wore a full set of armour—though made of something other than metal—and I felt like I'd walked into a convention for medieval cosplay. His silver hair was feathery soft and so straight it looked as though he'd ironed it flat.

"You're Ivy Lane."

"Yes…" Damn. Who'd told him my name?

"You're the one who closed the veil."

Shit. Maybe I do have a reputation.

"I had help." I reminded myself not to say anything that'd get me kicked out. Vance had a point… someone died here. The half-bloods policed themselves, but I'd never heard of any homicides on their territory. Admittedly, I did my best to avoid this part of town. "I'm here to talk about the death that occurred here yesterday, on behalf of the Mage Lords."

"Our concerns are not yours, human."

Figures. "They almost were. You nearly set this place on

fire yesterday. The Mage Councils give you permission to police yourselves, but considering the Mage Lord himself had to intervene last night, you're lucky nothing worse happened. Who died?"

"This would mean very little to you," said the half-faerie. "The name of the half-faerie was Verek. He was killed by Kairi, a Summer half-faerie."

So the killer had been caught?

"Rivalry?"

"Perhaps." The half-faerie looked me up and down. "We found traces of an unfamiliar substance in the attacker's blood."

"Wait. Where *is* the attacker?"

"Dead. He was trampled yesterday."

I fought the urge to groan. "You might have told me at the outset. So now *two* people are dead? Why not call the police instead of letting your people trample one another?"

The faerie's eyes gleamed. "You presume too much, human. Our rules are not yours."

"You live in *our* realm."

Big mistake. The faerie's lips pulled back from his teeth, giving him a feral appearance, and I thought he'd leap at my throat. Just as I wondered how *he'd* react to seeing my faerie magic in action, a shout behind him made us both startle.

"What?" he hissed.

"There's another one," called a second male half-faerie. Another medieval cosplayer wannabe.

The half-faerie guard shot me a glare, then turned around and followed the second one through the gate.

"Wait—"

I attempted to follow, but the gate closed on me. Literally. I yelped, withdrawing my arm, half-wriggling out. One more tug, and I was free. Blood beaded on my hand where I'd snagged it on the hedge.

Vance appeared in a swirl of autumn leaves. "Why is it whenever I leave you for five minutes, you're always bleeding?"

"Thanks for the help," I said. "Something else happened. When I tried to see what, the hedge shut me out."

"That can be dealt with." He raised his hands, and the gate sprang open like he'd frightened it into letting us in. I cast a wary look inside, but both half-faeries had disappeared.

"Nice," I said. "They'll be pissed with you."

"They shouldn't have left their gates unguarded."

Good point, and not my problem. Clearly, the only way to deal with my issues was to let the Mage Lord mow them out of the way. Which irritated the shit out of me. I was supposed to be an independent freelancer, not his lackey. How would we be able to get answers out of anyone now he'd decided to blow the doors open?

I sucked it up and walked alongside him, following the path into half-faerie territory.

The district looked different to last time, more like the world outside than its own private bubble of creepiness. Last time I'd been here, Summer magic had poured out of every corner, manifesting in eye-watering colours, smells and sounds. Now, though the sun shone, it seemed almost subdued, but not like Winter magic, either. Like a transition. Maybe they were preparing to switch over to Winter as the real-world seasons shifted. A chill lurked in the air, leaves turned brown and fell off trees, while flowers shed dead petals. The ground was a carpet of orange leaves, which stirred in a breeze I was pretty sure the Mage Lord's presence had intensified.

"Overkill on the special effects, much?" I muttered.

Faeries hid in every corner and under every stone. Even at Vance's side, the constant sense of being watched followed me around. The thick smell of decay filled the air. Dying flowers wilted in their flowerbeds, while every step stirred a fresh wave of leaves. I looked around, scanning the blocks of flats at the end. Nobody seemed to be around, but I didn't know how far the territory extended.

A rustling noise. Vance reacted so quickly I knew he'd been anticipating an attack. His blade appeared, slicing the air and knocking the attacker back several feet. The head of the mages really did have a flair for the dramatic.

"I wouldn't," he said quietly.

"Mage Lord!" gasped the half-faerie who'd appeared from thin air at our side. "I was told—an intruder—"

Vance's gaze swept over the frozen onlooker, as no fewer than five others appeared beside us. Must have hidden themselves using faerie glamour, which I hadn't spotted. So much for having highly attuned faerie senses.

"I'm here to see if you've managed to calm yourselves down after yesterday," said Vance. "Considering the current state of things, I'd guess not. I'm told two of your people are dead?"

What's it to you? I read the question on every face, but nobody dared ask it aloud.

"Three," spat the half-faerie who'd attacked. "Including the killer. A second murder was just committed."

"The first faerie who died… who killed him? Was there

anything odd?" I asked. There might not be a link between the two deaths, especially when the first killer was dead, but still.

"The killer was a Summer half-faerie. He flew into a fit of rage over a minor disagreement and stabbed the other half-faerie to death."

"And that's... out of character?" I managed to keep a straight face, with difficulty. I mean, I'd been grabbed, cursed at, bitten and kicked around by faeries on a daily basis since I came back from a stint in Faerie ten years ago. Violent seemed to be their default state.

"We operate according to the same Laws as the Seelie and Unseelie Courts," said the faerie guard from the gate, who'd also appeared from thin air at our side. "Nobody is allowed to harm or kill another faerie." He gave the Mage Lord a cold look. "No one invited you inside."

"No," said Vance, "but you clearly have problems within your ranks. With permission, I'd like to look at the bodies."

"They're dead." Even the half-faerie guard kept his distance from the Mage Lord. "Fine, but there's nothing to learn. We already know the cause of death, and the motives. This is an isolated incident."

"And the second murder?" I asked.

The half-faerie gave me a frosty look. "The killer has yet to be caught."

Oh, great. We were on the wrong side of the faeries' fence with a homicidal maniac on the loose somewhere. Wait, was 'homicide' the right word for half-faeries? I hadn't a clue.

Vance fell into step alongside me, and we walked down the path between flowerbeds of rotting buds.

"Do you have a tracking spell?" he asked me in an undertone. I gave the faeries a wary glance, but they appeared to be arguing amongst themselves.

"Yes." *Oh. He does have a plan.* One of Isabel's detection spells would detect any hidden magic around the bodies. Witch magic was accurate, if nothing else. But we needed to act fast before the half-faeries caught on.

We reached a small grove of red-leaved trees. The faeries moved aside to let us past—one of them tried to trip me, and I glared at him—through a curtain of ivy into a small clearing.

Two bodies lay on a carpet of leaves. The first looked like he might be sleeping, save for the deep wound in his chest, crusted with blood. No flies hovered around the bodies. The faeries had probably cast some kind of spell to stop anything feeding on their dead. Glassy blue eyes stared sightlessly at the sky.

As for the second body… ugh. His face was a mess of blood covering a clearly broken nose. He'd been trampled, I remembered, and not by humans. The deep wounds on his chest might have come from a kelpie or maybe a small troll. His wrists had been shattered, and the imprint of a giant footprint covered his chest. Dark blood soaked through his shirt, indicating shattered ribs underneath. His death had not been pleasant.

"Move quickly," said the Mage Lord in an undertone, sweeping to cover the view out of the clearing so the other faeries couldn't see us move.

I whipped the spell from my pocket—Isabel's spells mostly took the form of elastic bands—and activated it. The band spread into a circle around the bodies, and I leaned in. No magic remained, though. They were Summer faeries, but their magic had faded with their deaths.

So much for that.

Impulsively, I reached into my pocket for a small container. I always kept salt on me in case I ran into a wayward undead. Surreptitiously, I transferred the salt from one container into the other so I had one empty jar. Then I reached down to the body and let the blood flowing from the ghastly chest wound drip into the container.

I moved to the second body, reaching out, but the Mage Lord hissed a warning. He moved aside to let two warrior half-faeries walk into the clearing, carrying another limp body between them. This one had been stabbed, too, and vicious cuts marked his arms. Looked like wounds from a sword or knife fight.

"No idea who killed him?" I asked, before I could stop myself.

The half-faeries looked at me like I was dirt on their shoes. I shrugged. "Just trying to help out."

"You shouldn't be here."

The Mage Lord stepped to my side. "We were leaving."

So much for looking around. I edged closer to Vance, trying to hide my jacket. Blood stained my sleeve, and if the half-faeries looked too closely, they'd realise what I'd done. Carrying a sample of faerie blood in my pocket felt like wearing a brand.

A choking noise behind us made me whirl around. The half-faerie who'd been carried in gasped and writhed on the ground. *Holy shit. He's alive.*

Barely. The two guards descended immediately, while Vance and I moved behind them.

"Who did this to you?" asked the first guard.

The half-faerie choked out an unpronounceable name.

"Where is he?"

"He—not himself. He said he was—said he was immortal. I—" The faerie's body spasmed as he choked, the breath rattling in his throat. Then he went still.

I looked at Vance. *Immortal?*

Shit. The last time anyone had mentioned immortality, someone had broken open the veil. Didn't take a genius to see we were in trouble.

CHAPTER FOUR

"So," said Vance, as we walked down the street towards my flat. "It seems old rumours die hard. The faerie you fought—"

"Velkas," I interjected. "He promised pure faerie blood would give any faerie in this realm immortality. Obviously, it's total bullshit."

And this time, somebody had paid with their life.

"He might have been deluded," I added. "But considering what happened the other week… yeah. I don't think it's a coincidence. They're still hung up on what Velkas promised them. I mean, it's not like I can go into half-blood district and tell them all personally Velkas was a liar." I'd never thought to, either. Besides, he'd fed the same lie to pure faeries living in this realm. Like the Lady of the Tree. Technically, I owed her a favour, even if she'd duped us and sent us into a factory ruled by a murderous spider faerie.

"You have blood from one of the half-faeries?" he asked.

"Yeah. I didn't see any weird magic, but it fades after they die."

Which didn't help us. Besides, none of them had been killed by magic. Two had been stabbed. Sure, half-faeries were capable of flying off the handle and attacking one another, but two dying in the same way felt like a pattern. Maybe.

I let Vance into the flat, resigning myself to letting him see the state of the living room again. Isabel's witch paraphernalia covered the tables and one armchair—bottles, jars and other containers, along with a large number of pencils and elastic bands. The strong smell of herbs mingled with the scented candles burning on the windowsills, and particles of chalk drifted in the air.

Isabel herself stood at the stove. From the acrid smell, she was brewing up some kind of potion. She wore old jeans and a T-shirt, strands of frizzy hair escaping where she'd tied it back. Witch runes stood out against her brown skin, and chalk stains on her knees told me she'd been drawing spell circles again. Sure enough, most of the floor had symbols on it. I wouldn't be putting this faerie blood anywhere near a powerful witch spell.

"Hey," I said, reaching into my pocket for the jar of faerie blood. "Got a clear spot anywhere?"

"Hold on." She moved to the living room area to clear half the coffee table. "What's that?"

"Blood." I leaned over to the side table where she kept her store of spells, and picked out a detection charm—a yellow elastic band. "Mind giving me a hand with this? I'm trying to see if there's anything weird." I explained the situation we'd found while Isabel took over setting up the circle.

Isabel leaned over the spell circle she'd created on the table, frowning. Her witch eyes saw things nobody else did, but the way she was biting her lip told me she'd run into something she was unfamiliar with.

"That's not blood," she said. "Not pure blood, anyway. It's a formula, I'd guess. I can list the ingredients, but it won't be much use without knowing what it's for. It's like... a drug."

"Wait." I frowned. "He was drugged?"

"Not our drugs. Maybe a potion. Might not be connected..."

"It might be," I said. "This guy lost his shit and stabbed someone."

"The half-faeries are efficient at policing one another,"

said Vance. "Believe it or not. Anyone who lives in their territory follows the Chief's laws."

I blinked. "The Chief?"

"The title's a ceremonial one." Vance moved in to look closer at the spell, and I was acutely aware of how close he stood to my leg. "The half-faeries came up with their own system of governing when the Mage Lords ordered them to elect a representative in the early years following the invasion. That's why we gave them the territory."

"Learn something new every day," I said. I hadn't known, because I'd been absent for ten years after the invasion. I still didn't know everything that had occurred in the interim. "And can you talk to this… Chief?"

"I can, but he won't be any more accommodating than the others were. I certainly wouldn't be permitted to use a witch charm on their territory."

Isabel examined the blood. "Hmm. It's definitely a drug. I'll run some more tests."

Vance and I stood side by side as she paced the circle, throwing various substances into it to see if the blood reacted. When she threw a handful of white powder in, the edges of the circle flared up in white light, leaving a burning imprint on my eyelids.

"Whoa." Her own eyes widened. "That's... damn."

"What is it?"

She chewed on her lip. "I'm trying to figure out how to explain it in a way a non-witch would understand, but it's... volatile. I can't think of a reason anyone would have *that* in their blood. This was from the murderer?"

I nodded. "So he was drugged, and went on a killing spree?" Wait. "Dammit. We should have used a tracking spell by the second body. Then we might have caught the killer."

"The half-faeries would never allow it," said Vance. "However..." Two jars appeared in his hands. "I did take this from the crime scene."

"You used your displacing ability?" Each jar contained a spatter of blood.

"I'll get another spell," said Isabel, apparently unruffled by the jars' sudden appearance. Damn dramatic mages. Just telling me things was too straightforward for him.

"This one's from the first victim," he said, passing it to Isabel. "And the second is from the other victim. I don't expect you'll find anything unusual, but you might want to use a tracking spell, if the killer's at large."

Isabel nodded. "Can one of you set up the tracker?"

I was already on it, clearing a section of floor. I wanted to be the one to use the spell, so I could see this for myself. Why, I wasn't sure. I generally tried to stay far away from faerie-related drama. I couldn't say why it bothered me so much that three had died.

Generally, tracking spells were used to find someone's present location, but Isabel made a specialist branch of spells which let you see the immediate past of the person you were tracking. In other words, where they'd last been. As the ingredients were so expensive, we rarely used them.

The green tracker circle spread to cover a small section of the floor. Vance handed me the second container of blood. My fingers tingled a little where his brushed against mine. I ignored my reaction and unscrewed the jar. Three drops of blood into the circle. I leaned forward. Green light flared, spreading up my arms. I leaned further into the light.

Using a tracker was always strange. You were thrown into the perspective of the person you tracked like watching a movie in your head, but without sound, and with a weird double awareness of being in two places at once. Vertigo made my head spin even though the images unfolding in front of me remained steady.

Images. Walking through half-blood territory. The colours were muted in the vision, the edges blurred. The person I followed turned a corner.

A figure ran at them, wielding a knife. I leaned closer, willing my ears to pick up the sound. The knife-wielder's body language spoke for itself. More words were exchanged, then the half-faerie advanced on the other, a manic expression on his face.

The knife slid in quickly. Of course, I didn't feel it, but I still winced.

Out of the corner of my eye, I saw a blurred figure approach. They—she—came into focus, and she wore a terrified expression on her face. The knife-wielder, I realised belatedly, had disappeared. The female half-faerie spoke. Then she turned her back and walked away.

I blinked, realising why she'd looked familiar. Alain... I knew her. I'd helped her once.

Why had she spoken to the dying half-faerie then walked away?

"Ivy?" Isabel waved a hand in front of my face, breaking through the vision. "You okay?"

I blinked again, letting go of the spell. I shook my head to clear it. The living room seemed unusually bright after the fuzziness of the vision.

"What did you see?" asked Vance.

The last traces of magic faded from the circle. "That was really weird. I saw the victim's last moments, but… there was this other half-faerie. One I've spoken to before… kind of. Last time I saw her, her boyfriend set a kelpie on me."

"Oh," said Isabel, who'd heard the story. "Her. What did she do?"

I shook my head. "She spoke to the dying half-faerie. Then she wandered off. Doesn't seem a normal thing to do when you find someone dying."

"Unless she went to fetch someone," said Isabel.

"Did you see anything unusual in her body language?" asked Vance.

"She looked pretty scared," I said. "Damn. I'd speak to her, but I nearly got my foot chewed off last time I went near her flat."

"Ah." Isabel leaned forward to clear the spell's crumbling remains away. "That's… yeah. You don't want to do anything rash."

"I just did," I said. "How the hell do we explain what we know to the half-faeries? I saw the killer, but if I told them how, they'd probably flay me alive for stealing blood from recent murder victims and using it to cast spells. I doubt they'd listen to reason."

"No," said Isabel. "You have a knack for getting into situations you can't explain away. Is there anyone... one of the mages, maybe, who can talk to them? They'd never let a witch in."

"It's a pain in the ass," I said. "Your spells are more useful than faerie magic in situations like this. They don't have an equivalent to a tracking spell. We know more than they do."

"I know." Isabel returned to the spell she'd been using on the containers of blood. "This blood—the victim's—tests as normal, by the way. No traces of anything weird. Same with the other victim."

"So the drug was just in the killer's blood," I said. "I saw the murderer's face, but... you know I can't tell one half-faerie from another. They're probably hiding." Guilt gnawed at me all the same. I'd seen a murderer, even if I didn't know who they were, and couldn't warn anyone without getting myself locked away or attacked. "Damn. All right. We should go back—" I broke off as Vance pulled his phone out. He tapped the screen then held it to his ear, listening to the person on the other end with a slightly irritated look on his face.

His expression froze. "Yes. I'll be right there."

A beeping sounded as he hung up the phone.

"What happened?" I asked.

"They caught the person who killed the leader of the East Midland's mages."

"Wait, they did?" I suppressed a shiver at the sudden breeze rising up around him. "A half-faerie? Or human?"

"Half-faerie." His stormy gaze met mine. "This is no coincidence."

"Do you want me to come with you?" Part of me wanted to run for the hills when he wore his *I'm going to murder someone* expression. "Is the killer alive?"

"For now."

The threat wasn't so much implied as emphasised. I shivered for real this time. I had an inkling the killer, whoever it was, wouldn't last out the day.

CHAPTER FIVE

Vance didn't say a word as we walked to the door. His hand rested on my arm, and the next second, we stood outside the gates to the manor. A sleek black car was parked alongside the road, mounted on the pavement.

"Why not teleport us to wherever it is you planned to go?"

"Because it's outside the city," said Vance.

"And your range only goes so far?"

Drake had hinted as much, but I'd never got a conclusive answer about the limits of the Mage Lord's power.

Vance, however, didn't answer. Apparently he'd given orders to his other mages, because two of them approached and handed him the sword I'd seen him use a couple of times. I tried not to stare when he sheathed it at his waist. *Oh. We're going too far out of range of the manor.* His displacing power only worked up to a certain distance—which at least explained why he hadn't been able to call me last time, if he'd left his phone behind.

The single most awkward drive of my life followed. Vance's temper brewed like an approaching thunderstorm, and any ideas for small talk evaporated. I passed the time by messaging Isabel instead, as she uncovered the ingredients in the strange drug she'd found. I only understood half of what she told me, but she'd spoken to the coven leaders and they'd never found a formula like it before.

Weird. A drug that made half-faeries go apeshit and kill people? The Chief of the half-faeries was the person to tell, but it'd be impossible without admitting what we'd done.

I found myself fervently hoping we found out something useful when we spoke to the other killer. There might not be a connection, of course, and to be honest, it'd make my life a damn sight easier if these were random deaths. But nothing was ever random where the faeries were concerned.

An hour later, we arrived in Nottingham. Like where I lived, the outskirts of the city were a mess, a mixture of broken-down houses and overgrown forests which had sprung up when the faeries arrived. The mages never operated from the city centres, mostly because they were in a worse state than the outskirts. Before the war, all the mages had lived in hiding, operating under non-supernaturals' noses without anyone suspecting there might be people walking amongst them with the ability to conjure fire or start random storms.

We pulled up outside a nondescript brown brick building. Outside stood a group of cloaked figures. Mages, and not ones I'd met. I went tense as they all looked at me, suddenly self-conscious as the one person not wearing a fancy cloak. I met their stares evenly, refusing to be intimidated. I had every right to be here: the Mage Lord had invited me, and it was my job to deal with faerie-related incidents.

Or so I told myself. Whispers followed us inside, as everyone parted to let the Mage Lord through. They made comments along the lines of *who's she? She's no mage.* My hands curled into fists. Now I remembered why I'd hated mages so much. Their goddamned superior attitude, coupled with the assumption that they could say whatever they liked and never get challenged. I glared at them all.

Vance spoke with a few of them. Apparently the prisoner was alert and had confessed openly to the crime. A mage led us into a side corridor—it looked like this place was held for supernatural criminals, so it was run by mages rather than the regular police. Interesting. So joining the Mage Lords wasn't the only career option for mages.

The amount of magic swirling through the corridor,

threads in the air only visible to me, told me there was more than one half-faerie in this jail. Blue tendrils floated by, and most seemed to be coming from underneath one particular barred door.

The Mage Lord stopped. Though I'd half expected it, I jumped when his sword materialised out of thin air as the assistant unlocked the door. Vance stepped in, approaching the figure lying on the bed. He didn't look up when I followed Vance into the room.

"Javis," said the Mage Lord. "That's your name, isn't it?"

No response.

"Answer me." His command sliced the air in two. The half-faerie seemed to become aware there were people in the room and half sat up. His ragged clothes were totally at odds with his elegant, pointed face, but mud smeared him from head to toe. Mud, and dried dark blood. His eyes went wide at the sight of the Mage Lord.

"You're not—you're…damn. Dammit."

"Recognise me?" Vance moved forwards. The half-faerie's gaze darted towards the door.

"Yes, I killed him," said the half-faerie, his voice shrill. "It wasn't supposed to be like this. I was told—I was supposed to…"

"Spit it out," I said. "Did you mean to kill that Mage Lord or not?"

A moment passed. His head dipped. "I was told I was invincible. Wanted to test it out. The guy insulted me."

A hissing noise escaped Vance, and all the air in the room seemed to go thick, taut with energy.

"Who told you that you were invincible?" he asked quietly.

"Don't know his name. He came to the market last weekend."

"And he sold you something?" Vance had clearly come to the same conclusion as I had. "A substance that enhanced your magic?"

He shook his head. "Not magic. Faerie blood."

Alarm zinged through me. "To make you immortal. Right?" Damn. Would the rumour ever die?

"How'd you know?" The half-faerie's eyes flickered over to me. "The blood. It wasn't right. Something went wrong. I'm not all powerful. It's…" He shook all over, the back of his head resting against the wall.

"So you drugged yourself with a substance you thought was faerie blood?" said the Mage Lord. "Where did the seller get it from?"

If it was the real deal… but no. It wouldn't be. Plainly,

someone had tried to capitalise on the half-faeries' desperation after the veil closed and Velkas left. And now people were getting killed over it.

"I don't know."

The Mage Lord took one step forward. Careful, measured to show the light gleaming on the side of his blade. "You took the drug, then you stabbed the mage. Did anything happen in between? Did anyone else take it?"

The half-faerie's whole body flinched back at the sight of Vance's weapon. "Didn't see. Guy was at the market. He might have sold it to other people." He turned away from the Mage Lord to regard me with red-rimmed eyes. "What's with you? The magic's all over you."

I froze. Vance didn't look at me, but he moved forward until he stood between me and the half-faerie.

"Have you nothing else to say, other than that you had every intention of committing murder?"

"I—I—don't hurt me. Please."

"You murdered a Mage Lord," said Vance. "You didn't think you'd be let off with a slap on the wrist, did you?"

Frantic head-shaking. I knew what was coming, but didn't look away. The sword flashed out. Blood spattered the wall, and the half-faerie's head collapsed onto his chest.

"There are more pleasant ways to kill people," I said, swallowing. "You don't need to prove you're the scariest mage around. Everyone knows already."

He turned to me. "You don't think he deserved to die?"

"I think you should have pressed him further," I said. "Plainly, someone gave him the illegal substance. He might not have been acting under his own power. Not that it makes *murder* okay, but really, the person selling the drug's equally to blame."

"I'm a Mage Lord. My position leaves no room for second guessing. The Mage Lords have the weight of the entire supernatural community on our shoulders—and yes, that includes the half-faeries."

"They'll hate you now," I said. "Just saying."

Instead of responding, he made for the door. "I'm going to talk to the other mages. If possible, collect a blood sample, to make sure it's the same drug."

"If it is, it's travelled a long way," I said. "Like I said—we need to know who's selling it. Screwing people over is one thing, but making them go batshit insane is another." And there'd been one witness to the first killing… Alain.

I sighed. "I need to speak to Alain. She might have seen something. But I wasn't kidding about the kelpie almost eating me alive the last time I went near her place. I can't just waltz into their territory again, but nobody will give me permission to be there."

"I can," said the Mage Lord.

Great. Here I was, forced to depend on him again. But what choice did I have?

"You and I don't exactly see eye to eye on these things." Alain hadn't done anything wrong—at least, not that I'd seen. The image of her tear-streaked face flashed before my eyes, and suddenly I knew I couldn't let Vance go near her until I'd confirmed if she was guilty or not.

"I don't harm innocents." He cast a dismissive look at the dead half-faerie.

"Good to know." I walked after him, out of the room.

I pondered what we'd found on the long journey back, trying to figure out how in hell to talk to Alain without getting killed or maimed. A spell might help. Aside from truth serums, which were tricky to operate at the best of times and might not even work on half-faeries like they did on humans... Maybe if I sneaked in there without anyone knowing who I was.

Without anyone knowing I was human.

Illusion charms... Isabel did have some. But the

ingredients were hard to get hold of, and considering she used beautification charms herself, Alain might see through it. Odds were, I'd be better walking in as Ivy the freelancer and hoping I wouldn't get attacked this time. Apparently, closing the veil and saving all their hides didn't get me a free pass to half-faerie land.

I sighed inwardly and sent Isabel a message.

A response came: *I need to show you something.*

I frowned. *Show me what?*

I managed to separate the serum in the faerie's blood and tried a distant tracking spell on it. The results were a little blurry, but maybe you can make more sense of it than I can.

Wait, I messaged back. *You tried to see where the serum came from before that half-faerie injected himself with it?*

Tried to. It's the distant past, so it's pretty indistinct. I think someone sold it to him. I saw someone hand it over, but didn't see cash exchange hands. The details were blurry, though.

Sold it. Quickly, I told her what we'd discovered. And then, hesitantly, I told her my idea.

There was a long pause. Vance looked at me. "What are you doing?"

"Talking to Isabel," I said, shifting in my seat. "She tried a tracking spell on the serum. Looks like someone sold it to the half-faerie. Or gave it to him."

Vance looked preoccupied. "The same person? Or a collective? I've asked the mages in the other districts, and there haven't been any reports of similar incidents."

"Hmm…" I frowned. "Might be a local thing. Like the faerie equivalent of a drug dealer, promising immortality. That's messed up." But if we knew who was selling the stuff, we'd be able to stop it.

All I needed was a way to get into half-blood territory, undetected.

***

The following morning, I checked my phone and found no response to my messages. *Dammit, Vance.* He might be in another meeting, of course, but the guy could summon his phone out of thin air if he wanted to now he was back in the city.

I had bigger problems, anyway.

"I don't believe I'm doing this," I muttered.

"Keep still," said Isabel.

"I am."

I kept an eye on the edge of the circle I stood in, trying my hardest not to jump out of it. The edges swirled with red smoke, forming unreadable glyphs. I trusted Isabel with the difficult spell, but I'd been standing in the middle of the circle for twenty minutes and I looked exactly the same. The spell was meant to make me appear like a half-faerie—or a passable one.

I tapped my fingers against my crossed arms, watching as Isabel applied another layer of a faint blue powder to the circle, from a glass container. At least a dozen more lay on the side, filled with bright, glittering powders and potions. Words passed her lips, but I didn't understand a single one. The language was ancient, kept amongst historians and students of ancient magic. Only the witches used it, though I'd seen similar glyphs on the walls of the mages' headquarters and around the necromancers, too.

A tingling sensation ran up my arms. While faerie magic felt like a heady adrenaline rush and mage magic felt like a force of nature, witch magic generally seemed calm by comparison. The tingling wasn't unpleasant, more like a healing spell. Goose bumps rose on my arms. My head snapped up as Isabel gasped aloud.

"What?" My voice sounded strange. Instead of answering, Isabel crossed the room and went into her bedroom. She reappeared seconds later holding a small mirror. My heart began to beat faster, my arms dropping to my sides.

Isabel held the mirror up. For a second, it was like looking at a portrait or an illustration. The woman staring at me *was* me, but… altered. My face was more pointed, the cheekbones more pronounced. My eyes glittered, green as emeralds, and my brown hair had darkened to black, twisting into curls I'd never have achieved on my own. I was taller, too, and somehow even my tattered jeans and T-shirt looked good on me. Possibly because I was *glowing*. A blue-green halo surrounded my entire body, like I'd walked through a glittery waterfall. I winked, and the stranger in the mirror winked back.

Damn. I stumbled, tripping over the edge of the circle, and Isabel lifted the mirror, staring at me.

"Oh my god."

"Bad faerie!" screamed a voice. Erwin, our resident piskie, flew shrieking through the room, colliding with the far wall.

"It's only me," I said, but the piskie screamed again and flew up, this time hitting the ceiling. "Pull yourself together."

Shit. Even my *voice* sounded different. Like I was singing. Ugh. I turned to Isabel. "I hate this."

"Maybe I overdid it. I added in a couple of incantations to make you appear charming and divert suspicion. In case anyone starts asking questions."

"Pretty sure charm is a subjective thing." Which would explain my opinion on the Mage Lord, at least.

"Not waving your sword at people helps, too." She moved to start tidying the floor, like she was trying not to stare.

"Very funny." I paused. "It doesn't even matter if they see my magic. They'll think I'm one of them." Hands at my sides, I walked to the bathroom to get a closer look in the large mirror over the sink. I really did look like one of them, down to the pointy ears. Hesitantly, I raised my hands to touch them, and even the self-conscious movement somehow looked regal.

Assholes.

I smirked, putting on the expression of complete and total confidence all pure faeries seemed to wear. The lords, at least. I looked like a sneering elven knight. Yeuch. I kind of wanted to punch the faerie woman in the mirror on the nose, but even as a faerie, that'd look stupid.

I turned my back instead, suddenly glad the Mage Lord wasn't accompanying me this time. It'd be less conspicuous for me to get into half-faerie territory alone, and besides, he was stuck in meetings with the other mages, trying to get information about the murder. I still thought he should have left the killer alive, at least until they could properly question him.

And I really didn't want him to see me as a half-faerie.

Back in the living room, I found Isabel had managed to calm Erwin down. The piskie sat on the kitchen work surface, glaring at me with beady eyes.

"It's temporary," I said. "I'm doing some sneaking around—"

The doorbell rang. I hung behind, alarm ringing through me. Shit. *Please don't let it be Larsen. Or the landlord.* I didn't want either of them to see what we were up to. The landlord would kick me out, while Larsen would know we were messing with something illegal. Even if we did have the Mage Lord's permission.

Isabel peered through the keyhole. "It's Henry."

I breathed out when Henry Cavanaugh came into the flat, followed by four-year-old George.

"What are you doing?" asked Henry, eyeing the spell circles all over the floor.

"Er. Working on a case."

"Fancy dress?" asked George. "You look different, Ivy."

"It's a spell," I said. "I'm investigating on half-faerie territory and I don't want them to attack me."

"Right." Henry raised an eyebrow at me. "I wondered why

I smelled faerie blood."

"It's me, do you need to ask?" I asked, slightly uncomfortable. It was difficult to explain away illicit activity to a shifter with acute senses. Shifters didn't have any argument with the faeries, but after our flat had nearly burned down the other week, the Cavanaugh family had been asking every time anything remotely suspicious came near the building.

"Just wondering…" He frowned. "There's that scent again. Was a shifter in here?"

Oh, crap. The Mage Lord. Apparently he smelled like the most powerful form of shifter possible. I didn't smell anything beyond the tang of the ingredients Isabel had used to make the illusion spell.

"No," I said. "It might be from all the spells we were doing. We're looking into… uh, a possible faerie drug." I didn't see the harm in telling him. The shifters didn't mix with the half-faeries any more than the witches or mages did.

Isabel eyed me suspiciously, but didn't say anything. "Did the spell I put on the roof work?" she asked Henry instead. While they discussed the rain-proof spell—there'd been a hole in the roof for months, and the landlord had never bothered doing anything about it—I occupied myself staving off George's questions and keeping him away from the spell circles.

"You're very pretty," George said.

"Thanks, but this isn't me. It's a magical disguise."

"Still pretty. Like the elf lady."

I frowned. "Elf lady?"

"I sometimes see her on the corner of our road."

Crap. "What does she look like?"

"Pretty."

Hmm. Kids made up stories, but when it came to the faeries, caution won out. "Never talk to her," I said. "Don't speak to any stranger you don't know."

"I know *that*," said George.

I watched him uneasily. Sure, I knew I'd drawn the faeries' attention—and then some—when I'd closed the veil, but most of them didn't keep a close eye on humans. My magic wasn't obtrusive unless I was fighting, and besides, our house was now warded so thoroughly, any hostile faerie who came near would burn to a crisp.

When the Cavanaughs left, I turned to Isabel. "I already want to take this thing off."

"Shifter scent?" she asked me. "That's three times now he's noticed it around the flat. Faeries, I get, but super-powered shifters? Unless there's a client I don't know about or Larsen's finally shifted, the only powerful supernatural who's been here is the Mage Lord."

"Remember I told you he's part shifter?"

"Oh yeah." She frowned. "You said he was quarter-blooded."

"I don't know the details," I said. "Don't think he's on friendly terms with that side of the family. He can't shift into a full animal form, only partially. I've seen him do it when fighting."

"Damn." She blinked. "I knew he was powerful, but shifters are... volatile. Dangerous."

Dangerous. Yeah. Too bad common sense didn't always function the way it was supposed to when I was around the Mage Lord.

"Don't worry, he's perfectly in control." Aside from the time the faeries had unleashed magic on him and made him lose it and attack me. But Isabel had been unconscious for that part. "Anyway. Time to put this to the test." I put on a show of confidence, even twirling on the spot when I passed the hall mirror just to see what faerie-me looked like. Isabel snorted.

"You could start a new career as a ballet dancer. Half-faeries who go into the arts earn a fortune."

"No thanks," I said. "I've got a couple of hours, right?"

"Yep. Be careful."

"Always am."

I heard her say something like, *that's what I'm scared of,* as I left the building.

CHAPTER SIX

Walking through town as a half-faerie was… not what I'd expected. For the first time, the faerie-kind—dryads in the trees, piskies buzzing around the flowerbeds in gardens— looked right past me rather than flying up and trying to pull my hair or shouting obscenities at me. On the other hand, the few humans I passed glared openly. I was pretty much used to hostility by now, so I ignored them.

At the hedges bordering half-blood territory, I hesitated. My plan had seemed sound until I'd actually reached my destination. I'd get inside, pretend I knew Alain, and get her to talk to me alone. If I couldn't get answers out of her, I'd have to resort to threats. I'd only reveal my true identity as a last resort. No one would guess who I was. I doubted any other human would be stupid enough to deliberately walk into their territory, even in disguise. My stomach flipped with nerves as I approached the gate. I had no Mage Lord for backup this time.

The gate sprang open before I reached it. I stared, half expecting a guard to be waiting to oust me as human, but nobody appeared. Did my faerie magic give me a free pass? It couldn't be my blood or even my DNA—that was unchanged. Unless the faeries had security cameras or spies. I hesitated, scanning the hedge, but saw nobody. Odd. But not surprising. Faerie magic defied all logic.

Inside, the layout had slightly changed, the paths shifting to the opposite side of the grassy lawn. Autumn leaves littered the ground, and a river ran through the centre. Did the half-faeries rearrange the layout of this place on a whim? Based on my past experience in Faerie, I'd suspect so. Powerful Sidhe lords could wave a hand and conjure up a castle.

Or a torture chamber.

A shiver ran down my neck. I held my head high, not looking too closely at any of the faeries I passed. A group of half-selkies splashed in the river, while nymphs melted in and out of the shallows and gnomes ran through the grass. Groups of half-faerie teenagers lounged on the lawn on the other side of the river. Nobody gave me a second glance.

This was really weird. I felt like I wore an invisibility cloak, and actually had to look down at my body to check I was still here. Paranoia was so ingrained, I nearly jumped when two female half-faeries walked around the corner, deep in conversation. They passed by without even looking at me.

I paused, then turned back and followed after. "Hey," I said. "Er… do you know if they caught the killer yet?"

One of them, a stunning young woman with ivory-white hair and deep green eyes, looked at me curiously. "Yes. Where have you been?"

"Out," I said vaguely. I assumed the half-faeries had license to leave the territory whenever they felt like it. "I heard about the murders. Is he in jail?"

"He is, yes."

I didn't ask where the jail was, though I wanted to—the question might give the game away. Instead, I said, "Okay. Er… is anyone investigating a possible connection between the two deaths?"

Two pairs of confused eyes stared at me. "No. Why would they be?"

"No reason." Damn. I didn't want to make them suspicious. "Murder isn't common in here, right?"

"No, but everyone's been tense since the veil opened," said the second half-faerie, whose fair hair glittered like spun silk. "They're saying one of the Sidhe came here and opened it, somehow. Some people wanted to go back into Faerie, but the veil didn't stay open long enough."

Velkas.

I opened my mouth to ask if *she* wanted to go to Faerie, but the answer, clearly, was no. In fact, aside from their unnatural beauty, both of them wore plain T-shirts and jeans. Like modern-day human teenagers.

Weird. Definitely weird.

"Er, thanks," I said. Their confusion would turn into suspicion soon, and I didn't want to draw unneeded attention. "Just wondered. Er, is Alain around?"

"Alain Delian? Yes, she's at home."

I nodded. *Good.*

"Thanks," I said again, and they walked away. I shook my head, slightly disarmed.

It was only when I reached Alain's flat that I realised I'd just had a civilised conversation with two half-blooded faeries. *This is so weird.*

I braced myself to have to face her enraged half-troll boyfriend again, but when I rang the doorbell, nobody answered for a good five minutes. I fidgeted, catching glimpses of my reflection in the small window above the door. Every time, I had to remind myself the spell wasn't permanent. I'd rather be mortal than half a faerie.

After I rang the doorbell for the third time, a voice said thickly, "Who is it?"

"Alain?" I asked uncertainly. "I'm sorry to bother you, but I have something really important I need to talk to you about."

A pause. I crossed my fingers behind my back, hoping that bloody half-troll wouldn't answer the door. Instead, a golden haired young woman did. Alain. Like last time, she looked like she'd been crying. Her eyes were red-rimmed, her hands trembling as she opened the door.

"Hey," I said. "I'm really sorry about this, but I had to speak to you. You don't know me, but I hope that's okay."

"All right. Come in."

I blinked. "Uh. Your boyfriend isn't in there, is he?"

She burst into tears.

Whoa. I froze up. Call me insensitive, but I never have a clue how to deal with the waterworks. Especially coming from a half-faerie.

"What's wrong?"

Alain sobbed into her hands. "He's—he killed someone. I don't want them to take me away."

Oh. Shit. "He's the murderer they caught?"

Between sobs, she nodded, backing into the hall. I'd followed her in before I could stop and question what I was doing. The hallway looked normal enough, but rather than unlocking the door to her flat, she pressed a finger to it and the door melted away. The sound of birdsong rang out, and I stopped to stare.

Her flat looked, in short, like an imitation of Summer Faerie territory grown into one room. Wild grass took the place of a carpet. Bright pink and purple flowers grew in every corner, while several drooping blooms formed a cage around three toadstools. She threw herself down on one of them, sobbing.

I'd have made her a cup of tea—well, that was Isabel's way of dealing with a crisis—but the forested area covering the rest of her flat might hide anything. Hesitantly, I walked over and sat down on another of the toadstools. It was about as comfortable as it looked.

"Tell me what happened," I said, as gently as possible.

"He—he went to the Trials. Then he came back and he was different. Angry. He went out, and I didn't see him for days. Then... then I heard he'd been arrested for killing someone. I'm scared—they'll blame me. Nobody's talking to me. I—"

But that's not true. I saw Alain in the vision. She'd known what he'd done. Sure, he was her boyfriend, so she might jump to his defence, but still.

"So he... wait. Where did you say he went before he came back changed?" I asked.

"The Trials," she said.

"The Trials... I've not heard of them."

Alain's bloodshot eyes stared at me. "Who hasn't heard of the Trials?"

"I've led a sheltered life," I said.

She wiped her eyes. "Everyone knows. The winner of the Trials gets free passage into the Faerie Realm. They take place every night at twilight. I thought you were from there..." She squinted at me. "Weren't you there on the first night?"

Whoa. Not *legal.* Or possible. Who the hell was making these promises?

An image flashed through my mind of a faerie warrior wearing Avakis's armour. One who could walk through the worlds at will.

No. Velkas is dead.

Unless someone had decided to follow in his footsteps. He'd had help on this side of the veil. Maybe even from the half-faeries...

"Wait," I said. *'Where* in the Faerie Realms?"

"Does it matter? All the realms are the same. You didn't answer my question."

No. They're not the same. Half-blood territory played homage to Summer and Winter. They'd even thought Velkas was from Faerie. Did the half-faeries know the Grey Vale existed at all?

Damn. If they didn't, it explained a *lot.* For one, why they'd trusted Velkas. For another, why some of them were pissed I'd closed the veil. They didn't know what lurked on the other side would have likely killed them along with everyone else. Because nobody had explained it to them. The only half-faerie witnesses to what happened had been the ghosts who'd come back when the veil opened, and they'd disappeared once I'd closed it.

"How exactly are they promising to take you back?"

"Only the winner finds out." She sniffed. "Anyway—he won. But when he came home, he was different, and… and…" She burst into a fresh wave of sobs.

Damn. It sounded like someone at these *Trials* was ambushing people and handing out illegal drugs. Or selling them. Promising to take people to Faerie, though… either it was a trick, or someone was screwing around with the energy of the realms. Again.

Great.

"Er," I said, over her crying. "Did your boyfriend mention… if anything strange happened while he was at the Trials? If anyone, er, gave him anything, or promised…" I trailed off.

"Gave him what? Who've you been talking to?"

I think that's my cue to leave. "Nobody. It's just weird how his behaviour changed overnight. If that's not normal. Uh." Stop babbling, Ivy.

Alain stood, sweeping her golden curls over her shoulder. Even in this state, she was still gorgeous. "Who *are* you?" she asked. "You look like someone I've met before. You aren't from the Trials."

"You've probably seen me." I stood, too, as casually as possible. "I'm sorry for what happened, but I've somewhere I need to be."

I turned my back, and vines shot out of the floor, pulling me into the air. I yelped, hanging upside-down. "What the hell?"

Alain approached me, squinting. "Something's not right about your magic."

"I'm Summer." The green eyes were usually an indicator,

though my natural eye colour was pale blue.

"No," she said, moving her hands in a scything motion. "You're human."

Crap. Cover blown. Literally. A breeze swept me up and slammed me into the nearest tree, and I *felt* the disguise melt off my skin, revealing my human form beneath. My back struck against the bark, and I gasped as the air rushed out of my lungs. Drawing my knees up to my chest, I managed to land in a crouch.

"You took advantage of me, you bitch," Alain shouted. Tears streamed down her face, and I held my hands up in surrender.

"I'm sorry," I said. *You did invite me in,* I wanted to say, but that wouldn't be a wise move. "I'm leaving, I swear."

She raised her hands to the ceiling and a torrent of water shot towards me. I raised my arms, stupidly, but the deluge swamped me from head to toe. I spat out salty water, realising she'd turned her own tears into a weapon. What the hell kind of crazy Alice in Wonderland crap was this?

I pushed away from the wall, facing her. "Hold on," I said. "Can we talk—"

Another gust of wind hit me. This time, I braced my arms, trying to find my own magic. I still didn't fully understand the

Sidhe lord Avakis's power, but I did know it drew on negative emotions. And I was all kinds of pissed off.

Blue smoke curled around my wrists and formed a barrier between me and her. I moved forward, no longer in danger of being caught in a whirlwind. I'd never tried this before, but my magic seemed to be stronger here in the half-faeries' territory and reacted almost before I moved. I shoved outwards, pushing the shield at Alain, and she flew against the opposite wall behind a swirl of light blue smoke.

Alain screamed. "Bitch. Let me go!"

"Promise not to attack me again and I will." If it was too late to cover up what I'd done, I'd make damn sure I walked away with some answers.

"I'm not telling," she said, like a sulking kid.

"I'm trying to save lives!" I yelled back. "Because someone's selling a serum that turns people into murdering psychopaths. Whoever they are, they turned your boyfriend into a killer, and if you want to stop it from happening to anyone else, then I need you to tell me the truth. I know you lied to me when you said you didn't know he was the killer."

"How—how?" She gaped at me.

"Because I'm a witch," I said. "It isn't important. Who's the person selling this crap, and where are they getting it from? Are they telling you it's faerie blood?"

Her eyes widened. "That's what he said. He said it was a prize given to the winner of the Trials."

I swore. "Is there any other way to find out who gave it to him?"

She shook her head. "I don't know. He mentioned a private party for the winners. The whole point is that it's a surprise. Nobody knows where it is."

Damn. "The Trials... when do they take place?"

"One round each night," she said. "Last night was the final round of last week's tournament, so a new one begins tonight."

Oh, boy. All my thoughts went in a single direction. I couldn't trust anyone else to spy on my behalf. I'd have to sneak in somehow.

"Okay," I said. "Who can enter the contest?"

"Anyone," she said. *That means, 'anyone with faerie blood'.*

"And there's one winner?"

"It's one-on-one combat in each round," she said. "Starting with thirty-two entrants."

"Damn." So many people? Every week? Who the hell authorised this? Surely not the Chief... hell, faeries didn't play by the rules anyway, though. I should have suspected they'd have their own magical contests. The mages did, come to think of it. Annual Olympic-type shows of power and prestige. It wasn't illegal, but offering fake faerie blood as a prize sure as hell was. "Exactly where does this take place?"

"Mulberry Road. Number Twelve." She frowned. "Hang on. You didn't hit me with a witch's spell. Your magic's different."

Crap. "Don't tell anyone," I said warningly. "Not a single word. Otherwise you'll regret it."

I hated threatening someone who looked so beaten-down, but I didn't have much of a choice. Turning my back, I shoved the door open.

Wait. Shit. My disguise had gone. I had to walk through half-blood territory as a human.

Damn faeries. Bloody hell. I risked a peek through the keyhole and didn't see anyone, so I bolted outside. Then I speed-walked along the path towards the gate, inwardly cursing temperamental half-faeries to high heaven.

Miraculously, nothing blocked my path. The same subdued atmosphere surrounded the place, from the wilting flowers and dying plants, and the chill of autumn in the air. Maybe it was the faeries' shock at the deaths reflected in their surroundings. That kind of weird magic happened in Faerie disturbingly often. Like the night Avakis came back from hunting in a towering rage and the entire castle turned into a swamp. Faeries were capable of behaving like toddlers throwing tantrums. Even Sidhe lords.

I stopped at the gate, which didn't open for me this time. Crap. No disguise, no free pass. I tugged at the edges, but it didn't budge. I checked my pockets, but I hadn't thought to bring any unlocking spells. Dammit. *Think.*

Only one thing for it. I reached for my sword and sliced at the hedge. I held my breath, expecting someone to appear and attack me, but nothing did. Really weird. Suspiciously so. Maybe I'd used up my bad luck quota for the day. A girl could dream.

Didn't make climbing through the hedge any less messy. Once I'd cut a good-sized hole, I half-crawled out, my clothes snagging on branches. I pulled leaves from my hair and turned to look behind me. Half-faerie territory looked… kind of empty from this angle. Like everyone had left the area.

Not another death?

I didn't dare go back in there now, not without a disguise. So I sent Vance a message: *Did the killer mention anything about underground battles during the questioning?* I assumed someone had asked for the murderer's account of what happened, before the Mage Lord had skewered him.

No response came.

I really needed a drink. A night at the Singing Banshee sounded like heaven right now. Never had I needed to be around ordinary, imperfect humans so badly. Except that's not where I was going tonight. No, I intended to check out these Trials. Just to spy, not to interfere. The disguise had melted away, and I didn't want to waste all Isabel's ingredients in case I needed to use it again.

With all other options gone, it looked like I had no choice but to do some snooping around over at the Trials.

CHAPTER SEVEN

Please, please don't let this be a mistake.

I crept through the alleyway, inhaling the sickly scent of garbage mingling with something rotten. At first, it smelled like a dead animal, but then a familiar undercurrent joined it. The smell of decaying magic, tinged with the coppery smell of freshly spilled blood. Darkness shrouded everything, faint moonlight dimmed by clouds.

Pausing behind the squat red-brick building, I crouched underneath the windowsill, frowning. I hadn't seen any half-faeries use the front door, so there must be a hidden entrance. This had once been a mechanic's shop, which seemed a hell of a weird place to hold an underground faerie tournament. But the smell—and the lingering traces of blue smoke around the back—signalled this was where I needed to be.

Well. Where I probably shouldn't be, if I had any kind of sense.

Isabel had given me a cloaking spell she'd thrown

together, but it was like the cheapskate's version of an illusion. It blurred me around the edges and turned me into a human-shaped silhouette if I dialled it up high enough. Good for hiding in shadows and poorly lit areas, bad for hiding anywhere else. I twisted the band on my wrist, turning the spell's settings up to max, and my body went blurry around the edges. Not quite invisible, but good enough for me.

Tendrils of blue smoke clung to the damp bricks. A glimmer caught my eye, and when I looked closely, the outline of a door appeared, shimmering. *Gotcha.* My Sight probably wasn't as strong as a faerie's, but I could see through most glamours.

I reached to touch the door and it solidified, opening to reveal a staircase. I paused. Clearly, nobody was watching this one, but there might be an ambush lying in wait. Still, the stairs were dark, cloaked in shadows. The illusion would turn me virtually invisible unless I walked into a spotlight.

Unfortunately, it also made it damned difficult to climb downstairs. I took them slowly, squinting in the dim light cast by the faintly glowing magic around me, but I didn't dare use a spell. Of course I was properly armed this time, but even magic wouldn't spare me from a broken neck. Luckily, the stairs ended soon enough, and an equally dark corridor beckoned. I froze as lights sprang to life along the walls, but they cast plenty of shadow. Like a spy, I edged down the corridor towards the sound of voices.

A pair of blue-painted wooden doors lay open, revealing a room the size of an auditorium, with a big space cleared in the middle of the floor. Kind of like a night club, except nobody was dancing. Crowds mingled around the edges, sipping cocktails in neon colours, but the bare space in the floor's centre remained empty.

Had to be an illusion. The building I'd walked into was tiny. But then, every single person in this room was faerie-kind.

I slipped through the shadows around the room's edge. There were at least a couple of hundred half-faeries in here, but I didn't see who might be running the place. All were dressed as though going to a fancy dinner, which made the few who wore armour stand out. I counted a few of them, including a tall, handsome faerie warrior surrounded by females cooing over him. Were the half-faeries wearing armour the contestants? Maybe. I crept behind a group of gossiping female fey-kind, listening to their conversation.

"Is Hilla competing again?"

"No, she said she wanted to come back next week

instead."

Okay. I'd reached the right place, then. I listened to their debate over which contestant stood a better chance for a couple of minutes, then slipped away.

All the eyes in the room turned to the entrance as a huge guy stormed in. Half-troll, I thought. He was at least six and a half feet tall and half as wide, his huge fists swinging at his sides when he crossed the room. I watched, figuring he must be a contestant. One who probably didn't often lose. Then again, though, trolls didn't usually have much magic.

"I want to register." His voice sounded like tyres screeching on concrete, but he'd inadvertently given me a clue as to who ran the show. Surreptitiously, I crept through the shadows until I saw who he spoke to.

A short, ugly-looking faerie stood surrounded by thug-like half-bloods. I smothered a laugh. The faerie hardly came up to my knees. Not a brownie... a hobgoblin. The half-troll could easily have squished his head between the palms of his hands.

"Name?"

"Crusher."

I bit my lip, trying to hold in another wild giggle. *Hold it together, Ivy.*

"Noted," said the hobgoblin.

I hovered on tip-toes, debating. I looked human, aside from the shadowy illusion. I'd planned to throw my name into the hat, but figured I'd check out the competition first. I could always back out if there was a way to find the guy selling the fake faerie blood without having to take part in a magical tournament for half-faeries. If I dialled down the disguise a few notches and walked up to the hobgoblin, he'd see the shadowy outline of a person. Hopefully not enough to recognise me as human. There were weirder creatures hiding in the shadows.

Another half-faerie approached the hobgoblin, this one a more standard faerie—a young woman wearing silvery armour, with daggers strapped to her thighs. They wouldn't be iron, but the glittering sheen told me they weren't cheap.

"I'm Pixie, and I'd like to enter the Trials."

Were stupid nicknames a requirement? I paused, waiting for her to walk away, then took my chance.

The shadows moved along with me. Luckily, the room wasn't particularly well-lit, though I kept out of range of the artificial faerie lights hanging from parts of the ceiling. Instead, I called the faerie magic, while dialling down the shadow charm.

This time, the magic took a little longer to work. Fear was a powerful emotion, but not in a particularly helpful way. From my brief experiments since learning what emotions fuelled my power, anger was the most potent. Right now, I was more nervous than angry, but I thought about the deaths, the people the half-faeries had killed. Alain's tear-stained face rose in my mind's eye. My hands clenched. Blue smoke swirled around me, cloaking my shadowy form.

I walked towards the hobgoblin. He looked up at me, frowning. I hoped the combination of the shadow illusion and magic hid my otherwise human appearance. As far as most people knew, humans didn't—couldn't—have faerie magic. He'd never guess the truth.

"I want to enter," I said. "Give the name… Shadow."

I'd join in their silly game. The hobgoblin nodded. A symbol flashed in the air, then disappeared, as though blown away. Probably him making a note of my name. Faeries used magic as a substitute for nearly everything.

"You're listed. We have one opening left. Go and wait over there." He pointed to the shadows. "Half the matches will take place tonight."

I hoped I wouldn't get picked. My illusion would hold up for hours, but wouldn't be a great defence against a troll.

Crusher. Didn't quite seem so funny anymore.

Calm down. You can kill faeries in your sleep. I also had my sword, but couldn't use it. If the faeries got too close, they'd sense the iron and scream.

"When does a match end?" I asked the hobgoblin. Surely not in death.

"When one participant surrenders," he said. "Have you never come to the previous Trials?"

Shit. "I've been watching... from the shadows." The illusion masked my voice a little, making it lower than usual. Didn't sound like a faerie, but then again, as I looked around the room, there was a variety here. Gnomes, hobgoblins and brownies ran between tall faeries' legs, while sylphs hovered—literally, seeing as they didn't have corporeal forms—at the edges. Half-trolls stood like living boulders, while half-red caps huddled in groups, talking in shrill voices. Other faeries with more questionable shapes hung from the ceiling like bats or crawled up the walls with long-fingered hands. This place didn't look like it belonged to either Summer or Winter but an odd mix of both.

I retreated into my shadow and waited for the final contestant to arrive. Within ten minutes, one of the batlike shapes detached itself from the ceiling and landed in front of the hobgoblin. Long limbs spread out and it spoke in a language I didn't know. But the hobgoblin nodded, another symbol appeared, and I knew the spidery faerie had entered. I didn't hate spiders in particular, but those long, hairy legs made me shudder. I counted at least eight eyes on its head. *Hope I don't have to fight against that thing.* I wouldn't even know how to disable it with magic.

Crap. I really, really wasn't prepared for this.

Once the creepy spidery faerie crawled off, the hobgoblin walked into the centre of the open space on the floor. His voice rang out through the room, "We have our contestants."

Whooping, roars and stamping feet followed his words.

"I will draw tonight's matches." He waved a hand, and symbols floated into the air. I counted, and realised there was one symbol for each contestant. Once they'd settled into rows, high above his head where everyone could see them, glowing lines began to appear, connecting them.

Oh... damn. The symbols must be in the faeries' own language. Of course, I was the only person in the room unable to read it.

"The first match will place Crusher against Crawler."

Crawler. Might that be the spidery fey? A troll against a spider. That'd end well.

"The second match… Pixie against Lilac."

Not me. I breathed in and out, my heart thudding against my ribcage.

More announcements followed. I didn't dare relax until he said, "And the final match for tonight will put Sunbeam against Icer."

Thank god for that. My arms dropped to my sides, and I wiped the sweat off my forehead with my sleeve.

Okay. I had one day to prepare. To learn how to use magic against half-faeries without giving away that I was human. No big deal. Oh, and with no witch spells, not even protective ones. No daggers, or even my sword. Poor Irene would have to stay behind.

Me, and magic I hardly understood, against a bunch of half-bloods desperate to win a ticket back to Faerie. So, about as much of a recipe for disaster as a troll in a china shop.

Calm down. You've got time to prepare.

I debated slinking away, but before I'd taken two steps, the room changed.

Seats rose from the edges of the room, forming layers. I stumbled as the ground under my feet rose into concrete steps, halting near where the hobgoblin stood. My legs bumped against the step behind. Apparently nobody else had been taken by surprise, because they began sitting or standing on the steps.

Another rumbling sound came from under my feet, and at the edge of the lowest ring of seats, the ground opened. Brambles grew, forming a barrier between the people sitting down there and the now-clear opening in the middle of the floor. The arena. It was even bigger now the crowds had moved to the edges to take their seats, and the lights overhead dimmed until the one bright area covered the centre of the room. The hobgoblin walked out, flanked by two ugly, green-skinned brutes. Ogres. His bodyguards, most likely, in case the battles got out of hand. He stood facing the crowd, and spoke, his voice amplified.

"The first match of this week's Trials pits Crusher—" He paused, and the half-troll lumbered into the arena, swinging a club in one giant hand—"against Crawler."

There was a pause, then the spidery faerie's hairy legs carried it across the floor. Ugh. I shuddered a little, withdrawing into the shadows. Seeing the creature brought back memories of a crazy faerie squatting in an old factory in a nest of spiders and undead.

"Last faerie standing," said the hobgoblin, with a bloodthirsty grin. "Let the match begin."

Seconds later, the troll launched a flying kick at the spidery fey. The crowd howled and screamed, and the whole room shook when the troll landed, its huge feet hitting the floor. The spidery fey, however, had already crawled out of the way.

Knowing how clumsy and stupid trolls were, I'd bet on the spider winning the show. Sure enough, the troll spun on the spot, waving its club in the air, but the spidery fey kept scuttling out of range. Crawler's long legs moved swiftly, dodging one attack after another. Surely the fey must have some kind of weapon. Otherwise this'd go on forever, or at least until one of them tired out. Trolls were damned persistent when they wanted to be.

Crawler's steps moved closer to its opponent, weaving around the troll's club and scuttling in and out of its legs. Still, the troll couldn't catch it. A restless murmur went through the crowd. Shouts rang out. People were bored, and wanted more action.

The troll stomped and roared in frustration, stabbing the floor with the heel of its club. The spidery fey ran behind it again. With another roar, the troll swung the club in a full circle, very nearly clocking itself on the head. A few people laughed in the front row, but behind, things turned rowdy. I shuffled along the row, alarm ringing through me when someone in the same row threw a punch at the guy in front. The area beside me dissolved into a brawl, and nobody seemed to be paying any attention to the match anymore.

Get out of here.

I edged along the row, but found my way blocked by a half-ogre. Dammit. I looked at the arena, where the spidery fey had begun to weave in and out of the troll's feet again.

The foot came down. A spidery leg snapped. Yikes. I winced a little as the spidery fey screamed. The sound drew everyone's attention back to the arena, while I took advantage of their distraction to climb into the partly-empty row in front. I'd almost reached the door when a deafening thud shook the room.

The troll had collapsed onto its face, to thunderous noise. The spidery fey crawled on top of its body, waving long legs at the crowd, aside from the dead one hanging limp at its side. Whispers travelled through the crowd—Crawler's tail carried a poisonous barb. *Clever.* More so than I'd have expected from a creature whose face was entirely made of eyes.

Unfortunately, the end of the match brought more rowdiness. I stood pinned to the back of the seat as two half-faeries threw Summer magic at one another in the row behind. Blasts ruffled my hair, and a torrent of leaves materialised above me. I ducked, alarmed to see my own hands were clearer. The illusion had been knocked somehow. Or maybe it was wearing off. I needed to get out, asap.

Seizing my chance, I ducked under a half-faerie's arm and sprinted for the exit. I'd seen enough for now. Once I was home, I'd figure out my plan.

Nobody followed me from the room, but the darkness of the corridor slowed me down. The shadows hid me, but people passed in and out of the other doors. Looked like this whole place was an exclusive underground socialising place for half-faeries. I hadn't seen anything illegal yet, but neither had I found any clues about who might be giving fake faerie blood to the Trials' winners.

Hopefully I'd have better luck with my half-faerie disguise on.

The door opened under my touch, and I slipped out into the alleyway.

"What," said a silky voice, "is a human doing sneaking around here?"

I froze, turning around. I hadn't heard anyone behind me, but faeries had stealth magic I'd never hope to beat. With no sign of the enemy, I chanced another step forward.

"Not so fast."

Hands grabbed my shoulders. I tensed instinctively, attempting to break free, but their grip was impossibly strong.

"You can't run, you foolish mortal girl."

Laughter, melodic and awful. I struggled and kicked, but he held me, lifted me off the ground like I weighed nothing, and carried me away from the taste of freedom.

"Third time," he whispered. "You don't think I've been watching you? I think it's time I showed you how seriously I take your safety. You could get eaten alive out there in the forest."

I didn't speak. I'd gone limp, eyes wet with tears. Brambles snagged in my hair, and my hands were scratched. I stopped trying to break free.

In the present, I jabbed my elbows backwards in a move that would have winded a human. As it was, something solid—armour—crashed against my arms. I fought to escape the memories' grip, grasping for the magic just out of reach. *Come on, fear is a tool. Use it.*

A blue haze exploded across my vision and the grip finally let go. I whirled around, reaching for my sword. The half-faerie's faint form appeared, the glamour lifting to reveal a tall figure with a pointed face and silver hair cut to shoulder-length.

Strange… and vaguely familiar-looking. Then again, most half-faeries looked pretty similar, to me at least. He spun a sword in his hand, one that also looked familiar. Wait...

I froze, every muscle locking in place. The black armour he wore, the pale grey, wickedly sharp sword made out of carved wood, the blue haze of magic outlining his body... he wasn't from Winter or Summer. He was...

"Did you think you wouldn't draw my attention, Ivy Lane?" He gave me a feral smile, revealing perfectly white teeth. "You unleashed chaos in the Grey Vale."

I unfroze, slowly, as my own magic curled around my body like a protective coat. "I killed a dangerous Sidhe. What are you, half-Sidhe?" The Sidhe were the highest rank of faerie, but if his faerie parent came from the Grey Vale, I couldn't begin to guess what kind of magic he had.

"Half a Sidhe," he said. "You know which."

Oh. Fuck.

"Avakis." The name came out in a whisper.

"I've been interested to meet you. I didn't expect to find you hiding behind a spell amongst the half-bloods. I thought I'd have to seek you out myself."

Shit. How the hell had it slipped my notice? He looked just like him. Like Avakis. Aside from the silver hair, his appearance was more like his pure faerie father than any half-blood I'd met.

I kept my head high. "I'm not in the least bit interested to meet *you,* so unless you'd like to end up the same way as your father, I'd suggest you go back to the Grey Vale. Leave this realm alone."

"I live here, human." His too-handsome face twisted into a snarl.

"Really, now?" I gave him a derisive look to disguise the horror creeping down my spine. In my darkest nightmares, I'd never dared imagine some part of him might have survived. "What are you creeping around this alley for? Screwing with half-bloods, right?"

"It's amazing what outrageous lies will work on the desperate." He continued to watch me, his eyes like icy blue chips. "I heard your name. I know you closed the veil. I expected you to interfere."

"What do you want, a round of applause?" The more I talked to him, the easier my breathing came. He was like any half-faerie—desperate for attention. I doubted Avakis had been an attentive parent.

"Don't talk to me like that," he hissed.

"You don't get special treatment just because you're the son of a murdering lunatic." I pulled out my sword. "Stay away from the half-faeries. In fact, stay out of this realm altogether. We don't want you here, whatever your name is."

"It's Calder." His cold blue eyes flashed.

A snarling noise filled the air, and a layer of faerie glamour peeled away, revealing two huge furry shapes with giant paws.

Hellhounds.

I backed away, holding my sword. Wisps of magic flared around me, turning to light as dazzling as his own. Right on cue, the two hellhounds bared their teeth, sending a blast of fear-magic at me. But I was ready. My own magic formed a barrier between me and the ice-cold terror, my blade a smooth extension of my arm as I cut the first hellhound's throat.

My instincts sharpened. I spun around, slashing left and right until the hellhound was too dizzy to keep up. I felt Calder watching as I stabbed the beast through the roof of the mouth, then turned to engage a third opponent. As its huge form slumped to the ground, I used the momentum to carry me across the alley to Calder, and brought my sword in a wide arc.

He waved a hand, and a blast of icy air hit me, my back colliding with the alley wall. The magic he had must be a pale reflection of my own. I ought to be able to beat him.

The anger roiling in my veins fed into the blue smoke

swirling around me. I willed it to form a weapon, like when I'd fought Avakis, but it remained in smoke form. We were in the mortal realm. There must not be enough power here. Damn.

I tightened my grip on Irene instead. The iron would be more than enough to kill a half-faerie. My hands shook, all the same, my balance thrown off by the reappearance of my mortal enemy.

Fear was supposed to fuel my magic, but my legs shook as I stalked towards him. He waited for me to come, his own blade held casually at his side. Then he struck me with magic again. My feet skidded, my blade faltering. *No. For crying out loud, he's not Avakis. You can't let him intimidate you.*

My blade collided with his, and I bared my teeth. "This is your last warning."

"Don't you threaten me, human scum," he spat. "You're nothing. You killed Velkas by a fluke."

Magic coiled around me, but his was brighter, a blue halo surrounding his body. The same colour as his eyes. He raised his weapon-free hand and shot a blast of icy coldness over my head. The temperature dropped. The air around him hummed with magic. *It's not right.* His power shouldn't be so strong away from Faerie.

Was he feeding on my emotions? My fear? If his magic worked the same way as mine, maybe. My own magic faded by the second, more transparently blue than as bright as earlier. *No. Come on.* Sweat dripped down my forehead. His blade moved with ease, showing he'd had training, and a lot of it. But the way he wielded magic so casually was something else entirely. Swirling blue tendrils encased him. My grip slipped. I missed a block, then another. His sword's edge tore open my jacket sleeves, nicking my wrist. One more inch and he'd be at my throat.

I screamed and pushed everything I had left into my sword, striking and slashing until I'd regained the lost ground. But his magic swamped mine. Devoured it. Like he was drawing on *my* power.

It wasn't supposed to end like this. I can't die out here.

The blade clattered from my hands.

He smiled at me, a humourless, animal grin. "I thought you had some special talent. I thought that's why you killed him. But you're nothing at all, Ivy Lane. Nothing."

I couldn't move. My body had locked into place as his magic crushed mine. It even *looked* the same. Of course it did. My magic and his had the same source.

Baring his teeth, he swung the ash blade.

Blood spurted from my arm and side in a crimson haze. I collapsed, hardly registering the pain. My sight blurred. *I'm dying.* Blue smoke swirled before my eyes, blurring.

He'd turned away, like he'd heard something. Then he disappeared, far quicker than a normal human would be able to.

He was gone. I blinked, trying to stay conscious, and pushed myself up on my good hand. My head throbbed, though the real pain came from the wound in my side. I leaned on the wall to prop myself upright. *You… have to get out. You need to…*

Leaning on the wall, I staggered down the alleyway. Blood spattered the ground at every step, and the edges of my vision grew fuzzier by the second. I'd never make it home before I passed out, and then I'd be fair game for two hundred bloodthirsty half-faeries when they left the building.

Shit on a stick.

My hands fumbled my phone, shaking fingers racing down my contacts list. Call Isabel. No. She didn't know where I'd gone, and wouldn't get here in time. But Vance still hadn't answered my last message. Damn. I rested my other hand against the wall, my finger slipping onto the call button.

He wouldn't answer. The son of a bitch would leave me

here to die, because apparently he never bothered to check his damn phone. Anger made my hand shake harder, and I dropped the phone.

"Shit!" I said, aloud. I crouched, and that did it for my legs. They folded underneath me, and a wave of pain rocked me from head to toe. I threw out my good arm in time to break my fall, my head coming to rest against damp concrete.

"Ivy. Are you okay?" His voice sounded fuzzy, like he spoke from a crowded place. I'd knocked the call button.

"I'm bleeding to death in an alley." I tried to yell. It came out as a croak. "No, I'm not fucking okay, Vance." The world had gone hazy again. "I'm at Mulberry Road—an alley."

I didn't hear his response, because darkness rushed over me, and I fell into the black.

CHAPTER EIGHT

I blinked. I wasn't dead. Good start.

My second realisation: I lay on something soft. Like a bed. Maybe I'd dreamt it all. That'd be nice. No half-faeries, no idiot selling fake faerie blood, no morally dubious magical tournament…

No… *him.*

Fear rushed through me, though tempered by the bone-deep weariness weighing me down. Images from the fight flashed through my head—how I'd faltered, frozen in terror. My brain decided those thoughts were too much to bother with right now, and pushed them aside to focus on the present. I blinked again. Vance Colton looked back at me.

"Oh, it's you."

His brow wrinkled. "That's how you thank me for saving your life?"

I tried to sit up. A mistake. Pain lanced up my side. My vision swam, and I nearly fell into the dark again. My head hit the pillow. The world danced around a bit, then decided to stay where it was. I'd clearly interrupted Vance in the middle of a meeting, judging by the smart suit he wore. The sleeves were rolled to the elbows, and his forearms were stained dark red.

"Damn," I said.

"What did it this time?" Despite his flippant words, his expression was serious. I looked down at my injured arm, twitching my fingers. The movement didn't hurt, but my arm felt numb and heavy. Thick bandages covered my side, already soaked through with blood. The wound must be resistant to healing spells. Most likely, Calder had a bespelled sword.

"Hellhounds chased me," I told Vance. "Then…" After he'd ditched me, the idea of telling him about Calder… didn't appeal. Sure, I wouldn't be able to fool him for long, but I was too tired, too worn down, to slice open those emotional wounds again. My physical wounds were giving me enough grief already.

"You should consider getting a guard dog of your own." The Mage Lord stepped away, apparently satisfied I wasn't going to bleed to death.

I rolled my eyes. "Like a real dog would stand a chance

against… that was a joke, wasn't it?"

"She catches on eventually."

I feebly swatted at him. "Your bedside manner is appalling."

"You drool in your sleep."

"Oh, we're back to taking cheap shots?" I glanced down at the bandages again. "How long am I stuck like this?"

"I put on an extra coating of the healing salve. You'll fully heal in a few hours, but you'll probably find it hard to walk until morning."

"Morning." At last, far too late, it hit me. "I'm in your house."

"Looks that way, yes."

"In…" I looked around the room.

"This is a guest bedroom. I thought you'd appreciate the quiet."

"How very considerate." It was, actually. More so than I'd have expected… but what the hell did I know? "So you did have your phone switched on."

"Yes." His brow wrinkled again. "I was detained… for a significantly long time. The East Midlands mages had a disagreement over who to nominate to take the position of the new head mage. The two leading candidates decided a public duel was a way to settle their dispute."

"A duel? Is that normal?"

"Not unheard of." He waved a hand, and Quentin the brownie ran past, picking up something from the floor. I leaned over to see. More bloodstained cloths and bandages. Whoa. I'd been really lucky this time.

"So you have experience duelling with magic?" The words came out before I could stop them.

Shit. What was I asking? More to the point, *why?* He was the Mage Lord. He'd probably been duelling since childhood.

Wait, where was Irene? I scanned the room and saw my sword leaning against the far wall. Vance's eyes followed my gaze. "Yes, of course," he said, in answer to my question. "Why?"

I took a deep breath. "I may have entered myself into a magical tournament for half-faeries."

His gaze snapped back to mine. "What?"

I explained what I'd found out on my jaunt into half-blood territory, and on my investigation into the Trials. Except for my encounter with Calder. His name lay on my tongue, but I couldn't speak it. Nor how he'd completely crushed my magic. I couldn't begin to make sense of how he'd done it, and Vance wouldn't give me answers. Only pity I didn't want.

Yeah. Like lying to Vance Colton worked out so great last time.

His cool grey eyes studied me when I'd finished speaking. "You used faerie magic to kill Velkas," he said. "You're more than a match for any half-faerie."

"I was in their realm at the time, though," I said. "Magic's stronger there."

"And they're in *our* realm," said Vance. "The Trials are. Right?"

"Good point." *Idiot.* The blood loss was getting to me. The other half-faeries wouldn't be as super-powered as the son of a former Sidhe lord. They'd be weird creatures like that spidery fey. Creepy, but not invincible.

"You're over-thinking it," he said. "You're tough, your magic is strong. I don't see any reason you can't stand up to a half-faerie."

His unexpected expression of confidence in me made me blink. "One of them almost killed me right now." Calder, though, was half-Sidhe, a hundred times more powerful than a regular half-blood. I didn't know if any of the other contestants had the blood—and magic—of a Sidhe lord.

"Are you asking me to tell you it's a bad idea?"

"I was expecting you to," I said.

"I thought you needed a self-esteem boost."

Huh? "I really look that pathetic?" I moved my hands to the bandage on my side and gingerly poked it. Ow. Still not fully healed.

"Don't touch it yet," said Vance. "If you want the bandages changed during the night, call Quentin."

Wait. "Hang on, I'm staying here?"

"I don't see you going anywhere. Besides," he said. "I thought you implied you wanted me to help you prepare for this ill-advised magical bout." The corner of his mouth tilted up. "Have I risen one level in your esteem, Ivy Lane?"

"If you're going to be a dick about it, never mind. I'm tired." I closed my eyes, but arguing with him had made me more alert. And pissed off. "By the way, the bastard who did this to me is alive, and knows I'm human. So don't say I have no reason to fear for my life."

A pause. "I never said that."

I turned my head to the wall pointedly, keeping my eyes closed. Eventually, his soft footfalls told me he'd left the room.

Bloody Avakis and his mind games. I'd sworn never to fall for them again. Never to let one of *them* get underneath my skin. I'd only just begun coming to terms with my magic, once Avakis's, and accepting it as my own.

How did Calder smother my power?

Once I was sure Vance had gone, I pressed my head into the pillow, cursing. Damn the Mage Lord for making this harder than it needed to be. He was the one who nagged me not to fight against the faeries without backup. This was why getting involved with him was a bad idea. He was contradictory. Tempestuous. Inconsistent.

Possibly sleeping next door. Without clothes on.

Dammit, Ivy.

On the whole, I'd rather imagine Vance naked than think about Calder or Avakis, but neither would help me sleep. Instead, I tried to sit up and got a nice shock of pain through my left side. Biting down on a cry of pain, I watched the lights on the ceiling swim around for half a minute before the welcome blackness returned, pulling me under.

***

I moved through fog, chasing a voice. Melodic, enticing, it whispered, *"Ivy. This way."*

The fog smothered everything, preventing me from seeing where I walked, though I wasn't sure solid ground rested under my feet. More like... I was floating. Following the voice.

"Come with me, Ivy. We've been waiting for you."

Transparent, indistinct figures stared at me from the fog, fading every time I tried to get a closer look. I passed right through one, and an icy chill ran through my bones. So many... so many dead. Humans.

"Where—" I started to shout, then stopped dead.

Two figures floated in front of me. A man and a woman. Even though their features were blurred, the familiarity slammed into me like a heavy blow.

"Dad," I whispered. "Mum."

They watched me, slipping in and out of focus. I cried out as they faded, reaching as though I could pull them back into existence. My hand passed through thick yet insubstantial fog.

"Ivy," whispered the first voice.

The fog cleared, revealing trees—too tall to see the highest branches. They formed an unbroken canopy blocking all the light but a faint glow. Shadowy figures moved amongst the trees.

"Faerie," I said aloud. "The Grey Vale."

At once, memories filtered through to me. Avakis. His son. I was—

I snapped awake, raising my arms to shield my face from the sunlight falling onto the bed through a gap in the curtains.

Sitting up, I pushed sweaty hair from my forehead.

"He's not here," I muttered to myself. "He's not. His dickhead son thinks you're dead, and he only beat you by a fluke."

Concentrating on the knock to my pride rather than the horror that some part of Avakis survived, I peeled the bandages from my side. Blood stained them, but the skin beneath was unbroken. Another witch magic miracle. I slid off the bed, realising I still wore the clothes I'd fought Calder in. Either I'd been bleeding too much for Vance to remember to remove them, or he hadn't wanted to undress me while I was unconscious.

Hmm. I didn't want to read too much into *that*.

My jacket was hung over the back of a chair by a cherry wood desk. My shoes lay nearby, and my sword and other weapons were lined against the section of wall next to the door. A mirror over the desk reflected my sorry self back at me. Blood stained my injured arm, my clothes were a ragged mess, and my hair was damp with blood and dirt from where I'd fallen in the alleyway. When I opened the wardrobe in the corner of the room, I found nothing but dust and moths. Great.

The room had an en-suite bathroom, at least, so I could

wash my face and clean the worst of the blood off. Couldn't do a thing for my clothes, though. I'd have a proper shower when I got home. For now, I shoved my feet into my boots and picked up my daggers, replacing them in the pockets of my leather jacket. I froze when the tinkling sound of a piano reached my ears.

Every muscle in my body locked into place. *It's not them. It's not.* But my body reacted all the same—breaths coming short, an ice-cold sensation flooding me, and not of the pleasant, magic-related variety. The tune continued to play, eerie and haunting—too reminiscent of another. The faeries' orchestra had played without end, beautiful and deadly at the same time. Once you were caught in the spell, you danced until your feet were bloody, or until one of the crazed faeries sucked your life essence out, leaving you to rot in a corner.

"Stop," I moaned. "Make it stop."

My head felt too heavy to move, and panic spread through every inch of me even as I knew the music was no spell. I just reacted the same, after all these years, like I hadn't changed an inch from the kid they took into Faerie. Now the shock eased away, it didn't even sound like the faeries, more like an old piano piece, vaguely familiar. Seeing as I hadn't so much as switched on a radio since the faeries took me, I didn't know which it was.

The music stopped, abruptly. I remained hunched on the floor, shivering uncontrollably.

Fucking faeries.

The door opened a minute later. Out of my peripheral vision, I saw Vance.

Goddammit. The person I least wanted to see me in this state. I straightened upright with as much dignity as I could scrape together.

"What are you doing?"

"Nothing," I said.

"You're crying," he said, his expression bemused.

No way. I touched a hand to my face and it came away wet. *Dammit, Ivy.*

"What was that?" I asked. "Were you playing the piano?"

"Yes." His forehead crinkled. "I've heard my notation is sometimes off-key, but I've never made anyone cry."

"I hate the sound," I said.

He raised an eyebrow. "I'll keep that in mind."

"I'd like to be alone for a minute." More like an hour. Actually, I wouldn't have minded climbing out the window. So much for maintaining my professional reputation.

"If you insist." He gave me another scan, like he was

checking me for new injuries, then turned and left. "Call Quentin if you need anything."

"I have to go home," I said. "Isabel's probably... shit. Where's my phone?"

But he'd gone. Dammit.

I checked my pocket for my phone, then I spotted it on the desk. The battery was dead, which meant I probably had a dozen missed calls, but at least I hadn't permanently broken it when I'd dropped it in the alley. Shoving the phone into my pocket and grabbing Irene, I all but ran from the room. And then stopped at the end of an empty corridor. How the hell did I get downstairs from here?

Not only did I have no ride home, I had to walk around this maze of a manor in clothes that were falling apart. I'd already left my dignity behind in the alleyway, so I zipped my jacket and took off down the corridor. Three wrong turns later and I found a small staircase leading downstairs. I half-ran, finding myself in the corridor near the conservatory. Doubtless the Mage Lord would be in there, so I went the opposite way and promptly found myself lost again.

Vance probably had a hell of a fun time in here as a kid. A game of hide-and-seek would last for hours. Did he have friends? Most of his family had died in the invasion, so I guessed someone else had raised him. But this place seemed deserted. No sounds of voices followed me. This place was… kinda empty, really.

So empty, I didn't see anyone coming until I walked smack into Wanda.

"Shit! Sorry."

"Ivy." Wanda blinked at me. She was Vance's assistant, a frost mage apprentice with a kindly expression and her long dark hair pulled back in a ponytail.

"Oh. I know I look like shit." Apparently, my filter had gone walkabout along with my dignity. "I got stabbed yesterday and Vance disappeared before I could get a change of clothes. I'm heading home."

"I can lend you a shirt, if you like," she said.

I smiled. "Thanks, but really—I need to go. My phone's dead, and my flatmate will be worrying about me. Where's the way out?"

She pointed. "Left. You're almost there. If it helps, the main corridor goes in a square."

"Ah—okay. Thanks."

"What happened?"

"A half-faerie," I said, pulling my jacket tighter. "Thanks again."

"Let me know if you need anything," she called after me as I ran down the corridor.

I wondered how much she knew about the nature of my work for the mages. I was the only 'witch' employee, and it wasn't like I'd had ample opportunity to speak to the others.

I breathed a sigh of relief when I found the exit and slipped outside. Nobody seemed to be around, so I relaxed a little. I'd go home, properly clean up, and Isabel's magical cookies would make everything better.

Once I reassured her I was alive, and that I planned to have another battle with a half-faerie tonight.

CHAPTER NINE

The wards around our flat flared as bright as ever, but the door lay open. Not a good sign. I half-ran across the lawn, Irene at my side, and halted as Isabel came outside.

"My phone died," were the first, stupid words to come out of my mouth. "I'm sorry."

"I thought they killed you." She hugged me back, shakily. Her eyes were underscored with dark circles. "Where the *hell* have you been?"

"I'm sorry," I said again. "It was… a pretty bad job." I waited until the flat door closed behind us to unzip my jacket. Isabel gasped at the sight of my shredded clothes. "I need a shower, but I promise I'll tell you everything in five."

"You'd better." Her words followed me as I pushed my bedroom door open. I considered my wardrobe and grabbed a fresh outfit, and made for the shower. I shampooed my hair three times, scrubbing every flake of dried blood from my skin, but I still felt the taint of… *him*.

"I won't lose next time," I whispered, my words lost in the pounding of water.

I dressed and swept my hair into a ponytail, then went to join Isabel.

It didn't take too long for her to be shaking her head at me. "Ivy, I know you're reckless, but sneaking into an event for half-bloods only? That's…"

"Mad. I know." I took a half-hearted bite of the pasta meal I'd heated up in the microwave. "But people are dying. The leader of a mage council was murdered. And…" The words stuck in my throat. *And* his *son nearly killed me.*

Isabel looked at me curiously. "The leader of a mage council. Whoever it was, they probably got taken off guard. I can't see a part-shifter Mage Lord who can defy the laws of physics getting beaten by a half-faerie."

My mouth fell open. "Huh?" She thought I meant Vance might be targeted next?

"Ivy, if you're worried about the Mage Lord, I'm sure he has his own security team."

"I'm not worried about him." *Maybe I am, now.* It sounded like the half-faerie who killed the leader of the other mages had been half-crazed, drunk on the aftereffects of the drug. Didn't sound like he'd planned the attack, and Calder hadn't mentioned him either.

"You were at his house last night, weren't you? You don't have to hide anything from me."

Those words were the final trigger that burst the dam. I blurted out the real truth—everything from Calder attacking me, dampening my magic, and leaving me to bleed out in the alley. Her expression grew more alarmed with every second until she stood up to pace around the flat.

"Shit, Ivy."

Now I'd told her the full truth of my experiences in Faerie, she knew how much damage Avakis had done. How tenuous my grip on my own magic was.

"I'd drop out of the contest, but people are dying." I set my mostly untouched meal aside. "I can't let this slide."

"You nearly died," she said. "Do you know how it felt when you didn't come home? I thought they'd abducted you again."

"I'm sorry," I blurted. I'd already apologised twelve times, but guilt twisted through my guts. "I'm really, really sorry. I never expected I wouldn't make it back. The illusion spell worked perfectly, but I stayed too long. It was fading on the way out. I guess that's why he saw through it. He's half-Sidhe, too. But the way he used magic... it shouldn't be possible in this realm."

He maintained a level of control over his power I'd never seen before, because he'd had the magic his whole life.

Who trained him?

He'd looked just like Avakis when he'd faced me in the shadows, except... not. He had silver hair, not black, for one thing. His fighting style hadn't been the same. *You killed Velkas by a fluke,* he'd said. Not *you killed Avakis.*

"He met Velkas," I said. "Maybe they went to Faerie together."

He'd worn armour and carried a powerful tree-forged blade... neither of which was easy to get in this realm.

"Velkas had help, right?" said Isabel. "Not just from the necromancers."

Good point. "The people we questioned when we were trying to find out who took those kids kept mentioning a half-faerie with silver hair and an ash blade," I said. "A *half-faerie.* Velkas was a pure-blooded Sidhe. Maybe this guy used to be his lapdog." It explained a lot. He was carrying on with Velkas's lies. Immortality. Did he want to open a way back to Faerie, too? Most likely. Velkas's ultimate goal had been to build an army and make even Summer and Winter bow to him. He'd wanted to steal Avakis's power long before he'd set his sights on the mortal world.

Calder, on the other hand… he wasn't pure faerie. No matter how much control he had over his magic. If I wanted to beat him, I needed to learn the heart of my own magic and use against him. I wouldn't be blindsided again. Assuming I survived the Trials without anyone realising who I was, I might be able to sneak up on him.

I drew in a breath. Isabel watched me with a worried expression.

"He'll think I bled to death in the alley," I said. "If my half-faerie disguise is good enough, he won't guess it's me when I show up tonight. I can wear a costume. Some of the half-faeries did."

Isabel shook her head. "You aren't going to back down on this, are you? Can… can you at least not walk in there alone? The Mage Lord wants you to stay in one piece, right?"

"He'd never be able to sneak in," I said. "Unless you made two disguises, but I'll need one every night this week if I make it to the final round of the contest."

"I don't have enough ingredients for two people." Isabel shook her head again and crouched beside the spell circle set up on the floor. "I *might* be able to do you a fancier design, but you'll have to tell me what you want to look like."

"I will do. I should probably call Vance. I kind of freaked out this morning and ran home without telling him I was leaving."

She turned her head to me. "Hmm. You were at his house... alone?"

"In a guest room," I said. "And probably not alone. His place has enough rooms to host every mage in the whole town. I had to wait to heal up before I left. Nothing happened with us."

Nothing aside from him seeing what a wreck I really was, under the surface. Getting close to him, letting the lines between professional and personal blur... even if I was okay with it, part of me belonged to Faerie. Last night had reminded me just how deep its influence ran.

I walked to the kitchen to retrieve a batch of Isabel's cinnamon-and-awesomeness flavoured cookies and watched her reset the spell circle, muttering under her breath.

"Crap," I said. "I forgot... is there a way to make me be able to understand the faeries' language?"

Isabel looked at me. "What?"

"They use these glyphs," I explained. "Not like those— different ones." I indicated the book she'd left open on the armchair, with symbols drawn onto its yellowing pages. "In their own language."

"No," said Isabel. "Not that I know of. Spells involving words usually end up backfiring."

"Not for faeries," I said. "They can put a tongue-tying spell on to stop you speaking, or curse you to speak in riddles forever. Don't worry, there's nothing like that at the Trials," I added. "They're just duels. No permanent injuries allowed."

"Unless a creepy bastard fey ambushes you again." Her knuckles whitened, hands curling into fists. "I think you should sneak in an explosive spell or three. Just in case."

"Spells get knocked loose too easily," I said. "I lose enough of them. And daggers." The only reason I still owned a substantial collection was because I got a significant discount from the mercenary guild's weapons trader. And that might not last, if Larsen decided my working for the Mage Lord was a threat to his own business. Irene was the one weapon that had lasted me longer than a few months, and leaving her behind tonight would make me feel like I walked into the arena stark naked.

Isabel sighed. "I'll think of something. What do you want your disguise to look like?"

"I called myself 'Shadow' when I signed up," I said. "Guess I should have considered possible costumes first."

"I can work with it." Her brows pinched together in the thoughtful expression she got when she had an idea. If she hadn't been born a witch, I could have seen her working in fashion design. She never judged me for walking around in torn-up jeans and bloodstained leather jackets, but jumped at the chance to test out her skills.

My phone buzzed from where I'd plugged it in to charge. A message from Vance. *What are you doing?*

We're setting up the disguise spell, I messaged back.

Come to the manor. I need to talk to you.

Well. That was instructive. "Vance asked me to come to the manor."

"Good." Isabel paced around the circle. "Ask him if he knows a better way to catch the person selling the drug than sending you to your death."

"Will do." I slipped the phone into my pocket. "I'll be back in a few hours."

Saying goodbye over my shoulder, I grabbed my jacket and sword and left the flat.

CHAPTER TEN

This time, nobody waited outside the manor. I hesitated, half expecting Ralph to appear and shove me away, but the gate opened immediately. Mage magic. Shaking my head, I walked into the front garden and tried to figure out what the hell I was going to say to Vance.

Like the gate, the door opened the instant I rang the doorbell. Vance waited in the hall, dressed surprisingly casually in a plain T-shirt and slacks. It was the first time I'd seen him in anything other than a fitted suit. It threw me off, considering he'd been in uptight Mage Lord mode ever since he'd reappeared after being gone for a week.

"What is it?" I asked.

"You disappeared this morning."

"So did you," I said. "Literally. What's the issue?"

"Nothing," he said.

"You called me here for nothing?" What game was he playing this time?

"I called you here because you mentioned needing assistance preparing for your match tonight. We can talk in my office." He led the way, pushing open the wooden door with one hand.

"Thought you said I could beat off a faerie dog in my sleep," I said. "Your style of fighting isn't anything like faeries', anyway."

"Oh, really?"

The sword appeared in his hand so fast I jumped back. "Faeries can manipulate matter and take you by surprise." He spun the blade in one hand in a way that would be considered a safety hazard if anyone else was doing it.

"Are you challenging me to a duel?" I asked. "Because this is a long-winded way to go about it."

"Have you ever duelled with a half-faerie?"

I considered this. "Depends what you mean by 'duel'. I have the same kind of magic as they do, and more skill with a blade than most."

"And modesty."

"Hark who's talking." Honestly, I wasn't confident at all. The encounter with the blasted half-Sidhe had shaken me up. Didn't change the fact that I'd be fighting an adversary with unknown skills tonight.

"From what you said yesterday, you needed my help."

"You're going to hold it over my head forever, aren't you?" I groaned. "Tell me if you're challenging me to a duel or just being a pain in the ass. I've a faerie underground to infiltrate."

His smirk disappeared. "Not without preparing."

"Are you being a dick to give me an incentive to kick your ass? Because it's working."

"No."

"So you're just being a dick in general. Good to know where we stand."

"You're putting yourself in danger," he said. "I'm considering ways to mitigate the risk."

"Bulletproof armour? A Taser?"

"Ivy." He stopped. "I think you should wear a protective mark. It'd allow me to watch you from a distance and sense if you were in danger."

I gaped a little. He wanted me to wear… a mark? Those spells weren't the sort the witches handed out to everyone. He'd have bought a specially commissioned batch right from the head of the coven.

"If I can't be there in person, it's the next best option. Please," he said. "I'd prefer it if you wore the mark. If you needed me, you'd just need to touch it. I doubt your phone would survive a magical battle."

"It's survived plenty." The words came out automatically. I didn't know which surprised me more—the 'please' or the admission that he wanted to make sure I wasn't hurt again. I mean, what the hell was I supposed to say? "Is this normal?"

"No."

That's helpful. "If the faeries saw it, they'd know I was an intruder."

"I can mark you somewhere they won't be able to see."

"Er…" Whoa. Get your mind out of the gutter, Ivy.

The hint of a smirk touched the edge of his mouth. "Unless you're planning on stripping off in front of the half-faeries, there's no shortage of hiding places."

"You."

"What?" His eyes glittered with amusement. "The idea of me seeing you naked bothers you."

"Yes." My face heated up. Goddammit, he must have seen part of me naked when he'd bound up my injuries. The top half, at least. Oh, boy. I kept my gaze on his face. "Because it's none of your business. You're my boss." I said this more for my own benefit than his. A reminder.

"Right." He moved in closer, and I had to remind myself

to keep breathing normally. "Whereabouts would you prefer me to mark you?"

I hesitated. "My left shoulder." My right was the scarred one, but he'd probably seen my scars already while I was unconscious. I sat down in the chair he indicated.

His hands brushed against my collarbone, easing my top down. Goose bumps rose where he touched, his hands cool against my burning skin. He was so damned tall, even more so now I was sitting close. Too close.

Focus. You'll be duelling him in a few minutes. Could I best him in a fight? Maybe. I'd beaten bigger, more deadly opponents, but not those with the ability to manipulate space and make the world itself do as they commanded. To have such a power must feel like being a god. I shouldn't be surprised Vance always acted above everyone else.

I definitely shouldn't enjoy the sensation of his hand resting against the small of my back as the other drew the symbol.

"There." His face was inches from mine, his breath warm on my cheek. My heart, traitorous thing, stuttered. "Doesn't hurt a bit."

"No." I breathed out. If I moved a few inches to the left, tilted my head just so, our lips would touch. Even at this distance, shivers danced through my nerves.

Instead, I stood so rapidly, he moved out the way. "Thanks." I tugged my top up, covering the mark.

"Don't you want to look at it? I can fetch a mirror."

"It doesn't matter—" A flash of light, and he held a mirror in his left hand. "Now you're just showing off."

"Do you want to look?" he repeated, holding the mirror up.

The imprint of his touch remained on my skin, tingling. The mark, however, was only a faint red circle. Barely noticeable. "Thanks."

"You're welcome." The mirror vanished with one flick of his hand. "If you really want my assistance, I have the afternoon free."

"Wait, you do?" I squinted at him. "No top-secret meetings?"

"Apparently, the East Midlands mages managed to come to an agreement in my absence. They've chosen a new leader."

"Good." I faltered on the verge of asking how he'd become leader. Then I remembered how he'd told me he killed the last one. Hmm. Now probably wasn't the time to start digging into painful subjects. I still hadn't told him about

Calder. "So… about this training. Where—"

"Outside," he said. "If we're duelling with magic, the house has too many defensive spells on it."

"Okay." A dozen possible questions came to mind, but I was here to figure out my magic, not indulge my dangerous curiosity about the Mage Lord.

He turned and led the way down the corridor into the conservatory. At the back, a glass door led into the wide garden. Carefully mowed lawns extended into the distance, but the section of grass he approached bore the tell-tale marks of magic. The grass had mostly been burned or trampled, and remnants of spells buzzed in the air.

"Did you want to train with weapons or hand-to-hand? Not all your opponents will use magic, will they?"

"No, but it's all *I* can use, aside from hand-to-hand," I said. "Faeries don't fight with metal weapons in general. Same goes for half-faeries. The two I've seen so far were a troll and a giant spider. It's magic I need to practise."

"Against what?" A blunted sword appeared in his hand. "Some of the half-faeries will probably use weapons."

"Yeah. I guess so." I left Irene at the arena's side. The odds of me actually landing a hit on Vance were pretty low, but I'd rather use a fake weapon.

I considered him, this time through the eyes of an aggressor. I figured I'd pick out his weaknesses, only I wasn't sure he had any. His body was corded muscle, strong, toned and flexible. He'd moved fast enough to astonish me even when I'd been under the influence of faerie magic and operating on superhuman speed. But I didn't think he was superhuman—aside from the shifter blood. No, he was just unfairly perfect.

Let's face it. I was screwed. What the hell had I got myself into?

"Okay. We'll start with weapons." I needed to get my focus back, and duelling Vance would snap my head back into fighting mode.

"And then you want me to use magic?" Vance looked at me expectantly.

"*Not* displacing," I said. "I imagine you'd find it funny to teleport me to random places, but even the faeries in this realm respect the laws of physics. Most of the time."

He chuckled. "That wasn't the plan, but you're giving me ideas. Remember what I said during the fight with the half-faerie spirits?"

I nodded. "You said I used magic defensively, not offensively. But I *did* use it offensively to bring down Velkas.

I need to work out how to do so without access to the faerie realm. And without killing anyone. It's not allowed."

Since I'd killed Velkas, I'd been aware it'd take a hell of a lot of work to reprogram my old belief that Avakis's magic was a dangerous, alien thing, not a part of me. Even more so now Calder had *humiliated* me. The shame rolling through me had nothing to do with Calder being related to the dickhead who'd ruined my life and everything to do with the fact that I'd been thoroughly schooled.

"Magical combat," Vance said. "I'll see what I can do. Combat seems to be the key to turning your instincts from defensive to offensive."

"Yeah, because I'm usually fearing for my life. Or pissed off. It feeds on emotion."

"Most magic does, to some extent," he said. "That's why mages need to stay in control."

"Really?" I'd thought his shifter powers were the reason he was so uptight. Then again, carrying around the amount of power he did must have some side effects.

Maybe training with him was a mistake, but if anyone could give as good as he got in magical combat, it was Vance Colton. Problem was, if I spent too much time here, I might start getting other ideas about how to spend time with him.

Dangerous, appealing ideas.

I turned to the Mage Lord. "All right. Let's dance, pretty boy."

"Pretty?" Vance sounded insulted. He wasn't a faerie, that was for damn sure. He was probably the same height as one of them, but even the fey warriors carried a certain delicateness to their fine-boned features. Nothing about Vance Colton could be called delicate, from his broad-shouldered frame to the carved lines of muscle visible through his skin-tight shirt.

He raised an eyebrow at me. "Ready? You look lost in thought. Worried?"

"Worried about facing a horde of angry half-faeries? Me?" I faked a smile, readying my sword. We circled one another, neither willing to make the first strike. I knew as soon as I did, he'd block me, so I watched for an opening. There wasn't one.

"This is a duel, not a dance-off," I muttered, feeling like an idiot.

"A dance-off," he repeated, amusement flickering in his expression.

"Gah. Just hit me already."

I was prepared for the hit, but I staggered back several

steps as I blocked him. He grinned at me. "Regretting this?"

"Not a chance in hell." I stood my ground, already sweating. I'd sworn not to use my magic to give myself enhanced speed, but it was tempting right now.

Damn, he was good, even without using his ability. He moved fast, fluidly, fighting equally well with both hands. I held him off only because my style tended to work best when I was on the defensive.

The blunted end of his sword touched my throat. "Do you surrender?"

"This is where I'd use magic and blast you."

"And if I blocked it?"

I barely held back a flinch. Blocked my magic. Or smothered it. Damn Calder.

"Most faeries can't fight with swords. The odds of me coming up against one who can are pretty low."

"That's not a good attitude to have," he said. "Odds in your favour or not, you'd be dead."

"All right, Sir." I rolled my eyes.

"Just being honest."

I know, I thought, angry with myself for giving ground.

"Ivy? Want to try again?"

Damn him. "Sure."

I lost again because I was so rattled. And again. Finally, I threw the practise sword aside. "Hit me with magic."

"What? You're giving up?"

Magic rose, blue smoke wrapping around my arms. I'd never used it to attack anyone other than a faerie—let alone someone who wouldn't see my attack coming.

Aha. Call me petty, but I wanted to try this. "Hit me with magic. I meant it. Go on."

He searched my face, then tossed his own sword to the side. Unlike mine, it vanished before it hit the ground. "If you insist."

Solid air smacked into me, sending me flying, the magic slipping from my grasp. I skidded on the grass, struggling to breathe. The atmosphere tightened, like a storm was about to break over my head. Sucking in air, I pulled my tendrils of magic close to me again and focused on just how pissed off I was.

This time when he hit me, it bounced off the shield. *Oh, hell, yeah.* Looked like faerie and mage magic could face up to one another. Encouraged, I used the few seconds I'd won to gather more magic into my hands. The power came from *me,* and I didn't need to be in Faerie to use it.

Another hit from Vance knocked me back a few steps.

And again. My shield worked okay, but the magic refused to solidify for long enough for me to turn it into anything resembling a weapon. Dammit. I'd have to use my enhanced instincts until my magic decided to cooperate.

"Change of plans," I said. "Let's make this a free-for-all. Hand-to-hand, weapons, whichever."

"That's a mistake."

I waved a hand. "This bloody magic's refusing to turn into a weapon. I can't fight you with a shield."

"Ivy, I know you can do better than this. I've seen you."

"I'm not having a great day. Something about life-or-death stakes kills the mood."

"Then don't think about it."

I snorted. "Don't think about the life sentence hanging over your head. Sure. I can do that."

"Don't you remember what I told you? Offensive magic is usually the reflection of the defensive mode of a spell. I can't see your magic, but I've seen it before. I know."

I dropped my hands to my sides. "Yeah. Well, there was a shitload of death energy back when the veil was opening. All the half-faeries were crazily overpowered. It's not normally like that in this realm."

"You don't need to be overpowered. You just need to find

an opening."

"Like I said, I'm better at hand-to-hand combat." Or using a sword, but I wouldn't have one in the arena.

"Then I'll allow both."

Like you make the rules. I held my tongue. He didn't have to stand here taking crap from me. He'd walked away from a precarious situation with the other mages to save my life yesterday.

The warmth conjured by the realisation did emphatically *not* fuel my magic, so I turned my thoughts back to last night instead. Maybe fear did work as a tool after all. I could defend myself against hellhounds' magic, which was effectively a blast of emotion. What Calder had done wasn't all that different. I'd let myself get taken off guard, but I wouldn't let it happen again.

Vance nodded, apparently reading more in my expression than I'd intended to give away. Then the air shifted again. I stood my ground, dug my heels in, and let the magic flow to my hands. Without my weapons, there was no barrier between me and the blue light igniting around me. We were one.

I leaped forward, rolling to my front and grabbing the practise sword in the process. As I ran at Vance, my barrier smacked into the current of air stirring around him. So he was using a defensive magical shield, too. I let my frustration and anger simmer, and the blue light grew brighter, the shield becoming more distinct. I watched for an opening, certain he couldn't use his power indefinitely. The shimmering air in front of me seemed to be running on autopilot, which gave me an idea.

He was shielding, which meant if I got him to use his magic to attack me, he'd be wide open to a frontal assault. I continued to circle him, concentrating on the blue shield in front of me. *Come back,* I told it, and at the slightest gesture, the smoke crept up my hands, the shield's glimmer fading slightly.

Vance's eyes narrowed, telling me he'd been watching for exactly this kind of opportunity. He wanted me to attack him directly so my shield would drop and he'd be able to knock me down. Because he couldn't *see* my magic, he had to guess what I was doing. I must have given it away with my body language. I couldn't be sure the same would work for him, but one of us had to break first.

I put myself into the position I'd been in when I'd taken down Velkas. I'd wielded magic like a Winter Sidhe. Keeping both hands on the practise sword, I met his gaze, refusing to give anything away. At the same time, I concentrated on my simmering anger until my hands blazed, and the shield was barely existent anymore. If he attacked me now, no magic would defend me.

That wasn't my plan.

My magic crackled loose and slammed into his shield. As he raised a hand to retaliate, turning the displaced air into a weapon, I used my enhanced instincts to leap high—higher than he'd aimed the attack. *I knew it.* He could only displace one thing at a time. Before he could block me with another shield, I flipped and landed in front of him, pointing the sword at his neck. "Game over."

He stared. Then his mouth twisted in a smirk. "You said you wouldn't carry your sword."

"I'd punch you in the throat, then." I grinned back. "Or kick you in the crotch. Half-faeries have the same sensitive areas we do."

"I thought you weren't relying on the sword." He grabbed it from my hand.

"Hey!" I protested. "You can't steal away my victory—"

"Defend yourself with magic."

Air slammed into me, sending me head over heels. I yelped, landing on my back on the lawn, and Vance tackled me, pinning my legs down. "You didn't even try."

"You didn't give me a chance to." I tried feebly to get up, but he held me down with no apparent effort. He wasn't even using magic, dammit. Instead, I was very, very aware of his body pressing into mine, sending heat rushing to places I didn't need to be thinking about during a fight. Before I could shove him off me, his finger lightly brushed a strand of hair out of my face, lingering on the curve of my neck.

"Tell me what you're thinking."

I breathed in, unintentionally inhaling his thick, masculine scent, tinged with sweat and muskiness. His eyes darkened, a heated spark brewing within.

"I'm thinking you're stopping me from standing up."

"Something's bothering you," he said.

Of course. He wasn't trying to seduce me, only get information out of me. And it was working, dammit. I wanted to spill all my secrets.

"I'll tell you, if I survive tonight." I wasn't sure if I meant *I'll tell you about Calder,* or something else entirely. Like *I'm attracted to you. And that's a bad idea. The worst idea.*

He released me and stood up. "Tell me about the other contestants. Give me a better idea of what technique to use."

I shrugged. "An evil giant spider with a poisonous sting.

And faerie warriors. Summer and Winter ones. Unless we kidnap someone from half-blood territory, we won't be able to do an exact impression."

"I'm good at improvising," he said. "Let's begin."

CHAPTER ELEVEN

"How was it?" Isabel asked.

I closed the flat door behind me. "He's thorough, I'll give him that." I picked yet another leaf out of my hair. When I'd told him Summer faeries attacked using forces of nature, he'd thrown me into a hedge.

"Thorough, huh." She arched an eyebrow, and I threw a leaf at her.

"Get your mind out of the gutter." I tossed my coat aside and kicked off my shoes.

Admittedly, Vance was a good teacher. I could tell why he was in charge of the other mages' training in magic. It came as no surprise to learn he'd had tutors in swordplay all his life, too. Magic or not, skill with a weapon put you a cut above the rest—literally. So I didn't feel as bad about him beating me every round. Much. My competitive nature protested, but I hadn't exactly learned in an orthodox way. A fellow prisoner in Faerie had taught me how to kill, and by the time I'd come back into this realm and taken up a freelance position at Larsen's place, my instincts were stuck on "stab it until it stops moving".

Not so good when I actually had to leave my opponent alive tonight.

At eight, I stepped into Isabel's spell circle again and she set up the new disguise spell. This time, she held the mirror up so I could see my transformation. Shifting my feet from the circle's edge, I watched as a shimmering curtain dropped over me, distorting my reflection. Isabel muttered words in the ancient language while sprinkling a handful of a glittery dust around the circle's perimeter. Shivers ran down my arms, along with a sensation like water trickling down my spine. My reflection blurred around the edges, darkening until a weird shroud-like garment covered most of my body. My face beneath the hood came into focus. Blue, glittering eyes stared back.

This time, the person in the mirror was a total stranger. While the first illusion had been a Summer faerie version of Ivy Lane, the woman I'd turned into was sharp-featured and feral-looking, like a wildcat given human form. I held no weapons, but winter magic practically pulsed from my skin. The blue-green glow from before had sharpened to icy blue like a frozen lake, the same colour as my eyes.

I pushed the hood down and ran my fingers up the ears pointing between fine strands of black hair.

"Damn," I said. My voice came out soft, quietly cold, like the tinkle of fingertips on a piano. It creeped *me* out. "You outdid yourself this time, Isabel."

Isabel backed away from the circle. "Holy shit." She put down the glass container she'd been holding. "Now I get it. They're scary as hell. Are you sure you want to fight—*that?*" She pointed at the reflection in the mirror rather than at me, which I kind of appreciated.

"Don't worry," I said. "The half-faeries don't all look like this. I'm *supposed* to be freaky and intimidating. You really delivered on it." I climbed out of the circle. "I owe you for this. Big time."

"Save it for when you get back." Her hands twisted nervously. "Please, *please* be careful. I don't like that you have to leave your weapons behind."

"They'll detect the iron," I said. "Even last time, if anyone had touched me, they'd have known about Irene. Maybe that's how the half-Sidhe saw through the illusion."

I didn't say his name. Didn't dare think he might show up tonight. If he'd returned to the alleyway and found me gone, would he assume I'd survived somehow? A depressing number of deaths went unreported here in the suburbs. Especially humans. Non-supernaturals caught in a world they no longer fitted into.

And I was about to walk into its darkest underbelly. Again.

The doorbell rang. My nerves spiked, and I found myself shivering. *Show time.*

Vance's jaw hit the floor when I walked out.

"Don't say a word," I said.

He blinked a couple of times, shock evident on his features. "How's the mark?"

"Still there." I tapped my shoulder. It was weird touching a body that didn't seem to be there. "Where will you be?"

"Nearby. The mark will activate when you touch the exact centre, three times."

"Got it." I drew in a breath. *I can do this.* "We should go."

He nodded, resting his hand on my arm. I'd never seen him this hesitant around me. Faeries didn't scare him in the slightest.

"Are you ready?" he asked. I knew he didn't mean *are you ready to leave,* but *are you ready to fight them?* Our bout earlier had had mixed results, and I wasn't entirely sure I could handle my magic well enough to take on someone who'd used it all their life.

"I can fight," I said. "I'm more worried about being found out. It's not like I have an encyclopaedia of Faerie. If I get put on the spot and say the wrong thing…"

"You're masquerading as a shadow. Nobody will speak to you. They'll be too intimidated."

"They're half-faeries," I said. "Trust me, I'm like a fluffy kitten in comparison to some of the faerie-kind."

He half-smiled, shaking his head. "I said you were over-thinking it."

"Save the *I-told-you-so's* for after."

His hand tightened on my arm, and the hallway was replaced by a street. I inhaled the cool night air. We'd landed two streets down from the venue. I expected Vance to let go of my arm and disappear.

I didn't expect him to wrap his other arm around me, pulling me against his chest.

I froze. How the hell was I supposed to respond? Not by kissing him again. He'd nodded when I'd said we were employer and employee, but this position was anything but professional. Not least because I didn't even *look* like me.

He released me. "Good luck, Ivy."

I barely had time to blink before he vanished.

Whoa.

I half-ran to the alley, not stopping when I passed by the part I'd nearly died in. This section of town was abandoned, but someone had cleaned up the blood from last night. I averted my eyes and speed-walked to the back entrance. *I can do this.* Acting tough was part of my game. Nobody in here would recognise me in a million years. Maybe not even Calder. I *hoped* not.

Back into the dark. I moved swiftly, following the trail of voices into the auditorium. This time, it was already set up with the seats in place around the room's edges. I searched out the other contestants, my heartbeat kicking up. No hiding this time. I had to stand out in the open.

Seeing the hobgoblin, I stalked over to him, head held high. My shadowy cloak billowed around me, and more than a few heads turned in my direction.

"Shadow," said the hobgoblin. "You're intending to show your face this time?"

"Only if I lose," I said, in my new strange, cold voice. "And I don't intend to."

I eyed the other contestants, sizing them up. Aside from the spider and a short figure who looked like he might be part gnome, all the others were human-sized. But they varied from a tall woman in armour to a short redheaded guy who hardly looked older than fourteen, bouncing on his heels like he was eager for the Trials to start.

As the noise levels quietened, the hobgoblin directed everyone's attention to the centre of the arena, where glyphs had appeared in the air. This time, I knew what was coming.

"The first match of the night," the hobgoblin began, "pits Shark against Boulder."

A tall, grinning male half-faerie skipped into the arena, followed by a bigger, slower one. Half-ogre, I guessed, judging by his green, mottled skin.

"The second match," said the hobgoblin, "pits Shadow against Razor."

Razor, to my surprise, was a female Winter half-faerie wearing a mask over the lower half of her face. Her long, curly black hair was tied up and tossed over her shoulder, and she wore casual clothes rather than armour. I'd have to wait to see what tricks she had up her sleeve.

Once the other matches were announced, the arena cleared to make room for the first bout. Shark didn't appear intimidated by his half-ogre opponent, and circled him, grinning. Then he struck.

I winced inwardly as Shark ran headlong into Boulder's

fist, falling flat on his back. The half-ogre roared and pounced, pinning him flat and pounding his giant fists into the other half-faerie's face. Blood and spittle flew as Shark spat out broken teeth.

So much for an intimidating name choice.

Shark's head snapped back as Boulder punched him in the jaw. I winced a little. A normal human might have easily died. Half-faeries, however, were made of stronger stuff than mortals. Shaking his head, Shark spat out more teeth and attempted to roll to the side and throw the half-ogre off. He might as well have tried to move concrete with his fingers.

Boulder grabbed him by the throat and lifted him into the air, throwing him bodily across the arena. Ouch. The smaller half-faerie hit the dirt again, and cries of delight followed. The crowd wanted blood.

And they got some. When Shark pushed to his feet, Boulder punched him in the face again, which now resembled a battered piece of meat. His nose looked broken, and blood poured from his mouth. But he was still inexplicably grinning.

Then a pair of new teeth grew, right before my eyes, punching through his lower lip. A second set shot upwards, his mouth stretching unnaturally sideways. A ripple of surprise spread through the crowd.

Boulder stared at him, fists at his sides. Shark caught him totally off guard when he jumped, delivering a vicious kick to the knee that sent the half-ogre down. The still-grinning Shark caught Boulder's next punch and sank his teeth into the other faerie's hand... right through to the bone.

Boulder howled with pain. Shark's teeth bit deeper until blood bubbled up, and the half-ogre's wails reached a high pitch. He flailed his good hand, but couldn't land a hit. Crimson drops spattered the ground.

Shark let go, withdrawing his bloodstained teeth, and went for the neck.

Boulder froze, the other faerie clinging to his shoulders, teeth inches away from severing a vital artery.

I didn't hear his surrender, because the crowd roared, blasting my eardrums. They'd come for a show and got one, all right. Grinning a red-stained smile, Shark skipped away. If this hadn't been a contest, I had no doubt he'd have ripped out the half-ogre's throat.

The hobgoblin shouted over the noise, his voice amplified: "The second match will begin in a moment. Introducing Shadow and Razor."

Oh, boy. I'd witnessed the Trials in their brutal reality. But it was too late to turn back. I clenched my fists at my sides and walked into the arena.

Cheers and shouts trailed after me. I paid the audience no attention, too busy trying to figure out my opponent. Razor… why the name? She might not look impressive, but I'd be a fool to assume she didn't have a hidden plan.

So did I. Keeping my head high, I assessed her, planning my move. With magic-enhanced speed, I'd probably be able to take her down. She didn't carry any weapons. Her leather jacket would provide some cushioning if I knocked her to the ground, but not enough.

Magic thrummed through the air, reacting to my nerves. Here, surrounded by magic and shadows, I could almost believe I was *there* again. Rather than letting it paralyse me, I imagined the arena to be like a shadowy area of the Grey Vale. The clearing where I'd killed Velkas. The magic seemed to like that, growing brighter, flaring from my hands like blue fire, sliding along my body.

Razor stalked towards me, wielding magic of her own. Snowflakes began to fall over her head, and she hurled a handful of Winter magic at me. Icy shards split the air, and I rolled to the side to avoid them. My own magic remained in its unwieldy form, but I had no time to concentrate. She'd left her right side open, and I aimed a kick at her ribs.

Wintry air slammed into me, forcing me to flip and land on my feet. I pulled my own magic into a rippling shield and then directed it outward, but I hadn't drawn enough power in to do more than make her step back. I advanced on her, my feet moving with the swift speed the magic gave me. With one swipe, I swept her legs out from underneath her.

Razor's hands hit the ground to break her fall and a fountain of what looked like water poured out, crossing the floor. *Oh, shit.* I was forced to jump to avoid it, but the flood didn't stop at me. The icy water spread to cover the whole area we stood in, solidifying into ice.

Damn. I walked carefully, the ground slippery underfoot, cursing inwardly. I didn't dare do any fancy tricks with the floor like this. Irritation, anger, and fear churned inside me, and my magic appeared equally unruly.

Razor's feet left the ground and she leaped at me. I raised the magic in a clumsy shield and knocked her aside. Only then did I see the sharp edges to her boots. *Dammit.* Of course she wouldn't have given herself a disadvantage with the slippery floor.

I hovered on the balls of my feet and sent out a blast of energy she easily dodged. Hand to hand would be trickier with the floor this slippery, but not impossible.

Throwing another handful of magic, I let her dodge, anticipated her landing and jumped. I crashed into her, knocking us both off our feet. She wriggled beneath me, the ice helping her to roll free. Before she could pin me, I punched the joint of her arm hard enough to break it. She snarled, kicking out, and I saw the double function of those razor shoes. Damn.

She managed to break free of my hold and launched to her feet, aiming a kick at my knee. I dodged, skidding out of range. The half-faerie raised both hands and called up a torrent of magic. It glanced off my shield, and she snarled. I stepped sideways, my feet skidding again. When she launched another magical assault, I ran forward, using the momentum of the slippery ice to leap into the air, avoiding her attack. My fist struck her cheekbone, and I jabbed her in the ribs with another strike.

Razor went down, feet slipping from underneath her. The collapse took me by surprise, and I didn't react fast enough to stop her spiked foot coming up and hitting my arm. I felt the material of my jacket tear underneath the illusion and yanked my hand away.

Not fast enough. She moved sideways, sending me crashing onto my back, and her spiked foot came at my face.

With no time to move my head, I raised my hand. Pain exploded in my arm, the spike tearing through the flesh of my wrist. Swearing, I rolled aside, barely dodging another stab, and retaliated by kicking at her knee. My wrist burned with pain.

Pain. Wait. Avakis's magic fed on pain—I should get a boost. My shield brightened, blocking another magical assault. Her mask had torn free, and Razor bared her teeth at me, kicking viciously. The pain made me clumsier, too slow to dodge, and the sharp edge of her shoe ripped open the knee of my jeans. I felt warm blood trickle down my shin underneath the illusion.

I need to finish this fast.

Drawing on the pain, the magic's glow burned brighter, turning into a blue stream of energy. Pain… not just my pain. Wait. I could draw on the others' too. Boulder lay in a miserable heap at the arena's side, while Shark's mouth dripped blood. Razor herself moved awkwardly, like I'd cracked a rib. Their pain made my magic burn brighter, and this time, my attack actually knocked her flat onto her back. I approached, seeing my reflection in her eyes. A faerie warrior edged in blue light.

The crowd's whispers filtered through, especially the

other contestants. They knew something was screwy.

If I kept drawing on their pain like this, if Calder was here… he'd immediately know who I was. As far as I knew, nobody else had the same ability. I'd been an idiot not to realise sooner.

I continued to let the power flow through me, but directed it into forming a shield instead. Rather than hitting her with magic, I tackled her around the waist, knocking her flat. Her nose broke beneath my knuckles. Blood spurted between my fingers, and she screamed.

I twisted her arm behind her back, hard, and used my other arm to elbow her in the ribs. She broke free of my hold, blood dripping down her face, and tried to kick me again. Sharp pain ran down my leg, but I'd already kicked her viciously in the shin. She was forced to put weight on her uninjured leg, and her moment's hesitation gave me the chance to get in close and bring my knee up to strike her chin—hard enough for her teeth to bite into her lower lip. She fell, not quite unconscious, but halfway there. Blood dripped from her open mouth. Her head dropped to the side.

"Razor surrenders," said the hobgoblin.

"Damn right she does," I muttered. Ouch.

Not exactly how I planned to win, but I'd survived. I

limped to the arena's side, blood trickling down both my legs. I sat down on the nearest step, and a fresh bolt of pain lanced through both knees. My wrist continued to sting, too. I'd got lucky this time. Two guards carried the half-unconscious Razor to join the other injured contestants.

The next match pitted Crawler against the redheaded teenage half-faerie. The match was over in less than five minutes. Crawler's stinger went into the boy's foot, and he fell flat, writhing in pain. The hobgoblin's assistants carried him from the arena, where someone gave him an antidote. I guess that answered the question of whether the half-troll Crawler had stabbed last night had survived to tell the tale. If people died every night at the Trials, there' be nobody left to compete. From the whispered conversations I'd overheard, a fair number of the candidates had entered previous rounds, too.

Once he'd stopped foaming at the mouth, the teenage half-faerie ran from the arena, towards the exit.

A weird shivering sensation went through my body. Icy tingles ran up my arms—not from the cold. From a spell. Glancing over my shoulder, I saw the path to the exit was clear.

If I stayed for the final match, I'd get caught in the crush when everyone left at the end. I'd told Vance I'd get out as soon as possible. As no one was looking at me, this was my chance to slip away.

I crept along the front row—well, it did fit with my shadowy persona—and disappeared into the gap between the two ends of the seating area. Voices ahead froze my steps. I couldn't pretend to be part of the shadows this time, so I did my best to rein in the magic swirling around me. Reacting to something.

Was *he* here?

If he was, I needed to get out. Now. I took a few more steps, and spotted the two figures standing in the shadows. One was the teenage half-faerie who'd just lost the match. The second was a taller Summer half-faerie, judging by the greenish glow of magic around his hands.

"I'm sorry," gasped the boy. "I didn't know—"

"You saw Crawler fight yesterday, you pathetic excuse for a spy." The half-faerie slapped him. "You were supposed to win, you incompetent little whelp. What in the name of the Sidhe did you do with the charms?"

Damn. He'd cheated?

The boy yelped and stumbled over his own feet. "I'll try again next week."

"This is the last chance," hissed the other half-faerie. "The very last. Didn't you hear? You've lost your shot. We won't get glory *or* immortality."

I hung back, heart thudding against my ribcage. Immortality.

The half-faerie kicked the smaller guy again, then blasted him with a handful of Summer magic. He headed for the exit on light, quick feet.

I gave him a head start, then grabbed the teenage boy by the scruff of his neck and dragged him after me. I was improvising, of course, but I'd be a fool not to take the chance to question him.

My hand slapped over his mouth as he tried to scream. "Quiet," I hissed, stopping halfway down the corridor, just beside the exit. "Pipe the hell down if you don't want worse than a poisonous spike in your foot."

He stared at me with bulging eyes, and I slowly lifted my hand. "What the hell was that about?"

"I—I don't know what you mean."

"Someone put you up to enter the Trials, right?" I said. "What did that guy mean by immortality?"

"Nothing!" he squeaked.

"I'm interested." My heart raced, my pulse pounding, but

173

I looked for all the world like one of the half-faeries. He'd never guess my real motive. "Tell me, or everyone will know you cheated."

His pale face and watery eyes floated before me as my magic flared up, bright and cold. He leaned away. "Meet me after the matches tomorrow and I'll show you. I promise."

I released him. "If you're lying, I'll know." My menacing faerie voice rang in my ears as he pelted for the exit.

I followed more slowly, hoping I hadn't just signed my own death sentence.

CHAPTER TWELVE

I grimaced as Vance pressed a salve to my injured wrist.

"You were lucky."

I grunted. "Tell me about it."

I'd brought him up to speed on everything apart from the encounter in the corridor. Vance had transported us both to his office in the manor once I'd found him at the road where we'd agreed to meet. With the illusion gone, none of the half-faeries leaving the underground would have guessed my identity, even with the injuries. My knees were a bloody mess and I'd have to pretend the shredded holes in my jeans were a fashion statement, but it could be worse. Shark could have bitten through my hand, for example.

"It sounds like most are either shapeshifters or hiding something." Vance let go of my wrist. I flexed it, standing up from the office chair. Lamplight spilled onto the bookcases and desk, casting the corners in shadow.

"Yeah, but they're faeries. It's par for the course." I turned to him, glad not to be wearing a faerie's stupid face anymore. "Speaking of hiding things, I kinda scared one of the contestants into admitting he knew about the immortality drug."

Vance's gaze sharpened. "Tell me."

I quickly explained the encounter. "I'll have to sneak out early tomorrow again. It's not ideal, I know. Anyone might catch me. Still, it's an opportunity to get right to the heart of this."

Or end up face to face with Calder again.

I shivered. Damn half-faerie. I'd imagined blasting Razor aside with magic, but even in the arena, it was a pale shadow of what it might be in Faerie. Hell, even the other half-faeries' abilities were. Except for Calder. It bugged the hell out of me that I couldn't figure out what made him so powerful. Not just being the son of a Sidhe lord, surely.

"You can't go alone."

"I don't have much of a choice," I said. "Besides, if I can find a way to expose the illegal drug sellers, they might have to shut down the contest. I wouldn't have to participate in the rest of the Trials."

Vance studied me. "I'd tell you it's risky, but you know that already."

I nodded, kind of surprised how things had shifted so quickly. When we'd first met, he'd been incapable of not taking control, and the idea of me running around investigating behind his back grated on his nerves. Judging by his tone, he still wasn't fond of the idea.

"I really need to learn more about my magic," I said. "It's not traditionally Winter. I can't throw a blizzard or freeze the floor. I've heard some Winter Sidhe can freeze the air in a person's lungs and leave them to choke, or turn them into solid ice." I paused, thinking about what I'd done so far. Summon up a shield: check. Blast people with energy like I'd done to Velkas: check. Throw a bunch of fancy blue light around: yeah, but not particularly useful.

"You can fight with it," he said. "It's an elemental power, isn't it? Maybe you can train with Wanda. She's a frost mage."

I blinked. "I guess... but she doesn't know I have faerie magic."

He gave me a look I couldn't read. "The mages suspect your magic is unusual. They know you helped to close the veil, and it's a matter of time before someone asks you how you did it. I thought I'd let you come up with your own cover story."

I opened my mouth and closed it. *Damn.* I might have

eased up on the *don't tell anyone about Faerie and Avakis* issue, but the idea of word spreading like wildfire across the district's mages didn't appeal. After all, word might reach Calder. He might find out I was alive.

"If you continue to work with me, somebody is bound to ask you eventually," Vance said. "I wanted to warn you in advance. A few people asked questions at the summit."

"Damn," I muttered. "All right. We're going with what I first told you—I have faerie ancestors somewhere. Might be true, for all I know. I've never seen my family tree."

He gave a short nod, his expression pensive. Feeling sorry for me? The aching gap my parents' deaths had left was one problem amongst a thousand I'd had to deal with when I'd walked back from Faerie into a world changed beyond recognition. I thought about them sometimes, of course, but they were a part of the old world. My old life, before Faerie.

"Anyway," I said, suddenly aware of the short distance between us, and the tingling sensation his hands left where they'd touched the skin of my healed wrist. "I'll train with Wanda if she's okay with it."

Wanda herself once told me Vance had a protective streak, and wanted to look out for all of his mages. Guilt over what I'd withheld from him writhed inside me. I dug in my pocket for my phone. "I'll let Isabel know I'm okay."

"I can drop you off on your doorstep," he said. "Just in case." His eyes looked darker in the dim light, and a magnetic pull urged me to move closer to him.

You're deceiving him. He's your boss. A hundred excuses rocketed around my head, fading to a dull buzz with every step. A whisper of coldness brushed against the back of my neck like a caress. When he took my arm and pulled me closer, the tension thickened until I could hardly breathe.

I tried to say, *I thought you said our relationship was a professional one,* but the words disappeared on the way to my mouth. Vance leaned in, lips hovering above mine.

Giving in, I arched into him, daring him to cover the last inch between us. His tongue teased me, tracing my mouth, and then slipped inside. I responded in kind, nipping at his lower lip. A growl built low in his throat, and the breeze stirring in the air lifted the hair from my head. His cool, appealing scent slid over my bones, sending a frisson of heat through my body.

A rustle of wind later and we stood on my doorstep. For a moment, I waited, pressed against his warm, solid body. Safe, for now. God, I didn't want to move.

"You should get inside," he murmured, his cheek

brushing against mine.

"Yeah. I should."

Erwin the piskie flew past, shrieking, and I jumped out of my trance. Flushed and breathless, I threw a 'goodbye' over my shoulder and fled into the building. Panting, I shoved my key into the lock, but my hands were shaking too much to aim. The door opened, and Isabel jumped, concern flitting across her face.

"How'd it go?"

"Great." In response to her raised eyebrow, I added, "As good as it could possibly go, considering. I'm fine. Several half-faeries... aren't."

Her gaze moved to my bloody knees. "Injuries?"

"Vance took care of them." I followed her into the flat.

"Took care of you." She spun to face me. "I knew you looked weird. You're blushing."

"I'm not," I said. *Am I?*

"You look like someone just... no way, he kissed you, didn't he?"

My mouth parted. "Can we deal with this in the morning? I'm really tired."

"Nice try." She grinned at me. "I figured it was only a matter of time."

"Do I need to run through the reasons why this is a bad idea?" I checked Irene was where I'd left her, out of habit. "I'm fighting for my life to win a chance to confront somebody who nearly killed me once already."

"All the better reason to make the most of the good moments."

Yeah. Normally, I hoarded those moments, but the tumult of emotion roiling through me when I thought about Vance tired me out more than the idea of another day of training tomorrow. There was a reason I didn't get emotionally involved with anyone. Trust issues aside—not to mention the faeries' never-ending attempts to ruin my day—I didn't have room on my schedule for mind games. Though he might have justified his behaviour, Vance and I were on different wavelengths.

If it's just a short time... I shook off the thought. I couldn't afford to be distracted. With Vance's help or not, if I didn't figure my magic out, there was no way I'd survive another confrontation with Calder.

***

I hit the dirt. Again.

Vance shook his head at me. "You didn't even try this time."

"I tried to block you with a shield," I said. "Didn't work."

"Evidently." He stood apart from me on the grass outside the manor, where we'd been for the best part of the past hour. Apparently, he'd put Drake on the front desk as his replacement to deal with clients while he worked with me.

Tension simmered, but more of the *oh shit, I have to fight another magical battle against a half-faerie tonight* variety. That was enough to deal with without considering what had happened between us last night. I wrote it off as a moment of weakness after surviving the first match, and to my surprise, Vance hadn't mentioned it since I'd arrived. In today's training session, I'd managed to form the magic into an unwieldy weapon, but didn't leave so much as a scratch on Vance. He'd swatted me aside like a fly. Several times. I could hit him in hand-to-hand combat or swordplay—occasionally—but magic remained elusively out of my grasp.

Trickery was my only option left. It might get me through the Trials, but wouldn't help me if Calder showed up again.

"Okay," I said, back on my feet. "Hit me again."

This time, I managed to hold my shield in place when he sent a torrent of displaced air slamming into me. I could have let the magic sharpen my instincts and speed, but didn't. Calder had dampened my magic when we'd fought, and if we battled again, I needed to be ready to fight someone with supernatural instincts while operating on normal human speed.

Needless to say, it wasn't going well.

For one thing, Vance only needed to snap his fingers and the air would knock my feet out from underneath me. I'd told him to stop it with the cheap tricks, but he seemed to have an infinite supply.

Air smacked into the back of my head and knocked me onto my front. I landed on my elbows in the mud, wincing.

"You left the back of your shield open."

"Damn you." I lifted my head and pushed to my feet.

"Faeries aren't past using trickery," he said. "You know that."

"I'm not an idiot." I brushed grass from my jeans with my palms.

"I'm aware, but faeries won't wait for you to prepare a plan before they hit you."

I narrowed my eyes at him. "Again."

This time, I made sure to yank my shield into place, covering every inch of me. The air rippled and I jumped, rolling to the side. I circled him as he threw attack after attack at me, every dodge bringing me closer to breaking through his defences. Without my magic enhanced instincts, I moved slower and tired faster, but inch by inch, I gained on him. When he sent a particularly strong blast of magic at me, I knew he'd need a few seconds to recharge. I launched into a forward roll, now close enough to strike at him.

Unsurprisingly, he blocked my punch with his forearm. I tried another with my free hand, the magical shield shimmering around me. He watched me, figuring out I didn't intend to use my enhanced speed, and I could see him ticking it over in his mind.

His slight hesitation was all I needed. I'd figured out his fighting style—knock the enemy down before they could slip through his defences. I'd done exactly that, and he usually didn't expect an adversary to get within close range. Considering he could skewer people on the opposite side of a room, this came as no surprise.

With magic useless against my shield, he was too focused on blocking my hits to get in a strike of his own. A gleam entered his eye. He was *enjoying* this, damn him. It had probably been a while since he'd met his match.

The problem was, I'd tired myself out spending so long breaking through his defences, and without the magical boost, my stamina was fading fast. Eventually, Vance swept my legs out from underneath me. I rolled to my feet before he could pin me and smacked into a wall of solid air, falling flat on my back. I lay there, the breath knocked out of me.

"I thought you'd stopped using magic," I managed to gasp out.

"I didn't want you to tire yourself out," he said.

I feebly lifted my head. "I'm fine."

"Hmm. I've never seen you fight like that."

I half-sat up and shrugged, my shoulder protesting at the movement. "I don't want to rely on magic."

His brow furrowed. "I thought you wanted to understand it."

"I do." I got to my feet and scrambled for my excuses list. "But in the arena yesterday, I realised my magic isn't like other Winter faeries'. It's from a Sidhe lord. If anyone there worked it out, I'd have to answer a bunch of questions."

He arched an eyebrow. "I thought you didn't intend to speak to anyone. You're not obliged to answer questions. Besides, it's hardly unheard of for Sidhe lords to abandon their offspring in this realm."

I froze. Abandon their offspring... had Avakis *left* Calder here? I hadn't asked. Obviously.

Was Calder a changeling?

Vance watched me curiously. I stammered, "I guess not, but... Avakis. If any of them know who he is, they might recognise me using his magic."

I didn't blame Vance for giving me an incredulous look. "I doubt it," he said. "Your own doubt isn't helping matters. The magic is yours: own it." He glanced at the manor. "I should probably check on Drake and my clients. I'll send Wanda your way, if you'd still like to train with her."

I nodded, and he walked away. Sitting on the grass, I rested my elbows on my knees and brought my head into my hands. Dammit. I'd been as subtle as an ogre rampaging through a glass door. Was I really stupid enough to think I could fool the Mage Lord?

I considered his words instead. *Your magic is yours: own it.* Exactly what I'd done when I'd faced down Velkas. It wasn't just the death energy, the echo of the pain Avakis's captives had left behind. The strength, in the end, had ultimately come from within me.

"Hey." Wanda waved at me, walking down from the house. She wore workout clothes rather than her usual secretary getup, her long black hair tied back. We were around the same height, but she was rail-thin, while I had the kind of muscles you got when you spent ten years swinging a heavy sword around.

Behind her walked Drake, Vance's second-in-command. The red-headed mage grinned at me, a flame dancing between his palms. "I'm here to watch the show, not participate, don't worry."

I returned his smile to hide my nerves. At this rate, everyone who came to the manor would know my magic wasn't normal for a witch.

"Vance mentioned you wanted to duel with magic," said Wanda.

I gave a sheepish shrug. "Yeah... long story short, my magic's not exactly conventional. It's similar to frost magic, so he thought we'd be a good match."

"No problem."

We stood apart and I let her make the first attack. Wanda raised a hand and snowflakes filled the air, pelting at my face. I quickly flung up my shield and they glanced off. This time, I let the magic rush over my skin, cool and familiar. *Of course it's familiar. It's* mine.

The magic seemed to hum in response, the shield becoming more solid. Now I needed to turn it from defensive to offensive... somewhat difficult while trying to stop a snowstorm from beating at my head. Wanda threw twin streams of snowflakes at me and I had to raise both hands to block them. I paced around her on quick feet, using the magic-enhanced speed to my advantage. To attack her, I needed to let my shield drop.

I jumped, reeling in the shield at the same time so her attack missed. Landing on both feet, I pulled the shield closer to me and willed it to dissolve into streams of energy. Like in the Grey Vale—and on half-blood territory, too.

An attack shot from both of my palms. Wanda wasn't quite fast enough to turn and block it and the energy caught her in the back, sending her staggering.

"Whoa." She blinked at me. "You're fast. I didn't see your attack."

"It's… kinda invisible." At least, to people without the Sight.

"I did wonder," said Drake, who lounged against a nearby wall. "My turn next?"

Figuring I might as well get in practise while I could, I faced him. My magical shield hummed, back in place, the flood of energy still racing through me. *I finally did it.*

Drake's style was wilder than Wanda's or even Vance's. He threw streams of fire from both hands, which glanced off my shield and scorched the grass. I moved faster thanks to my enhanced instincts, but I had to throw myself to the ground every time he hurled a fireball. I was sure he'd reined in the heat so it wouldn't burn me on contact.

We stopped when Drake set the hedge on fire.

"I'll get it." Wanda shot a handful of ice at it. The ice melted. "Oh…"

I smothered a laugh. Behind me, I felt Vance's presence as he walked down the steps to the lawn, waving a hand. The burning section of the hedge disappeared.

"Where'd you send it?" I asked.

"An empty field somewhere."

"You're impossible." I shook my head. "What if you set someone's garden on fire?"

Drake snickered. "It's been known to happen. Vance was in charge of mentoring me when we were teenagers. He was supposed to keep me from going off the rails. Both of us knew that was never gonna happen."

"Really?" I couldn't help swinging my gaze around to Vance, who stood not a metre away from me, wearing his smart suit again. "Been in another meeting?" I asked.

"Not yet." He looked down at me. "Can I talk to you for a moment?"

Damn. Aware of the others' stares, I followed him into

the hallway.

"By 'not yet', do you mean you're going away?" My heartbeat quickened.

"I'll be back by this evening," he said. "You weren't joking when you said you intended to speak to this half-faerie who planned to win the fake faerie blood, were you?"

"No," I answered. "I know it's risky, but it's all I've got. I'll call you if I need help."

"You have a knack for ending up in trouble if I'm not there."

"Yeah, I might do something stupid like enter a magical tournament for half-faeries." I rolled my eyes. "I get it. Danger is my line of work."

"Take your sword. Sneak it under the illusion. Can Isabel put a disguise on it?"

"On *Irene?*" I blinked in disbelief. "Maybe, but it's made of iron. Faeries can sense it. Even half-faeries. At best they'd kick me out if they found it."

At worst, two hundred enraged half-faeries would trample me flat.

"This magical drug business sounds like the work of a collective, not an individual," said Vance. "There'll be more than one person involved, and if they all turn on you at once—"

"I'll call you," I cut in, tapping my shoulder underneath the mark. "Unless you want Isabel to put a shadow illusion on you, you'll have to sit this one out."

Frustration bubbled under the surface, both unwanted and irrational. I'd come closer to understanding my magic than ever, and while I understood why Vance didn't want me meeting the drug dealing half-faeries alone, it didn't mean I was happy to be condescended to.

A pause. "You ran away from me last night."

Huh? He chose *now* to bring that up, when I was already angry with him? "Can't it wait, Vance? I've another fight in a few hours. I can't think about anything else."

"I know," he said. "But you're acting oddly, and if there's anything that might impact your performance tonight, I need you to tell me. I don't want you walking into the arena tonight if there's a problem. I *especially* don't want you tailing magical drug dealers."

"There is no problem," I ground out. "Thanks for your concern."

I brushed past him and headed outside, determined to get more practise in before the next match.

CHAPTER THIRTEEN

The crowd roared.

Another bloodthirsty bout had just come to an end, and the evidence was strewn all over the arena. Several security guards carried the limp form of Sabre—imaginative name there—past the screaming front row of rowdy spectators. The victor, a horrifying mass of tentacles who'd spit slime all over the arena and nearly drowned its opponent, transformed back into the innocuous form of an eight-year-old girl.

I wasn't entirely sure the last ten minutes hadn't been a hallucination. Supposedly, 'Lilac' was a chimera faerie who could transform into whatever animal she felt like. So she'd picked a poisonous land-dwelling octopus and left the crew a hell of a mess to clean up.

One of the hobgoblin's faerie guards moved in, waving a hand, and the slime disappeared. *Thank god for that.* Fighting on an ice rink would be preferable to fighting knee deep in slime. I'd been put up against a Summer half-faerie known as

Raptor. I'd watched *Jurassic Park* as a kid and was pretty sure I knew what to expect.

The hobgoblin called the match, and I stood up at the same time as Lilac skipped past.

"Might see you in the next round," she whispered to me as she passed. Creepy.

Raptor was a raven-haired male half-faerie who wore both armour and a bird-shaped mask. The armour would make it hard to land a hit on him. I'd need to use magic first.

I faced him across the arena, already tugging my magic into place. It seemed restless tonight, keeping up an ever-burning glow that would have drawn attention had it not been for all the other magic pouring off the crowd. They'd worked up into a frenzy, and as this was the last match of the night, the noise climbed to a fever pitch. Drunk on glamour and faerie cocktails passed amongst the crowd, they screeched and shouted after me, expecting a good show.

Raptor's face was entirely hidden by the mask so I couldn't see his expression. I studied the armour instead. It covered his body from shoulders to knees, leaving his arms exposed. I could work with that.

His hands flexed, and long claws sprouted from his fingers. Bird's claws. Oh, shit.

He launched himself at me, and I spun around, ducking his outstretched hands. Since he hadn't used magic, I risked dimming my shield down and turned it into offensive mode instead. Streams of blue energy rippled from my palms, forcing Raptor to dodge to the side. I'd practised earlier—a lot—but the last time my magic had been this unruly was in Faerie.

Hope that's a good sign.

Raptor spun around, claws outstretched, and ran at me again with the speed and agility of a faerie warrior. With magic humming through my veins and manifesting in swirls of blue energy around my palms, my own instincts were equally sharp. I fired a blast of energy at him which knocked into one of his clawed hands, sending him sideways. Raptor made a snarling noise, and wings sprouted from his back.

Crap.

Even with magic enhancing my speed, I couldn't jump high enough to catch an opponent when he was in the air. Raptor shot up like a rocket, out of range. Swearing, I fired magic at him and missed, and yells from above told me I'd nearly hit the crowd. As I prepared to fire again, Raptor came soaring down at me.

I raised my hands, magic forming a shield, but too late.

My body took the full impact and he slammed into me, knocking me onto my side. I bit back a yell, my legs crushed beneath his armour, and his claws sank into my skin.

My left leg ignited, and I screamed half in pain, half in rage. My magic reacted, flaring up in layers of blue light. Though he pinned my legs down, I caught his other clawed hand before he could stab me again, and twisted his exposed wrist. With him pinning me down, I punched him with my free hand, catching the elbow joint. Another punch, a snap, and a yelp. One broken arm.

I used his moment's distraction to throw him off me, though my bleeding leg wouldn't be standing up anytime soon. Instead, I rolled over and grabbed his other arm, snapping the wrist. His clawed hand twitched feebly at me, but I punched his face with my free hand, yanking the mask off.

"Give it up," I hissed in my most menacing Shadow-voice.

He groaned, his expression glazed with pain, and feebly tried to kick me. I punched him in the throat, hard enough to make his eyes roll back in his head.

"Surrender."

He choked out some incomprehensible faerie-tongue. The hobgoblin's amplified voice rang out: "Shadow is the winner."

Shadow could hardly walk. Laughter drifted over me as I struggled to pull my limp leg upright. The claws hadn't pierced to the bone, but dull pain thumped through me, making my head spin. I wouldn't be sticking around for the rest of the show.

I nearly smacked myself in the forehead for stupidity. Isabel had given me a small healing spell to carry in my pocket, but it might not be strong enough to heal all the damage. I could hardly show up at the meeting with the half-faerie with a bleeding leg. Great thinking there, Ivy.

Limping from the arena seemed to take forever. Every step made blinding pain shoot through my leg, and the world grew fuzzy around the edges. I stumbled down the corridor, searching for an empty room—any room. Somewhere to activate the healing spell in peace. A lot of faeries had natural healing abilities, but the spells they generally used were a different sort to the witch remedies I carried with me. I also had my phone, in my padded inner coat pocket. And the mage mark, but that was for emergencies only.

Healing first.

I pushed open the nearest door and practically fell into the room, on top of a naked couple who screamed shrilly at me.

I yelped and tripped over my own feet, letting the door swing shut.

The second room was empty, thank god. I threw down the spell circle and stuck my leg into it. The worst of the pain disappeared, but like I'd feared, a dull ache spread through my leg when I put weight on it. I'd have to limp out and find Vance before I went hunting after half-faerie drug lords.

Now my head had stopped spinning, I noticed the weird way my magic continued to behave. Swirls of blue danced around me, agitated, and a chill bit at my skin underneath the disguise. I limped from the room, making sure I hadn't left a trail of blood. That was a risk I hadn't thought of—my blood was pure human, with or without faerie magic. If anyone found traces and tracked them to me, I'd be in trouble. Luckily, half-faeries had no substitute for tracking spells. Or any concept of forensic science, for that matter. They had no reason to suspect a human had sneaked into their games.

I followed the corridor to the end and tripped over something solid at the foot of the stairs. No, some*one*. A person.

A body.

The redheaded half-faerie kid I was supposed to meet later. He was dead. His arms had been ripped open from wrist to elbow, exposing bone, muscle and pink flesh. A similar wound cut through his chest, where crushed ribs covered the place where his heart used to be.

I'd seen some fucked-up things in Faerie, and even I wanted to gag. Who the hell would murder someone like this? It wasn't even magic. This was sadism. Swallowing bile, I walked around the body, averting my eyes from the mass of gore at the base of his neck. His face was the worst, though— eyes stretched wide in terror and agony, mouth open in a silent scream. He'd been ripped to pieces by an animal. No way could a human have done this.

The image of a hellhound flashed before me.

Calder?

Why the hell would a Winter faerie—even one from the Grey Vale—rip someone to pieces like this?

He's Avakis's son. Sadism is in his nature.

In three years as Avakis's prisoner, I'd seen my fair share of torture. He'd kept piskies in cages so he could tear their wings off when he needed a quick magic boost from their pain. He'd once cursed three humans to dance until they died. But this wasn't just torture. The killer had left the body out in the open. Like a message. A threat.

A familiar tang hovered in the air, cold and menacing.

Hellhounds. The chest wound... I'd bet it came from a hellhound, all right. Or a shapeshifter faerie. The contestants, however, were still inside the arena.

I tried not to inhale the decaying scent of magic as I tiptoed around to his other side. When faeries died, their magic decayed along with the body. As a half-faerie, this guy wouldn't just fade away. He'd cross over the veil, like other half-faeries who died.

I might have magic with its roots in death, but I was no necromancer. I couldn't bring his spirit back and question it. Nor did I have a tracking spell with me. Goose bumps prickled my skin, and the icy sensation in the pit of my stomach grew by the second. *I can't stay here.*

Someone would find the body eventually. I wasn't stupid enough to touch it, illusion or not. My magic swirled in blue clouds, agitated, as though reminding me I stood at a crime scene. I climbed over the body, onto the stairs, and fled as fast as my throbbing leg would carry me.

Once outside, I limped down the alley, sending Vance a message. With the kid informant dead, my chances of meeting the drug lords—or Calder—were shot.

Unless Calder was here. Watching me.

I limped faster, changing my message to ask Vance to

meet me on another street instead. My magic was a dead giveaway even with the disguise on. Around the corner, I broke into a half-run. My leg protested at the movement and I knew I'd lost a lot of blood, but I couldn't meet Vance right next to the alley in case Calder really was spying on me.

The few people walking on the streets stared as I hurried past. Shit. With my disguise active, they wouldn't be able to see the blood, but a limping half-faerie wasn't a common sight. I kept my eyes on my path, surrendering every last trace of dignity. Finally, I hobbled around a corner and found Vance waiting. He raised an eyebrow, but closed his hand around my wrist without commenting.

A rush of air, and we were in his study. I fell into his office chair, flipping the disguise spell off.

"What happened?" Vance asked, his hands on my leg. The claws had made a mess of yet another pair of jeans, tearing bloody furrows into the fabric.

"Healing spell wasn't strong enough." Before I'd finished speaking, a spell appeared in Vance's hands. "Also, someone murdered the kid I was supposed to meet. Tore him open."

My teeth chattered together. Of course Calder had done it. I couldn't keep this a secret any longer.

I took a deep breath. "I need to tell you something."

He quietly listened as I told him exactly how my encounter with Calder had transpired, and my suspicions about the death of the other half-faerie.

A long pause followed. My heart beat loudly in the silence.

"I suspected you were keeping something from me," said Vance. "I also suspected this to be the work of an associate of Velkas."

"They met," I said. "I'm almost certain. You know when we were questioning people about the missing children, and they all mentioned seeing a half-faerie with an ash blade?" What with Velkas, and everything that had transpired since, I'd forgotten that particular detail. "We thought they meant Velkas, but he was a full-blooded Sidhe. Maybe it was Calder all along. He has a blade that looks like it might be made out of ash. And armour. Just like his."

"I see," said Vance, his voice dangerously calm. "I suspected Velkas had help from the half-faeries. I insinuated as much during my last meeting with the Chief, and I suspect that's the reason he refused to let me enter his territory."

You never told me. I didn't dare accuse him of hiding information, though, when I'd admitted to doing worse.

"So," I said, aware of the awkward silence looming over us, "I reckon he was Velkas's personal servant or something.

I'll bet *he* was the one who spread the rumour amongst the half-faeries in the first place. They might not have met Velkas at all."

"They didn't," said Vance. "The Chief had no idea who he was. Unless he used a disguise, which is possible, of course."

"And Avakis? Did you mention him?"

Please, no.

Vance's gaze softened a little. "No. It's not my story to tell."

I breathed out a little, but my chest tightened. "Calder can't live on half-blood territory, then," I said. "He must be hiding somewhere else. I'd say he came from the Grey Vale, but he—Avakis—never mentioned a son. Most half-faeries—like you said, they're abandoned here in this realm. Their faerie parents don't give a crap. But Calder acts so much like Avakis. They must have met." Or batshit-crazy ran in the family.

Vance studied me. "Perhaps. The way to the faerie realm is closed. Calder is working from this side."

"Unless he inherited the talent for crossing over the veil," I said, my heart lurching. "Damn. I never did find out how Velkas learnt to do it. *He* didn't have magic like Avakis."

"He was a Sidhe lord," said Vance. "They have the unique ability to cross between realms when they choose. But you're right—if the Grey Vale is another realm entirely, and can only be reached through Death…"

"Maybe Velkas only left the realm a couple of times," I said. "Just enough to spread his rumours. He acted through other people, mostly—like Calder. But he was definitely pure faerie."

"No half-faerie can walk between realms," said Vance. "This entire plot hinges on fooling the half-bloods into thinking there's a way back, doesn't it? Instead, they're being fed a lie." Anger rang through his tone. "This Calder. Did he say he was behind the plan to share the drug with the other half-faeries?"

"He as good as did," I said. "Amongst other vague villain speeches. You know how dramatic faeries are." My tone came out steady, though the anger in his voice shook me a little. He didn't *look* as angry as I'd feared considering I'd lied to him for days, but the humming power in the air made me forget the odd behaviour of my own magic. The blue haze had died down a little now I'd switched the disguise off, making me more aware of the Mage Lord's arresting presence. I did my best to hold his stare.

"Tell me what else Calder said."

"He implied he was working with others," I said. "More than one person… he said they noticed I'd caused chaos in the Grey Vale when I killed Velkas. I asked if he planned to invade us. He said he wasn't interested in this realm."

Vance's eyes flashed. "I suppose not," he said. "If he's an exile."

"All half-faeries are exiles," I said. "Or… or changelings." Even the one left in my place when I'd been taken to Faerie. Hell, *Calder* might have been left in my place.

His magic had been all over that kid's body. He'd killed him, and left the body there as a threat. To me. He'd probably tortured the kid into admitting he'd agreed to meet me. I'd been wearing my disguise at the time, but perhaps he'd guessed.

I should have come up with a better plan.

Vance's expression said as much. That, and *you'd better have good reason for not telling me.*

I looked away. "Is there a record of half-faeries anywhere? Surely their Chief would know. Shit. That reminds me." I turned to him again. "I don't think most half-faeries even know the Grey Vale exists. They've been shut out since birth, so they can't know *that's* the place Velkas meant when he promised they'd be able to return to Faerie. It's why they're so mad I closed the veil. They think I denied them the chance to go back to Summer or Winter."

"They don't know you likely saved their lives." Vance nodded, a gleam I couldn't read in his eyes. What was he scheming? "I intend to talk to the Chief again myself."

Whoa. "Wait," I said. "If you mention Calder, he probably won't believe you. And if Calder himself finds out..." *He'll come after you.* He'd been responsible for the death of one Mage Lord already.

"Do you think keeping quiet will dissuade him from carrying out his plan?"

The hint of disgust underlying his voice pierced right through me. I didn't need his anger, not after the night I'd had already. Seeing that dead kid had filled me with enough guilt for both of us, even though I doubted I could have stopped Calder. Not without dying myself, for real this time.

It made me really, really mad.

"So call me a fucking coward, then," I spat. "It's the reason I'm still alive after three years in Faerie. I killed Avakis because I didn't confront him until I had the upper hand. That might have been cowardly, but it kept me and the other captives alive. If a handful of people find out about Calder, he'll kill them to keep them quiet. If everyone in town finds out, he'll unleash whatever he's plotting against humans and half-faeries alike." I paused to breathe. "What would happen if he gave this drug of his to every half-faerie at once? They'd be more inclined to believe his offer of immortality than believe me if I told them about the Grey Vale. It'd be a bloodbath." I met his stare defiantly. "Go ahead and call me whatever you like."

"I didn't call you a coward." His voice was dangerously quiet. "But it's your job to inform me of any threats to the population of this city—human or supernatural. This dangerous individual has caused many deaths already."

"I know." I also knew I'd pissed him off, because Vance only reverted into formal Mage Lord mode when he was angry. "But even if I'd told you, the odds of catching a powerful faerie who doesn't want to be found are pretty low. He nearly killed me, and I have Avakis's magic. I couldn't even touch him with my sword." The excuses poured out even as the twisting sensation in my chest dug deeper. I didn't need Vance to lay on the guilt trip, too. "Telling the whole universe will open up a can of worms we're not ready for. The supernatural community will panic. The half-faeries will accuse us of lying. I'll bet Calder would *love* that. We'd cause chaos without him having to lift a finger."

Vance's sharp gaze bit into me. "You seem to have given this a lot of thought, Ivy. Did you really think I would be foolish enough to announce the presence of a dangerous half-faerie to the human public?"

I opened my mouth then closed it. "I guess not." Arrest warnings might be how the mortal police alerted the public to dangerous criminals, but supernaturals played by different rules. "If word reached him, though…"

"He'd kill more half-bloods? That child would have died no matter what. He chose to work with Calder."

"If you're implying I'm weak for failing to kill him the first time—"

"I said nothing of the sort," said Vance. "Anyone with the blood of a Sidhe lord has magic most mortals cannot hope to match—including most of my mages. As for me, I intend to search him out myself."

That's what I'm afraid of. My guts twisted in knots. "Don't. Vance, don't." My voice came out a whisper. "He—he wants *me* to find him. This is a sick game, I know it. He'll have picked it up from Avakis himself."

"Game or not, we can't let him walk away alive."

I crossed my arms. "What did you think I expected to

happen tonight? I figured the kid would take me straight to him."

"And you planned to go alone."

I continued to stare him out, though my eyes began to water. I was sick of fighting with my allies when Calder had slipped away. "I can beat him with Avakis's magic. Don't you dare say I can't. I've had a shitty night and I'm not in the mood for any more of your crap."

I turned away, and his hand rested on my arm.

"If you'd let me get a word in edgeways," said Vance, "I never implied you couldn't beat Calder on your own. You need to stop letting your injured pride cloud your judgement."

My eyes burned. *That's not the problem.* "Injured pride? His father made my life a living hell. I've seen proof of what he can do to a person—tonight. He's the same as Avakis, and if he so much as gets a hint that you're searching for him—well, he's killed one Mage Lord already." I stopped as he flashed me a dangerous look again.

"I'm searching for him," he said. "And I intend to find him. You needn't concern yourself with my safety. Calder is hardly unique amongst rogue supernaturals, and I'm certain a large number of people would happily see me dead. You don't end up in my position without making a few enemies."

Now he said that, I realised how stupid I'd been. "Okay, I get it. I wanted to tell you. I told Isabel, but she's not likely to wander off and try and poke holes in him."

"He's in for a worse fate, when I find him." A chill wind swept through the room, and the dim light made Vance look more menacing than ever. "He's no Sidhe lord."

"I don't give a flying fuck who he is. It freaked me out because he looks just like Avakis and jumped at me out of nowhere. And his magic."

"He's half-human," said Vance. "Think about the other half-faeries you know. Even if he thinks he's on the same level as a Sidhe lord, he isn't."

"I guess not, but that doesn't mean he won't have something nasty up his sleeve if you hunt him down. He's been hiding all this time. Maybe in plain sight."

"Not for much longer." Vance moved closer to me, and the tension simmering around us tightened. "I'll take you home, and we'll discuss this again tomorrow."

I nodded, not willing to get dragged into another debate. Vance clearly wasn't budging on this one, and who knew, maybe we'd be able to come up with a better plan together.

His hand closed around mine, icy-cold and rough, like he

was seconds from shifting. The chill in the air made me certain I wouldn't be getting a goodbye kiss this time. I'd well and truly fucked up.

It shouldn't bother me. At all. But I had to blink tears back when he left me on my doorstep, disappearing immediately without another word.

Shit. I was in trouble.

CHAPTER FOURTEEN

"Almost show time," Isabel muttered, applying the finishing touches to the spell circle at the foot of the stairs. Vance stood watch at the top, while I'd thoroughly checked all the rooms inside the basement of the old building, including the auditorium where the Trials were held. Mercifully, this time I didn't stumble upon horny half-faeries *or* a dead body. An improvement on yesterday already.

No traces remained from last night. No blood, either, and I'd been too rattled to pick up a sample. Isabel, with her usual forethought, had found some on my shoes where I must have trodden in it on the way out. A tracking spell would be able to show me the half-faerie's last moments, and maybe hint at where Calder was hiding.

Of course, the dickhead hadn't left any traces at the scene. I'd been too out of it last night to really look, and aside from my erratically behaving magic, no sign of Calder had remained behind. You wouldn't think there'd been a brutal supernatural contest here last night, either. The place looked abandoned in daylight.

I hated the idea of bringing Isabel to a murder site, but she refused point-blank to be left out of the investigation. While Isabel continued to check the spell circle, I walked up the stairs to join Vance. Today, he didn't seem in a particularly talkative mood. He watched the spell circle with narrowed eyes.

"What is it?" I asked.

"Are you sure you want to do this?"

"See the spell? I have every right to. I'm certain he killed the half-faerie kid to get to me."

Vance's grey eyes met mine. "I meant the Trials."

"Don't really have a choice, do I?" I forced a laugh.

"You're risking your neck. You might have died."

"I knew what I was getting into."

"No," he said. "You didn't."

I didn't argue with him. He was entirely right. Even though the three of us knew who the real bad guy was, by mutual assent, nobody mentioned Calder by name.

Isabel looked up at me with worry written all over her face. "I've set up the spell." Her expression also said, *Are you sure about this?* No, I wasn't sure. Watching the play-by-play of the last moments of a half-faerie's life had *not* been on my plan for my free day.

"Okay." I walked back downstairs to the spell circle, refusing to let Vance see my hesitation in case he stepped in himself. This was a long shot, I knew, but short of hiring a necromancer, we had no other way to find out if Calder had been here.

I took a deep breath, and prepared to relieve the half-faerie's final moments.

As my hands touched the spell circle, my magic hummed in response. I nearly jerked my hands away. The blood in my veins seemed to freeze underneath the glyphs spiralling up my arms. My head dipped forward, and images flashed into my head. It took a moment to orient myself and realise I was looking into the corridor as it had been last night—dark and shadowy. I squinted, trying to focus on the scene. Figures drifted past, climbing the stairs. These were the half-faerie kid's memories—or the echo of them—so he must have hung out here for a while instead of watching the fights in the arena. Maybe waiting for someone.

The crowds died down, suggesting the first match had already begun, but the person whose eyes I watched through didn't move. The view remained too dark to see much besides shifting shadows, until the bright glow of faerie magic descended the stairs.

It's him. Every muscle locked, and it took all the self-control I had left not to flinch and let go of the vision. Calder descended the stairs, looking much the same as he had the other night. His tall form was wreathed in blue threads of magic. His mouth moved, but of course, I couldn't hear a damned thing.

Calder gestured, something in his hand. Not a weapon. A paper bag, emblazoned with a vaguely familiar logo. He held it up, and the half-faerie's hands reached out to take it. Calder held it out of range, an expression of rage distorting his features.

The half-faerie turned to the side, and a huge, furry body materialised, teeth sinking into my—his—arm.

I didn't need to hear the sound to know the half-faerie was screaming. Calder watched, not moving, and the world blurred into a confusing mess of claws and blood.

I jerked back into my own body, gasping, tasting the echo of his fear on my tongue. Vance and Isabel both watched me, both wearing equally concerned expressions.

"Yeah, it was him," I said. "He set hellhounds on that kid." I withdrew my hands from the circle, wiping my sweaty palms on my jeans. He'd stood right here and watched someone die.

"Anything else?" asked Vance.

"I think he offered the guy the drug, but I can't be sure. He had a paper bag... shit." I stopped. "I know where I've seen it before. I'm certain the logo on the bag looked like one of the witches' places. It was a stylised letter "E"."

"Edith's Apothecary," said Isabel. "It's the only place you can get certain herbs... damn. I have half the ingredients in our flat, and I never considered..." She ran a hand through her curly hair, a distraught expression pinching her face. "But does that mean one of the coven members knows who he is?"

"Probably not," I said, pushing to my feet. "He could have used glamour and lied."

Isabel didn't look convinced. "I want to talk to them. I can stop them stocking the herbs as long as it takes for this to end."

"Bet he already has the ingredients," I said. "And as for what he's planning to do with them... no clue. It doesn't make sense." Frustration burned in my blood. "He's hiding this drug and giving it out to a couple of people at a time. That suggests he's testing it."

"Because he doesn't know the full effects," said Vance. "And he doesn't want to draw attention."

"Maybe not, but what's his goal? Stir up every half-faerie in this realm?" I paused. "I keep thinking he has a plan, but if he's anything like his father, his goal's to incite chaos. Avakis didn't have a goal when he kidnapped a bunch of humans. He just liked the power and dominance."

I looked away from Isabel and Vance, not willing to acknowledge their pity. I was *through* with being the victim.

"His goal might be to anger the half-faeries," said Vance, "but I'd guess he seeks a way back into Faerie himself."

"Probably," I said. "I'll bet he wants to take over what's left of his father's kingdom." The armour he'd worn must have come from there. Half-faeries couldn't usually cross over, so maybe Velkas had taken him or given him the armour in person. Maybe he intended to pave the way for another invasion, as Velkas had… but again, I kept thinking there might be some form of rationality behind this. Avakis had been everything *but* rational. I'd spent three years at the mercy of his whims, wondering when it'd be my turn to die.

"One thing's for certain," said Vance. "There's no longer a doubt he was responsible for the deaths." The air hummed with power, while Vance wore the darkly dangerous expression he usually reserved for when he killed someone. *Oh.* The other mage. He wanted to punish the person behind the drug and avenge his friend. Probably by poking holes in the culprit.

"Pretty sure he'll have erased his traces everywhere else," I said. "Sure would help to know where he's hanging out, though."

He must live somewhere in this realm. With the veil closed, there was no way Calder could have walked out of the Grey Vale into our realm without anyone noticing over at necromancer HQ. Certainly not after the other week. Every inch of the Ley Line was under close watch.

Had Calder even *met* his father? For most changeling half-bloods, their faerie parents rarely bothered to come over for a visit. The Sidhe who screwed with mortals didn't go in for the whole regular family thing.

Isabel pocketed the remains of the spell circle with a nervous glance over her shoulder. "What even *is* this place? Can't you shut it down?" She addressed Vance.

The Mage Lord approached the doors to the auditorium. I followed, one hand on the sword strapped to my waist. I missed Irene like crazy when fighting in the arena.

"There's nothing in there," I said. "I checked. If you shut

the place, Calder will know I told you."

"I'm aware," said the Mage Lord. "As I said, it's my intention to speak to the Chief of the half-bloods and find out if he's aware *this* is going on." He indicated the empty arena. "I didn't bring the subject up at our last… *meeting.*" His voice dropped on the last word. "I'll bring him proof this time."

"It's not illegal," I said. "Like, you know, human street fighting. It's a thing."

"Is it, now?"

"I thought everyone knew." Except the mages, apparently.

A shout from behind, accompanied by a familiar chill, made me whirl around. Isabel backed away from a giant, furred beast, which paced the top of the stairs, preparing to jump.

Like hell. I'd get there first. Magic flooded my veins as I grabbed my sword and ran for the stairs.

Even with enhanced speed, I narrowly avoided tripping downstairs when I landed, bringing the blade in a wide arc. Blood spurted above the hellhound's gaping mouth and I ducked to avoid those deadly jaws. My second swipe got it in the neck.

"There'll be more of them," I warned the others. "We should go—"

Howls echoed downstairs.

"—outside," I finished.

With no choice but to run right into the hellhounds' path, we made for the stairs, and the exit. Growls and scratching noises told me at least one prowled right outside the door. Vance moved in front, blasting the door wide open and knocking the hellhound aside. The second beast recovered, directing its fear-spell at us. At once, iciness spread through my limbs, but my magic pushed it back.

Vance raised a hand and sent the hellhound flying into the alley wall, apparently unaffected by its spell. Before the beast could regain its footing, a sword had materialised and pierced it in the neck. The sword reappeared in Vance's hand. Isabel and I scrambled upstairs to join him. I scanned the alley for more hellhounds.

"They might be using glamour," I said. "There's usually at least four per pack. And they feed on death energy."

"Lovely," said Isabel, holding an explosive spell in each hand. "This Calder character keeps them as pets?"

"Pretty standard for the Grey Vale," I muttered. Avakis had kept over a hundred hellhounds shackled around his manor, ready to bite into anyone who dared to attempt escape. "They're rejects from the Wild Hunt. Too wild for Summer or Winter."

A blue shimmer caught my eye. I moved towards it, sword at the ready, directing the blue threads of magic to form a shield around me in case I got jumped from behind.

Turned out my instincts were on the mark. A growl reached my right ear, followed by hot, stinking breath on the back of my neck.

I whipped around with magic-enhanced speed and my sword flashed out. Behind the hellhound's collapsing body, Isabel and Vance confronted another of the beasts. I kicked the hellhound's body down, approaching the blue light. *Is he here?* Or had he sent his hellhounds to root out potential trespassers? Might he be using glamour?

Avakis couldn't use glamour.

The realisation flashed through my head at the same time as yet another giant hellhound appeared, this one twice the size of the others. Damn creature. Bloody teeth snapped at me, making me flinch—did this creature kill the half-faerie kid, or had it been snacking on humans?

Iron met flesh and the hellhound collapsed, its bloody mouth inches from my feet. Behind me, Isabel and Vance had brought down the last one. Vance appeared to be on his phone. Probably calling the mages to clean up the mess. *Oh, no. They can't come here.*

"Ivy?" Isabel waved me over.

"Look." I pointed at the hellhound's stained red teeth. "He didn't chew on me. I reckon that's our killer."

Isabel blanched, but she passed me a small container. Nausea rising in my throat, I took a blood sample as quickly as possible and straightened up.

"I think we got the last of them," I said to Vance. "I reckon that one killed the half-faerie."

"I'll set up a tracking spell, but not here," said Isabel.

"Yeah… you didn't call your mages, did you? We can't let anyone else near here."

"I'm not letting this incident slide by, unpunished," said Vance, his voice low, dangerous.

"Won't be, if we find him." I waved the jar of blood. "Unless he left this behind on purpose. I wouldn't put it past him to have set up a trap."

Hell, I was pretty much counting on it. By this point, I'd be disappointed if he didn't.

"I'll bet those hellhounds were a message," I said. "For me. He knows I'm alive."

"The spell," said Isabel, a nervous tremor in her voice. "Are you sure you want me to use it?"

I nodded. "Best get it over with. Er... not here." I looked at Vance. I'd never seen him transport more than one person at a time, but he nodded to me, understanding my idea. I turned to Isabel. "Don't panic—"

Vance transported the three of us away before I could finish my sentence.

CHAPTER FIFTEEN

Isabel broke away from me, making a small noise of fright. "What the—?"

"Sorry," I said, giving Vance an accusing look. We stood in a field behind a row of dilapidated houses. A fence lay between us and the nearest overgrown garden, though large sections had collapsed. From the state of our surroundings and the unnatural quiet, this place was one of the areas that had been abandoned during the war.

Isabel turned around on the spot, staring at the grey sky. "Are we even still in the city?"

"Just outside it," said Vance. "This is a field owned by the mage guild specifically for the purpose of using spells without being traced. We have several areas." Vance moved to a spot where former spell circles had burned all the grass away, revealing cracked earth beneath. "Here will do."

Isabel blinked at him, then me. I gave her a shrug that said, *yeah, he gives everyone orders all the time. You should probably get used to it.*

While Isabel crouched down to set up the tracking spell, I approached Vance. "So hellhound fear spells don't affect you?" I didn't know anyone, human or faerie, who could resist that spell. Avakis had used hellhounds as pretty effective guard dogs.

He hesitated a moment before answering. "No. Shifter blood is immune to most spells of that nature."

"Really? I didn't know. I thought it was a kind of faerie magic."

"Hellhounds are hybrids," said Vance. "Faeries summoned with necromancy. I'd guess their magic is of a hybrid nature as well." He paused. "For this Calder to be controlling so many suggests he's buying necromancy supplies. Lord Evander tells me his necromancers are under close watch after Velkas infiltrated them."

I groaned. "Damn. I should have figured. The necromancers were right at the centre of Velkas's plan. I don't trust a word *Lord* Evander says."

"Hellhounds can switch loyalties," said Isabel, who was listening in. "When Velkas left, they might have flocked to join Calder. The coven's watching the Ley Line, too, and we'd know if someone had tried a mass summoning."

"Hmm." That made sense. Hellhounds obeyed the biggest dickhead, generally. "Maybe talk to the necromancers. I'm definitely not welcome over there, though."

"I intended to speak to them anyway, as Lord Evander has a lot to answer for." Vance looked sideways at me. *Oh. The money.* This week had turned into such a shitshow, I'd forgotten my dire financial situation.

"So does Calder," I said. "But you said you were going to speak to the Chief of the half-faeries tomorrow."

"I'll do both."

"Might as well piss off all the supernaturals in one go, right?" I flashed him a quick smile, wondering where we stood after last night. Maybe I'd blown my last shot at gaining his trust. "I want to come and meet the leader of the half-faeries."

"He might recognise you. Your magic is distinctive, as you told me."

I gave him an incredulous look. "What? I didn't think it mattered. You said Calder would notice either way. Besides, what are you even going to tell the Chief? He refused to speak to you before, right?"

"I intend to tell him one of his half-faeries has gone rogue," said Vance. "Not every half-blood is obligated to live in his designated territory, but he's the person responsible for any problems they cause, even the ones that live amongst humans."

"Hmm." Few did. Most wanted to *avoid* humans, but a handful still lived with their mortal families rather than moving onto the half-faeries' territory. "Can't see Calder doing that. Wonder where he lives…" He must have grown up somewhere here, if not in Faerie itself. Not that I should be in the slightest bit curious about the childhood of a cold-hearted killer.

"Guys." Isabel waved me over. "This is all set up."

"Gotcha." My heart began to thump against my ribcage. I almost hoped we *wouldn't* find him… but that was a coward's thought. I'd committed to taking down Calder now, or die trying.

I closed my eyes, taking deep breaths. Then I reached into the circle. Once again, I fell down the torrent of memory.

Seeing through a hellhound's eyes turned out to be in black and white, which combined by the darkness of the setting, made it impossible to see where I was going. An open field spread in front of me, but not one I recognised. Trees and a footpath told me it was a park. Several other hellhounds appeared, too. Several were fighting one another. I winced inwardly as one hellhound tore at another's throat.

Behind them, a faint glow spread. A figure stood within it, watching the fight. The light and the lack of colour distorted my vision, but I recognised the person. He stood wreathed in bright light—probably blue—thick tendrils streaming from the body of the fallen hellhound.

Shit. He'd set them to fight one another to give himself a power boost from their pain. If he had an infinite supply, no wonder he'd been so strong when I'd fought him.

The hellhound whose eyes I watched through prowled around the fighters until it stood right next to him. Calder looked down with an expression of anger mixed with something else. Fear? No way. Even though everything was black and white, the shimmering brightness flowing to him could only be magic. He glowed all over.

Calder's face twisted and he shouted at the hellhound. His mouth stretched in an expression of absolute fury, and I froze, my body trembling. I'd seen that look on Avakis, too many times.

Calder kicked at the nearest hellhound, still shouting. The hellhound's head dipped and I caught sight of a spell circle, a defunct one. Calder's foot stamped down on it, over and over. His face came into view again, and this time I read the words on his mouth—*Not enough. It's not enough.*

I fell back into my own body. "He's not here—or in the alley. Also, he's a sick bastard." Like I didn't know that already. "He had the hellhounds killing one another to boost his own power."

The question was, what did *not enough* mean? Had the crazy strength he'd shown when we'd fought been a temporary boost? If *that* was the source of his power, it wouldn't last forever. What the hell was his game?

"So he feeds on pain, then?" asked Isabel. "I know you explained, but—how's his magic different?"

"From his father's?" I shrugged, looking at Vance. "It's the same, but he's only a half-Sidhe. If he was full-blooded, I guess he'd have some weird hybrid of both parents'. I think one side usually dominates. You don't get Winter-Summer hybrids."

"So who was his human parent? Is there any way you can check?"

"No," said Vance. "I'll ask the Chief of the half-bloods, but they don't record births. It'd be too complicated, with some being born in Faerie and carried here later."

"Abandoned," said Isabel. "No wonder he's so messed up."

Messed up. Yeah. He'd been in control when he fought me, but the Calder I'd just seen was more like Avakis in one of his uncontrolled, irrational rages. Faeries didn't age, and Avakis had likely been hundreds of years old, but his son couldn't be older than nineteen. I kept thinking of him as ancient and invincible, when he wasn't. Not at all.

Not enough...

"He has Avakis's blood." I stood, brushing grass from my knees. "Unless we have time for a chat, I probably won't get answers. Guess he didn't intend me to track him. I've no idea where the park I saw is, anyway."

"I'll send mages patrolling."

Damn. Should have figured he wouldn't leave well enough alone. He'd as good as said most mages wouldn't stand a chance against Calder.

"Vance." I gave him a pointed look.

He met my stare, stony-eyed. "We'll discuss this later," he said. "I need to get back to the guild and check everything's running smoothly. I'll let you know if anything changes."

I nodded. I couldn't do anything else. Calder wasn't naturally stronger than me, at all. He'd been artificially boosting his power all along. To have so many hellhounds required a summoning circle or a really good hiding place.

There was only one place in town where you could hide a powerful spell and not be detected: the Ley Line.

***

The following afternoon found Isabel and me on the wrong side of the law again.

Vance had been gone all day, after reassuring me he wouldn't tell anyone outside of his immediate circle about Calder unless he struck again. Apparently, saying *I know who the killer is and I intend to catch him myself* was an appropriate alternative to letting the rest of the council know what was going on. Perks of being head mage.

He'd gone to the necromancers first, and sent me a message after Lord Evander had insisted none of his necromancers were involved this time. Worse, the half-faerie Chief had flat-out refused a meeting, again, arguing the Trials were perfectly legal. I'd have liked to have introduced him to my sword, but Vance had insisted on confronting him alone. I fully intended to go there later, but right now, Isabel and I had bigger problems.

We hovered in the corner of Edith's Apothecary, waiting for the other customers to leave so we could talk to the owner alone. The middle-aged witch behind the counter glowered at us for hanging around near the glass cases containing expensive charms.

"We look suspicious," I said out of the corner of my mouth.

"Not much choice." Isabel pretended to examine a glittering pendant. I flipped through an ancient spellbook open on a pedestal between the shelves. This was for display—the witches kept their real magic hidden away in places only the covens could access. I'd never seen one myself.

"Maybe he ordered them," I muttered, not daring to say Calder's name in here. "Does this place do home deliveries?"

Isabel's head snapped up. "To custom clients. Can't hurt to ask." She glanced over at the desk. The last customer had finally left, door swinging shut behind them. "I'll do it," she added. "She knows who I am."

Isabel casually approached the witch at the desk, while I examined a shelf of luminous potions. Witch spells had different effects on half-faeries, and since the two groups didn't mix, nobody knew what those effects might be. No wonder Calder had got away with his plan. Half the city's problems would probably be solved if the different supernatural groups just *talked* to one another.

Isabel walked over, beckoning me behind a nearby display.

"There was a bulk order of mandrake leaves, but she refused to tell me where."

"Oh, no." I knew that look. "I've sworn off breaking and entering," I said as quietly as possible.

"Shadow spell."

I groaned quietly. "Fine." I glanced over my shoulder, but the old woman at the desk didn't appear to be looking our way. "You didn't bespell her, did you?"

"Minor diversion spell."

"You're evil." I said this without malice, taking the shadow illusion spell. One click and I turned more or less transparent. With daylight streaming through the front windows, I had to edge around the shelves to find a clear route behind the desk, somewhat helped by the owner's distraction.

Crouching down, I searched her desk for the document where she'd have recorded shipments. I paused as she glanced to the side, but the shadows kept me hidden. So this was why Isabel had spent yesterday evening making a new batch of illusion spells.

Several nerve-wracking seconds later, I'd snatched the right document out from the desk. I crouched awkwardly in the shadows, skimming through names and addresses. Only two mass orders of mandrake leaves had been put through in the last few weeks. I memorised both addresses, replaced the paper, and ran to join Isabel. We hurried out of there like hellhounds were on our tail.

Outside, the main shopping district was as crowded as usual on a weekday at late afternoon. Mostly humans, though some might have been witches or shifters. Here, the crowds mingled in the streets of the small shopping district, and the apothecary lay nestled between a grocer's and a chemist's. It did make sense. Witches used human shops, and it wasn't unheard of for humans to seek out witch remedies or hire someone to perform a spell.

One bumpy bus journey later and we'd reached the road near our flat. I checked out of habit to make sure nothing followed us, but the house was swamped in wards, iron, and Isabel's instant-trigger magical tripwire spells.

"Warn me next time." I led the way to the building. Then stopped. Several small bodies lay outside the gate, right next to the new layer of wards. "What the...?"

"Piskies," said Isabel. "They must have flown into the tripwire spell."

"Ouch." They appeared unconscious, not dead. I counted at least ten of them. "Crap. It's the ones who escaped from the shed."

Isabel crouched to pick one up. Its arms flopped over her arm. "Why would they come here?"

"Very good question." A suspicious chill went down my back. *He* hadn't sent them, had he? No. If he knew my address, he'd have sent hellhounds. Even piskies couldn't break our defences, at least.

I stepped over the boundary and approached the door. "How many new wards are there, anyway?"

"Seventeen," said Isabel. "Anti-faerie spells, anti-undead…"

"Anti-undead?"

"The Cavanaughs figured out you were in trouble with the necromancers.

I sighed. "Yeah, if the necromancers and I were on speaking terms, I'd be able to find out if anyone's messing with the veil."

"Like I said, nobody in the coven's noticed anything. I think he's stuck on this side."

"Well, *Calder*—" I pointedly used his name, determined not to shrink away from it anymore—"is an elusive pain in the ass. Hopefully one of these addresses will work."

"More than one?"

"Two. No recorded names." I turned the key in the lock and stepped into our flat, Isabel on my heels. Once inside, I rattled off the addresses.

Isabel checked her phone. "Abandoned," she said. "Both of them. Maybe it's a setup. Calder might have been too clever to leave a trail."

I thought of the temper tantrum I'd witnessed through the hellhound's eyes. "Perhaps." I took out my own phone and messaged Vance. To my surprise, a reply came immediately. "He's coming—"

The doorbell rang.

"—here," I finished.

"He's awfully quick to respond to your messages." Isabel smirked, laying her own phone on the coffee table.

"Yeah, because I gave him grief about ignoring me for a week while the necromancers took all my cash." I deflected her pointed stare. "Not now."

"Later, then. You're not off the hook. He likes you, Ivy Lane."

"Enough," I said, through gritted teeth. Yes, I knew I needed to make sense of the situation, fast, but Vance made it difficult to think clearly. As for telling him what I felt? Either he'd ditch me and leave me jobless, or he'd reciprocate and—what? Did we have a future, with the faeries stalking my every move?

"You didn't give me the chance to reply to your message," I said, opening the front door. "I might have been busy."

"You aren't." He crossed the threshold into the flat, letting the door swing shut behind him.

I rolled my eyes. "No, but we found out where the orders for the drug ingredients came from. Two empty addresses."

Vance ran a similar search on his own phone, frowning. "They're both near half-blood district."

"What happened back there, anyway?" I asked. "Have there been any more attacks?"

"No," he said. "The Chief, however, is almost as irresponsible as Lord Evander." Irritation rolled off his words.

"Well, they're half-faeries," I said. "By definition, they're capricious and unreliable. The Sidhe lords rule on power and heritage alone, and like to put curses on people they disagree with rather than settling anything like responsible leaders. As for the half-faeries, they're just as bad. Did I mention one of them transformed into a giant octopus and flooded the arena with slime yesterday?"

Vance looked at me. "I'm going with you tonight."

I held up my hands. "Oh, no."

"You rightly pointed out that I'm incapable of being in several places at once," he said. "It stands to reason, however, that the one place where there's trouble happening is where *you* are."

A snicker came from behind me. I shot Isabel a glare. "You can't just walk in there."

"I'll wear a cloaking spell. You mentioned you had some spare ones."

I groaned. "Fine. But for the love of hellhounds, stay out of the way of the fighting and don't draw attention."

"I planned nothing of the sort."

"Vance, you knock the doors down, ask questions later. Don't deny it."

The hint of a smile touched his mouth. "Maybe."

Isabel cleared her throat. "I'm going to a coven meeting tonight. Be careful."

"Same to you," I said, turning to Vance. "What about those addresses? You aren't seriously sending your people there, are you? If Calder's there… he doesn't take prisoners."

"No," said Vance. "If nothing happens at the Trials tonight, we'll make a new plan tomorrow."

"If nothing happens tonight?" I raised an eyebrow.

"Calder will invite me over for a friendly tea party first."

I walked back to Isabel, ready to put on my half-faerie disguise again.

CHAPTER SIXTEEN

Knowing Vance watched somewhere in the audience did absolutely nothing to ease my jittery nerves. Eight of us remained in the game. Four of us would walk away.

The hobgoblin called my name, along with my opponent's—Lilac. Yeah, I was up against crazy octopus girl. I narrowed my eyes at her. *She'd better not spit slime on the arena floor again.* Being poisoned would give me away as a human, because we didn't respond to the same healing remedies as faeries did. Lucky Vance was here, really.

Lilac smiled benignly at me, but I wasn't fooled for an instant. She had bubblegum-pink hair today, and wore a dress in an equally eye-watering shade. The crowd, however, had seen her fight more than once already. They knew she had no end of tricks up her sleeve.

Unfortunately, this made it impossible for me to tell her weakness upfront. I settled for pulling a magical shield around myself instead, preparing to dodge whatever she threw at me.

Lilac bounced on her feet, still smiling. Ugh. Her faerie parent was probably the sort who tore the limbs off humans for fun. With no attack forthcoming, I risked getting closer, readying for a strike of my own. She'd transform if I hit her directly, but maybe my magic could knock her down first.

I sent a blue stream of energy at her face. She didn't move or dodge, and I stared in disbelief as the attack hit her dead on, sending her skidding several feet on her back. Laughter rippled through the crowd, though with a nervous undertone. Even the faeries were creeped out by her cute little-girl act.

Lilac stood up. I pressed my advantage and fired a second attack, knocking her down again. And again. I moved in closer, though I was pretty certain she was trying to lure me in so she'd be able to get at me. I didn't have much choice, because my attacks from a distance weren't strong enough to force a surrender. I drew on my growing frustration, feeding it into the magic building around me, but didn't dare tap into the other contestants like I had last time. I threw another attack, half expecting her to let it hit her again.

Lilac launched into the air, limbs spread wide, like a puppet pulled up by the strings. Her limbs lengthened and widened, her body arching and stretching, and fur grew all over her body. Throwing her head back, she roared, landing on four padded feet with enough force to shake the ceiling.

Well, shit. She'd turned into a lion.

Okay… change of plans. Hand-to-hand combat against a lion would likely involve *losing* a hand, so I'd need to rely on magic or force her back into her normal form.

The lion shook its head, waving a considerably scaly tail. Definitely not a regular lion.

I paced around, putting more distance between myself and the beast. It could probably move as fast as I could with my senses boosted, and I didn't want to take any chances. *It's just another stupid hellhound,* I told myself.

The trouble was, I'd never beaten a hellhound—or another faerie creature—without my sword. Vance had said he'd fetch Irene for me if there was trouble, but it'd be kind of conspicuous for him to appear in the arena and hand me my weapon.

I glared at the lion, letting the magic from the shield move to my hands instead. A magical shield wouldn't repel a giant monster. I'd need to go on the attack from here on out.

Or alternatively, do the sensible-person thing and run away.

I did neither. Magic flowed down my arms, forming

streams of blue energy, and I sent the wave right at the lion's back. The lion moved to avoid it, stomping those huge feet. Its mouth opened wide, jaws unhinged, and a jet of fire shot at my face.

I threw myself flat, knees and elbows scraping the floor. *Holy shit. That's no lion.* I'd met a real-life chimera once before and barely escaped with my head attached to my shoulders.

The chimera roared, spewing a torrent of fire. I continued to crawl along the floor, not caring about the crowd laughing at me. I needed to find a weakness somewhere—or a way to force Lilac out of her chimera form.

The chimera's blast of fire evaporated, giving me a few seconds to scramble to my feet. Shock had made me drop my magic, but now it flared up again. I leaped into the air when the chimera breathed a fresh stream of fire that very nearly torched the front row of the audience. I slammed down on its back, to its obvious anger. The chimera roared and tried to buck me off, but I dug my hands into the sides of its head.

Shit. What am I supposed to do now?

Answer: hang there like an idiot. The chimera's fire couldn't hurt me here, but my fists did no more damage than throwing an apple at a troll. I punched the side of its head and damn near dislocated my wrist. Wincing, I searched for a weapon—any weapon. Whichever dickhead made up the rules—or lack thereof—for this bout deserved to meet with Irene.

I crawled to the top of the chimera's head, trying to recall how the other half-faeries had bested shapeshifters. Shark's teeth would be useful right now.

Teeth. Its teeth had a poisonous bite—at least, if it was like wild chimeras.

Oh, boy. This isn't gonna be nice.

I lay flat on the chimera's back, gripping with my legs, and lurched forward, throwing all of my energy into a punch at the side of its jaw. The chimera snarled and attempted to throw me off again. I gripped tighter, edged forward, and fired a stream of magical energy. I missed wildly, and this time, its movement sent me flying over its head. I landed on my back, the wind knocked out of me.

Fire flared above, too fast for me to dodge. I screamed, rolling over in pain, hoping to god I wasn't literally on fire underneath the illusion. My legs burned, throbbing with every movement, but a second stream of fire sent me running. Anger and pain fuelled my steps and my magic, which shone brighter than before. Oh, right. Pain boost. This might come in handy.

I threw beams of energy after the chimera, relying on the speed boost from the faerie magic to push past the pain. It worked—for now—and I got in behind the beast. My next magical assault slammed into the backs of its legs, sending its knees buckling. I kicked it for good measure, regretting the movement when a nauseating wave of burning pain shot through both my shins. The chimera had clearly hurt itself when it fell forward, because it barely reacted this time I climbed onto it. My legs burned with pain and I used my arms to pull myself forward instead until I'd reached its shoulders.

Magic pulsed into my hands and I aimed at the side of its head, missing wildly. The chimera's huge teeth snapped, and I went with my original plan, using magic to strike at its mouth.

It took three blasts to knock one of its giant teeth loose, but by now, the chimera had crawled to its feet, snarling in pain. My magic must have done more damage than I'd thought. Then again, my legs hurt like absolute hell. Light-headedness swept over me, and I blinked the fuzziness from my vision, grasping its tooth in my hands.

Stupid idea, Ivy. With my hands free, the chimera managed to throw me off again. Once more, my back hit the floor, though mercifully not my injured legs. Gasping for breath, I snapped back to life as another burst of fire singed my jacket underneath the illusion. I rolled over, still clutching the bloodstained tooth, certain my all-too-human body would give out and collapse on me at any moment.

No. I'll win first. I have to.

The chimera's huge body lumbered to its feet, but before it could pull itself upright, I'd hit it with another blast of magic in each of its front legs. Then another, in its bleeding mouth. Legs burning, sweat streaming down my forehead, I ran through the pain, shooting it with magic until its side hit the ground.

I leaped, stabbing down with the tooth. Skin and flesh gave way and blood spurted over my hands, crimson and blue.

The crowd's roar echoed in my ears, turning into a ringing sound. I swayed as I stepped back, holding the bloody tooth.

Hell, yeah.

I punched the air. Eat that, shapeshifter dickheads.

My legs folded, the magic fled, and I passed out.

***

I woke up, to my astonishment, in my own bed. Blinking at the ceiling light, I twitched my feet. No pain. No shoes, either. I gritted my teeth, figuring I'd get the worst part over with and see how much damage I'd taken under the illusion.

I pushed the covers off my legs and winced. Red marks stained my shins, where someone had cut my jeans below the thigh. A spell circle surrounded the bed, along with the scent of healing salve. My head hurt a little, but I could sit up.

Vance Colton came into the room. I damn near jumped out of bed.

"Holy shit. You're in my room."

"Well observed."

I opened my mouth, but no witty response came to mind. Or even the observation that I'd left underwear on the floor and hung bras on the wardrobe's doorknobs. I kind of wished I was back with the chimera.

I groaned. "How bad?"

"Not as bad as it looked when I got you out of there. How did you stay conscious for the rest of the fight?"

"Probably the magic," I muttered, hissing in a breath when he reached to apply another layer of healing salve to my shins. Magic-related injuries always healed slower. "Ow."

Vance moved back and bumped into the bookcase. I smothered a laugh. My room was the size of a cupboard and contained everything I'd owned for the ten years since I'd come back from Faerie. All my spare weapons lay on the desk, while bills—some paid, some not—were shoved haphazardly into drawers. I'd never let anyone aside from Isabel come in. Even the guys I'd dated—the one who'd come to our flat had left when Erwin the piskie pulled his hair out.

Vance, however, didn't comment on the mess. "You were lucky."

"I get nine lives, right? Reckon I've got about five left."

"Ivy." His gaze was stern. "You don't have a match tomorrow night."

"How do you know?"

"I listened to the announcer."

"The hobgoblin. He drew tomorrow's matches?"

"Yes. Half the contestants were unconscious, so I'm not sure how many took his message in."

"Who am I fighting?"

"Someone named Chameleon."

"Could be worse," I muttered. "Jesus, you'd think breathing fire in the arena would be illegal."

"Yes," said Vance tightly. "I was tempted to give the organiser a warning."

A chill came with his words, which to be honest, was welcome on my burned legs. "Keep doing that."

Confusion crossed his expression. "Doing what?"

"Making it go all cold."

He frowned. "I am?"

"It's when you put on your scary-ass mage voice. Look." I indicated a stack of papers on the desk, which fluttered in the breeze that had entered the room. "No window in here."

"Hmm." Apparently, being scary came as easy as breathing to him. Maybe I shouldn't have been surprised.

Cold hands touched my legs. I yelped. "Okay, that's too much."

"Really." The corner of his mouth tilted up.

"Ivy?" Isabel's voice came from the other side of the door. "You okay?"

"I'm fine," I said.

The heat came back, and my head thumped. Ow. Even the healing spell didn't change the fact I needed a solid twelve hours' sleep to recover from this one.

"Why here?" I asked stupidly.

"Isabel insisted," said Vance. "Also, there are a large number of mages at the manor. I'm hosting an event there tomorrow."

"You are?"

"The ceremonial election of the new head mage for the

East Midlands is tomorrow afternoon."

"Oh. At your place?"

"No, I'm hosting… I suppose you could call it the after-party. I hoped you might join me."

I blinked. "Oh, no. I don't do fancy events." Seriously? "What the hell would I even wear? This?" I indicated what was left of my jeans.

The corner of his mouth curled up. "You could."

I leaned forward and hit him in the arm. "I'm not showing myself up in front of your snooty mage friends."

Oops. Any hint of humour from his expression disappeared. "I thought you'd find it preferable to investigating a murder or fighting against shapeshifter half-faeries."

Fair point, though I had considerably more experience fighting crazed faeries than I did with fancy parties. Especially ones where he was the host. Did he really think I'd fit in amongst high society mages?

Okay. Maybe I needed to chill—well, I *had* narrowly avoided getting burned to a crisp. This might be my chance to rebuild our relationship—our *professional* relationship, that is.

"Okay," I found myself saying. "I'm not exaggerating

when I say I've nothing to wear." Or any cash to buy new clothes with.

"Don't worry about it. Sleep for now."

"Hey, wait—"

Too late. He'd vanished.

Isabel appeared in his place. "Shit, Ivy. What did you face?"

"A fire-breathing lion."

Her eyes said, *holy shit.* "That contest will be the death of you."

"Only two rounds to go." I sat upright. The marks on my legs had almost faded, though the jeans were a lost cause. Unless I cut them more neatly and turned them into a pair of shorts. Hmm, that could work. When you found yourself with a significant lack of cash, improvising came naturally.

"Did I hear him inviting you out?" she asked.

"There's a fancy event on tomorrow at the mages' place," I said, standing up. My legs barely stung. "But he doesn't seem to realise I literally have nothing in my wardrobe suitable to wear without being laughed at."

"I'll see if I can find something," said Isabel, a glint in her eye. "What I said—I meant it. He looked so mad when he brought you in here. Like I mean, it was scary as hell, but kinda sexy."

"Since when did looking like a serial killer qualify as a sign of him being romantically interested in me?" I knew exactly what she meant, though. "He's my boss. If I hook up with him and then he disappears again—"

"So you're considering it, hmm." She tilted her head. "I don't think he'll disappear. Especially now he's inviting you to his social events."

"All employees are invited," I said. "I'm the only non-mage. Anyway, where's my sword?"

"Where it's always been," said Isabel, stepping aside to let me pass into the narrow corridor between our rooms. Irene rested against the wall beside the door.

I sighed in relief. "Next time a chimera tries to torch me, I'm breaking the rules and bringing my sword."

Isabel approached me from behind. "I found something else today." She indicated a glass case on the side table. A small winged figure lay curled up asleep inside it.

I walked closer. "Er... why's Erwin trapped in there?"

"It's not Erwin," said Isabel. "It's one of those piskies who escaped from the garden shed. You know the ones who tried to break the wards?"

I blinked. I'd forgotten all about that—unsurprisingly.

"Why've you trapped him in there?"

"I knocked him out," she said. "I ran into him near the coven meeting site and he tried to chew my ear off. I know piskies are hyperactive, but they aren't normally aggressive, so I brought him here to find out why." She looked at me intently. "He had the drug. And I'll bet the other piskies did, too."

I gaped at her for a moment. "But… damn." What had they been—a test run? The piskies had been running amok for weeks, I remembered—the owners of the house had waited until the last second before reporting them. "The explosion in the shed… was that the drug?"

"I wondered," said Isabel. "So I sneaked back into their garden and used a tracking spell. Someone set up a trap. It was dark in the shed so I couldn't see much, but I'm certain it was one of *them*. A half-faerie. I saw them in the vision."

Calder? Why would he bother with piskies, even his lab rats? "Okay. I don't even know what to think. Why wind up piskies?" I walked to look closer at the glass case. "I'd be careful. Calder is still wandering around, and I wouldn't put it past him to have people tailing me. If he figures out we know one another, like Velkas did…"

"Don't worry about me," said Isabel. "I carry a dozen anti-faerie spells. He'd regret it if he tried anything."

I opened my mouth to argue and decided better of it. At this rate, I'd turn into Vance and expect to be in ten places at once. Considering I didn't have the advantage of a teleporting ability, it'd be a hell of a lot trickier for me.

I have to kill Calder. I shut the thought away for later, but it remained, beating at the doors in the back of my head.

Isabel moved the sleeping piskie to join Erwin on the windowsill. "Now the *Ivy nearly dies* part of the night's over, want to watch me test-drive some more tripwire spells?"

I smiled. "Oh hell, yes."

CHAPTER SEVENTEEN

The following morning, I slept in long and late, and woke up to blessed silence and the knowledge that I had one day free from fighting in the Trials.

And then I remembered I'd accepted an invite to one of the mages' social events, headed by Vance Colton himself.

"Great," I muttered, rolling out of bed and unplugging my phone from its charger. No messages from Vance.

I considered my ripped jeans and threw them next to the door. Then I picked up every loose article of clothing from the floor, tossing any lost causes into the 'throw away' pile as well. Not because Vance might come into my room again. I'd needed to tidy the place for months. Also… I had an impossible task ahead.

My wardrobe consisted of a combination of cheap, jumble sale clothes that ripped or gained permanent bloodstains on the first outing, and the occasional more durable, expensive purchase like my leather jacket. I went for practicality, not style. I didn't accept invites to parties, human or otherwise.

I kicked the wardrobe door closed and made for the shower. Even after the healing spell, landing on the floor so many times had done a number on my back, and I'd acquired fresh scars to add to the ones I already had. I scowled at my reflection. Assuming I managed to find something to wear, the amount of skin I showed depended on whether I wanted to draw people's attention to my scars. There'd been no healing spells in Faerie, so every mark stayed on me like a brand.

"Ivy." Isabel rapped on the door. "Mailman's here with a delivery for you."

"I didn't order anything." I finished dressing and I tugged a brush through my hair, tying it into its usual ponytail. "No money, remember?"

"It's in your name."

Huh? I unlocked the door and went into the hallway, then grabbed my sword. Our wards were in top working order, but I wouldn't put it past Calder or the other faeries to find some new way to get to me.

The postman flinched away at the sight of my sword. Instead of asking me to sign for the package, he all but fled the doorstep, leaving me blinking. "Oops."

"What is it?" asked Isabel.

"Good question." An unlabelled box was a red flag if I ever saw one, but it had made it through seventeen layers of wards. I knelt and tugged at the packaging. Isabel joined me, ripping the cardboard open.

"It's clothes."

I looked. She was right. "Well, shit."

"He didn't." Isabel's face split into a grin. "You told him you didn't have anything to wear. Right?"

"Oh my god." How the hell was I even supposed to react to this? "How—shit. I can't repay him. He knows I don't have any money. There's no way."

"Doubt he expects you to." Isabel picked up the box. "Let's see what we've got in here."

She carried the box into the flat, leaving me standing on the doorstep like an idiot. My mind was a blank of shock. Did Vance think I'd been asking him for help? *Jesus.* No matter how dire things got, I never asked other people for help. Pride didn't allow it.

He likely knew, and had done it anyway. *Dammit, Vance.*

"He gets your style." Isabel deposited the box on the sofa, disturbing a sleeping Erwin. The piskie took flight with a shriek. I stepped around a chalk circle on the floor and stared into the box. He hadn't just bought me an outfit for today, he'd replaced my jeans… several times over. I pulled article after article of clothing from the box with growing horror. "I'd have to save for six months to pay for all these."

"He can afford to throw money away." Isabel examined some of the tops with an appreciative expression. "Don't worry about it."

"It's the principle," I muttered, ineffectually. A new leather jacket lay near the bottom, complete with inside pockets exactly the right size for my daggers. "Now that's unfair."

"Like I said, he knows you." Isabel pulled out the last two items—dresses. Not open-backed. He'd seen my scars already, of course. I buried my head in my hands and groaned.

When I opened my eyes, the clothes were still there. Isabel held up the two dresses. "Blue or black?"

"Either." I shrugged.

"Blue," she said. "It matches your eyes."

"All right." He'd won, damn him. If I objected, I'd be ungrateful. He couldn't know how it felt to constantly struggle for money, and the pride and anger that came from it. It wasn't fair to blame him for not understanding something he'd never experienced.

Like what Avakis had done. How it had chewed me up inside and changed me.

"Ivy?" Isabel waved the dress in front of me. "You okay?"

"Yeah. I'll be fine."

"You'll be more than fine." She placed the dress in my hands. "You'll look stunning. Count on it. If Vance wasn't already smitten with you, he would be after seeing you in this."

"If you say so."

"If you want make-up, I have some. Or we could use a spell—"

"No," I said, warningly. "Absolutely no spells. I've had enough of running around in masks."

If Vance wanted me, he could have me the way I was. If there was one thing Faerie had taught me, it was that every illusion came with a cost.

***

The dress, as it turned out, didn't even come down to my knees. I wobbled to the mages' front door in the ridiculous heels I'd borrowed from Isabel—she'd given me a scandalised look when I'd suggested wearing my boots—and carried a pair of flat shoes in my bag for backup. I hated not having my sword, but I'd been able to fit two daggers in my shoulder bag. They'd have to do.

The door opened, and Vance grinned at me.

I scraped together every piece of dignity I had left. "Thank you for the delivery today."

He raised an eyebrow. "You're welcome."

"Did you expect me to throw it back in your face?"

"Part of me thought you might." His eyes raked over me, gleaming with obvious appreciation. "You look delectable," he said in an undertone, sending warm shivers down my spine. He didn't look half bad himself, though I'd seen him wearing a suit a dozen times.

"How the hell am I supposed to repay you?" I hissed. "I haven't even solved one case yet."

"You will." He glanced over his shoulder. "I need to take care of something. Wanda and Drake are here. I told them you were coming."

And that was that. Hesitantly, I made my way towards the source of the noise. Twin glass windowed-doors led the way into a huge hall. Tables had been set up around the outskirts, leaving the centre clear for dancing. A beat I didn't recognise filled the air. Not my taste, but at least it didn't sound like piano music.

The mages knew how to throw a party, that was for sure. As for me, I stood there like I'd walked into the arena again. A few people glanced at me, but I didn't attract any derogatory stares this time. I looked like one of them, after all. I scanned the crowd, searching for someone I knew. Instead, my gaze zeroed in on Vance again, who stood talking to two other mages.

I almost wanted to hate him for dragging me into this. I hated crowds, and the bright light of the chandelier made me want to back away into the shadows. I took a glass of champagne from one of the passing servants, since I'd never tried it before. I gingerly took a sip. Yeuch. Maybe not. I ditched it on a nearby table and debated making for the door.

"Ivy!" Wanda approached, smiling at me. She wore a strappy red dress and had her hair styled in curls that I could never hope to achieve. I'd just tied mine back, as usual. "Why are you lurking near the door?"

I gave an awkward shrug. "Social situations aren't my thing."

"Vance invited you."

"He invited everyone." I indicated the room at large. "Seriously, I'm going—"

"Ivy!" Drake appeared at my side, not looking terrible

himself in a smart suit. His coppery hair was unruly as ever. "Glad you could make it."

"Yeah." *I'm not.*

Drake clearly knew everyone here. Within seconds he'd disappeared onto the dance floor, dragging Wanda along with him. I laughed at her expression, and didn't notice Vance behind me until he leaned over and whispered, "Dance with me?"

Yes. "No."

"You owe me one," he said quietly. Oh, shit. *He did it on purpose.* He had me cornered.

"I have two left feet."

"You're lying. I've seen you fight." He rested a warm hand on my arm. "It's enchanting. Almost enough to make me drop my guard."

"Oh please," I said. "I bet you use that line on all the girls."

"No," he said, "I don't." He drew me closer to him, raised my hand to his mouth and pressed his lips to it, leaving the skin tingling.

Then before I'd quite regained the use of my mental functions, he'd swept me onto the dance floor.

It came as no surprise that the man could dance. We fell

into a rhythm not unlike when we fought, but a different kind of energy filled the air. This was no struggle for dominance. I didn't even *like* dancing. But the outside world melted away as though a bubble formed around us, and there was nothing but his hand around my waist and the electrifying closeness of his body. Heat blossomed underneath my skin. Damn him, and damn my stupid body for responding to his touch.

"This is ridiculous," I hissed between my teeth.

He chuckled. "Indulge me."

"If you insist."

He leaned closer, hand resting on my shoulder as the rhythm slowed. "Were you really worried about my safety?"

"No. Yes—goddamn you."

"You're blushing." He smirked. "Anyone would think I flustered you."

"Anyone would think I'm not about to kick you in the kneecap right now."

"Someone's twitchy today."

"Can't have anything to do with my next duel to the death, can it?"

His smile faded. "You aren't going to die. Not if I have anything to do with it."

I stopped moving. Met his grey eyes. "You don't have to

pull the act on me. I can fight by myself."

"You can't blame me for worrying about your safety."

At the end of his sentence, I heard, *especially when you're so worried about mine.*

Sweet Jesus, I was in trouble. His stubble brushed against my cheek, his lips inches from the delicate spot behind my ear. "That dress is making me crazy."

I exhaled. Finally. He'd admitted he wanted me. And I, fool that I was, stood there like I'd lost all ability to speak. Even to say, *I want you too.* Or *I'm falling for you, Vance.*

I said neither, mostly because people were watching. Of course they were. I'd been staring into his eyes like an idiot the whole time we were dancing.

"Ivy." His voice was barely a breath.

"I want out of here."

The next thing I knew, he'd pulled me away from the dance floor, to the doors into the hallway. Then his hands were either side of me, pinning me to the wall.

Vance's mouth found mine, fierce, demanding, stopping my breath. My teeth nipped his lower lip and the growl that escaped his throat told me I had at least some effect on him similar to the one he had on me.

His hands moved to my thighs, below my dress. His

mouth claimed mine again, fierce, heated. His fingers inched higher, feather-light against my skin, slipping under the hem, towards the heat building between my legs. I bit back a moan.

"Ivy," he growled in my ear. "Do you—"

A scream rang through the corridor.

He jerked away from me and I steadied myself against the wall. "What the hell—?" he snarled, spinning around.

Another mage ran past, shouting, "There's been a security breach."

"Of what sort?" Vance demanded.

"Brawling half-faeries."

Vance followed, me running after him. Damn. Had more half-faeries fallen under the drug's control? Within seconds, the heat igniting in my body turned to ice as the temperature dropped. A breeze ruffled my hair, and Vance's stony expression told me he was the source, and the culprits would pay for interrupting us.

I had five seconds to be thoroughly flattered, then all hell broke loose.

CHAPTER EIGHTEEN

Several other mages ran out of the building alongside us. Smoke filled the air, bringing the smell of burning grass. Fire imps ran screaming through the garden, hurling fireballs which mostly bounced off the wards on the manor's front. Nobody attempted to catch them, because all the mages were clustered around the main path, where several figures brawled. I grabbed the nearest imp and tossed it headfirst into the fountain.

Who the hell had brought down the wards outside the mages' headquarters? They were even more sophisticated than the ones on my flat. I moved quickly along the path, cursing these blasted heels. The crowd parted a little, showing me one of the fighters.

Ralph.

The mages' guard writhed and yelled, punching and kicking anyone who came near. His opponent, a wiry teenage half-faerie with green hair, fought alongside a female half-faerie who I vaguely recognised as one of the eliminated contestants. Plainly, Ralph had left the gates unlocked and started a fight on the doorstep.

Vance, undeterred, swept the crowd aside with a wave of his hand and pinned the three brawling part-faeries to the pavement in three seconds flat. Even held in place by the strength of the Mage Lord's magic, they continued to struggle.

"Knock them out," he said through clenched teeth. "Somebody knock them out."

Apparently it cost him a lot of power to hold down three people at once. Several other mages ran over, hauling two of the squirming half-faeries upright. One was Ralph, who continued to flail, hands clawing, spit flying from his mouth.

"Bring him in," said Vance to the mage holding him. "As for the other two—" He moved to grab the third half-faerie, locking an arm around his throat—"We're taking them with us."

Two mages restrained the second half-faerie, while the one Vance held slumped into unconsciousness under the pressure Vance's arm put on his windpipe.

"What're you doing with them?" I'd started to severely regret wearing heels. Not to mention leaving my sword behind.

"Taking them back home."

I swore. "To the half-faeries' territory? I want to come with you, but I'm not going dressed like this."

Vance handed the half-faerie over to another waiting mage. "I'll take you home."

"Wait—"

Too late. Vance's hand took mine, and the manor disappeared.

I stumbled down my own hallway, cursing. "You can't leave me out of this, Vance—" Before I'd got the words out, he'd vanished.

"Fucking hell." I added a number of other expressive curses.

The flat door opened. "Whoa." Isabel blinked at me. "What happened?"

"Faeries." I kicked off my heels, carrying them into the flat. "Of course, the bloody faeries ruined everything."

I ran into my room, changed in twenty seconds, and grabbed my sword, shrugging on my jacket. "I'm going in there as Ivy, not in disguise. This is Calder's work, and that bloody over-confident Mage Lord is probably walking into a trap." I considered calling him using the mage mark, but I'd planned to go to half-blood territory either way.

"Hang on," said Isabel. "Fill me in. He's where?"

"Half-blood territory, carrying a pair of drugged idiots who started a fight outside the manor." My phone vibrated in my jeans pocket. *It's him.* I tugged out the phone and stared, heart sinking. "Oh, fuck."

"What?"

I looked at her. "The Chief of the half-faeries is missing."

We'd been stupid. Of course Calder wouldn't restrict his plotting to within the time the Trials took place. We'd let our guards slip and now Calder had struck right where he wanted to. With no leader, the half-faeries would turn to the next available person.

Especially when he offered them their wildest dreams.

Screw the disguise. Calder knew I was alive. There was no point in pretending.

"Please stay here." I backed towards the door. "I'll meet Vance." My hands raced across the on-screen keyboard.

A muffled scream made us both spin around. The piskie Isabel had trapped beat at the sides of its glass prison with its tiny fists. Screams followed, setting Erwin off, too.

"Isabel," I said. "I know it's a long shot, but if you can figure out how to counteract the drug, it might save lives.

Calder's probably used it on the half-faeries' Chief." Or killed him and taken the leadership. Either way, we were screwed.

She dipped her head. "Yeah. I actually asked the coven for ideas on how to calm the piskie down." She indicated the raving piskie's container. "I've been testing all our usual anti-spell solutions, but none have worked so far."

"Tell the coven," I said. "If Calder's not already out in the open, he will be. Everyone should know about that drug."

Isabel nodded again. "Ivy... *please* be careful."

My phone buzzed with Vance's reply. "He's outside. I— you be careful, too." We hugged briefly, then I turned my back on the screaming piskies and went to meet Vance.

"What happened?" I asked immediately, closing the door behind me.

Instead of responding, Vance took my arm. In a flash, we stood outside half-blood territory.

"Hey—wait." I stared ahead at the deceptively quiet-looking grounds. "Do they know?"

"They suspect," he said. "A number of other half-faeries are also missing. There are rumours."

"Crap," I said. "I should have known Calder would strike us where we least expected. Isabel's looking into making an antidote for the drug. If Calder uses it on a lot of people at once, though…" I shrugged helplessly. "What's the plan?"

"Calder has left no traces," said Vance. "Apart from those two addresses, and they turned out to be dead ends. Unoccupied houses."

"Your mages looked into it?"

"They're patrolling half-blood territory." He indicated the street ahead. "There's one place left to look, but I wanted it to be your choice."

One place. I nodded, swallowing my fear. "Back to the Trials."

I'd been a fool to think Calder would wait until the final round of the contest to strike. He might have offered the drug up to the winners, but the Trials were a means to an end. And that end… was most likely opening the veil.

"I wish I knew where I saw him in the vision," I said. "It looked like a field in a park, but the details were blurry. He summoned the hellhounds there. It must be near the Ley Line, wherever it is."

Vance gave me a sharp look. "The Line's under close watch, too, as is necromancer territory. I've alerted Lord Evander, but he insists hellhounds aren't his area."

"They will be if they tear his throat out." Would *nobody* in this town take some damned responsibility? Aside from

Vance and the Mage Lords, of course.

"No activity is currently reported on the Line," said Vance. "If there was, I'd suspect Calder waited for us there."

"No, he'll be in the arena. Dramatics. Like father, like son. I think you're right. We should go there first. Kill him, take care of the mess he left behind later."

"Kill him." Vance's tone told me how very much he wanted to bury a blade in the half-faerie's throat. But I trusted he'd let me deal the killing blow.

Vance's icy cold hand gripped mine, and then we were in the alley, hellhounds on either side.

"Shit," I said, eloquently.

My sword came out as the nearest hellhound's teeth snapped at my face. Vance's blade sliced into it, stopping the momentum before the beast tore my head off. I swore and hit out with my own weapon, catching its throat and spilling arterial blood down my arms. Damn. My new jacket had lasted all of five minutes without acquiring bloodstains.

I spun around to help Vance and found he'd caused a pile-up, sending three hellhounds crashing into one another. Two swords whipped through the air, delivering killing blows and reappearing in Vance's hands.

"Bastard's brought half the Wild Hunt," I muttered.

A spray of blood darkened the brick walls. I stabbed another hellhound, moving closer to the back way into the arena. The doors lay open, screaming, *this is a trap, Ivy*.

Yeah, I knew. I also knew that unless I killed Calder, asap, he'd unleash his magical drug and tear the city to pieces.

My speed quickened, magic flooding my veins. Wait— could I feed on the hellhounds' pain? I'd never tried it on a non-human. My sword cut into a hellhound's flank, and I envisioned the pain flowing through to me. Nothing happened. Maybe my sword blocked it.

Or maybe Avakis's ability only worked on mortals.

My hesitation damn near cost me a limb. Cutting the offending hellhound's throat, I caught sight of a familiar flash of blue inside the opening to the stairs. Taunting me to come inside.

Calder. I knew it.

"Vance," I said, out of the corner of my mouth, "he's in there."

Vance finished off the hellhound he was fighting, kicking its heavy body aside. "He is?"

"I can see his magical signature," I said. "It'd throw off his game if we set the whole building on fire."

Vance's expression showed no amusement. His hands and

wrists were coated in black scales around the twin blades he held, but his gaze was steady. "I suspect the building is warded."

"Maybe."

Vance walked past me, towards the open door. I moved in behind, heart thudding. "Hold on—" *It should be me,* I would have said, if Vance hadn't stopped dead at the top of the stairs.

"Bastard," he said through clenched teeth. Damn. The place was warded, all right.

"Let me…" I trailed off, heart sinking to my feet. The air above the stairs shimmered blue. Like my magic did, when I turned it into a shield. Only visible to people with the Sight. "Dammit. He wants me to fight him alone." I held Irene up, willing my hands to stop shaking. "I'm going in."

A pause. Vance watched me, eyes unblinking.

"Don't argue with me," I said. "Seriously. Go back, help Isabel with the cure for the drug. Or just throw knockout spells at the half-faeries causing the most damage. Stop them. I'll kill—"

He cut my words off, leaning in and covering my mouth with his.

Oh. *Oh.* His tongue touched mine, his lips surprisingly

soft. His hands were rough, cold, but the way they held mine said more than words could. "Be careful, Ivy."

"Same to you." My voice was barely a whisper, and the pain when I turned away from him turned into a physical ache. I took one step towards the entrance, then two. No barrier blocked my path. Only people with faerie magic could pass through here.

The darkness closed in on me. A clunk behind me told me the doors closed of their own accord.

The faint glow of magic lit my way downstairs, through the corridor. At their end, the doors to the arena opened, revealing a room cloaked in shadows. The ground had turned to earth, while tall trees surrounded the outskirts of what had turned into a wide clearing the size of the arena.

"Impressive." The echo of my voice bounced down the corridor. "How long did it take you to set up?"

No answer. I held Irene up, magic suffusing the air and lighting up the gloom. Not enough to see the creature in the shadows until it pounced at me. I ducked, and a bundle of snarling, spiked green fur leaped past my head. I spun around, blade in hand. The creature had disappeared.

Crap. This was Chameleon—my next opponent, and presumably controlled by the magic drug. Or just coerced.

No doubt Calder didn't have to try hard to garner obedience. He'd dangled immortality in front of the half-faeries, and they'd taken the bait. Hell, maybe even the Chief had, in the end.

I had to kill Calder's minion to get to him, then. So be it.

Rather than waving my sword around like an idiot, I used my magic to light up the area around me. Calder was probably hiding somewhere. If he was even here. I didn't put it past him to set up a trap and then leave... but I'd got the impression he wanted to kill me in person.

Bring it.

Magic cloaked me in shimmering blue. I'd do better to use it as a shield to keep from being jumped, at least until I figured out where the creature was hiding. Problem was, then I'd be stuck crouching here until it made a move.

Go on the offensive. A little tricky when I couldn't *see* the enemy. I moved forward, right into the centre of the arena, and risked a look up at the balconies. No sign of Calder up there, either.

A shuffling sound. I glanced down and saw a patch of grass running along the floor. *Aha.* If I stood here, nothing would be able to sneak up on me without making a noise. Taking a deep breath, I let my shield of magic drop, flowing to the fingertips of my free hand, and lashed out with my blade, hitting thin air. The shapeshifter faerie wouldn't be able to come near me without reacting to the iron.

When nothing appeared, I shot a blast of magic up at the ceiling, lighting the whole arena. The flash lasted a second, but enough for me to see the outline of the shapeshifter faerie creeping up on me. Gotcha.

I swung the sword around with magic-enhanced instincts. A pained scream sounded, and Chameleon appeared, my blade buried deep in his side.

The half-faerie slumped down. Applause sounded, and my head jerked up.

"Enjoy the entertainment?" I asked. To my relief, my voice didn't shake, even though I knew who watched me. The sick bastard who'd set up his own version of the Trials.

Calder stood tall, carrying a sword in one hand and wearing the same black-and-silver armour. I turned to him, my own blade held at an angle to show the blood dripping down it. *I'll bury my sword in your heart.*

"That wasn't much of a show," he said, almost petulantly.

"I'll give you a show, all right." I approached him, blade humming in my hands. My whole body shook with the force of the magic rolling through my veins. Not dampened this

276

time. I wouldn't let it be. *Avakis's power belongs to me. The magic is mine.*

The magic burning around Calder seemed dim by comparison, not bright like last time. I moved in closer, readying myself to jump. Then I lunged forward.

He barely dodged my blade. The air turned cold, but not icy. Maybe because the hellhounds were outside. Calder swung his own sword to block my next attack. I had him on the defensive. His bright blue eyes were furious, but his magic had turned transparent, the way mine had when his fed on mine.

I didn't know why, but I'd take every advantage I could. Blue smoke rose around me, encasing my body. My blade slashed and swiped, nearly making contact several times. He was definitely slower than last time. Like *his* power had been dampened rather than mine. Calder kept moving backwards, as though he was letting me drive him to the arena's edge.

I stopped. Not fast enough. His magic grew bright, sharp, as threads of light poured into him from the body of the fallen shapeshifter. It was still alive, feebly stirring, and he'd drawn strength from its pain.

Calder lunged forward with speed equal to mine. Our blades clashed with a clang. He bared his teeth in a snarl. I glared back.

"Don't get too close to the iron," I hissed, pushing my blade down on his. It didn't give. Must be the real deal—like Avakis's sword, forged from the heart of a tree in Faerie.

My blade inched towards his exposed hand. *Come on.*

Calder's other hand moved, and sent a blast of icy energy at my chest. My shield shattered into a thousand fragments.

Irene flew from my hand. My body was flung into the air, the breath frozen in my lungs. He'd hit me with pure Death energy. My vision swam, and I swore I saw transparent figures in the corners of my vision. *No. I can't be—*

I hit the ground. Pain exploded in my skull, and the world faded out.

CHAPTER NINETEEN

I woke when a punch nearly dislocated my jaw. The pain sent me spinning to the side, my head colliding with a damp, solid surface. Brick.

"Wake up," said a harsh voice.

I groaned. "Give me another hour."

Another punch rattled my jaw. Apparently he didn't find that funny. I spat out a mouthful of blood, and glared at Calder.

He moved in closer so I could see every inch of him leaning over me. He really was the spitting image of his father, albeit with silver hair rather than black—he didn't even have the rounded ears of a human. He was so pale, his skin glowed in the dim light of the… cell. Figures.

"So you decided not to kill me this time." I half sat up, my back brushing against the cold wall behind me. From the protesting aches all over my body, the floor wasn't a fluffy mattress. Not that I saw much beyond the eerie blue glow surrounding Calder. He must have boosted his magic in the time he'd been unconscious, because he blazed all over. Didn't do much for the nonexistent lighting in here. I saw the dim outline of another person slumped nearby. Dead or alive, I couldn't tell.

"Ivy." His eyes gleamed, blue as icy chips. "We didn't have the chance to talk."

"Yeah, because you stabbed me and left me bleeding to death." I attempted to stretch my stiff neck. Since my hands were tied behind my back, this proved difficult. "Doesn't really make for friendly conversation. And for the record, I'm not interested in talking to you." I wiggled my hands. The movement stung, like he'd tied me with string embedded with spikes. Ow.

"Don't bother," said Calder. "You won't break free."

"Thought you wanted me dead."

He shrugged. The movement looked odd on him. "You're more useful to me alive right now. I don't think you understand what a gift my father gave you."

"I took it from him," I said.

"I know. I'm glad you lived, Ivy." His hard, flat tone echoed off the walls. "I knew you killed my father, but I didn't know you took his magic yourself. You're human."

"I won his magic when I killed him. Just like I'm going to kill you. What the hell did you think killing the Chief of the half-faeries would achieve?"

"I deserve to be in his place. Besides, I didn't kill him." He indicated the other figure slumped against the wall. Now the light from Calder's full-body glow illuminated the far corner, it became clear the cell's other occupant wasn't dead after all. The man appeared to be unconscious, but faint traces of magic hovered around him.

I turned back to Calder. "Going soft? Or do you prefer making other people do your dirty work, like your father did?"

"I'm not him," said Calder, the trace of a snarl underneath his voice. "I have every intention of killing you myself, after I pry every secret from your tongue."

"That's a big statement." I shifted forward, fighting a wince at the pain in my wrists. "So you didn't like your father, then."

His mouth twisted. "You don't understand, do you? You were taken into Faerie. A changeling was left in your place. A half-Sidhe. Me. He abandoned me like I was some pathetic human."

"So you *are* a changeling," I said. "You've never been to

the Grey Vale."

"Thanks to you." He spat out the words, kicking me viciously in the knee. I managed to turn my yelp of pain into a gasp. Damn, that'd leave a bruise. "You left us stranded."

"I saved your ass, you ungrateful dick," I said. "The Grey Vale is where exiles go. I'd gladly send you back there myself if it meant not having to listen to your *woe is me* speech. It might have escaped your attention that life's a bitch whether you're human or not." I was babbling, fingers scraping for a way to undo the ties. Based on the stinging in my fingers and hands, he'd tied me up with barbed wire or thorns. Maybe I could use magic—

Calder's eyes flashed blue, and a shock went through my limbs. I yelped, my body suddenly icy cold, and the magic slipped out of reach.

"Like I said, I'm more than you are. I'm the son of a Sidhe lord, not a pathetic human. The other Sidhe lords are fools if they think they can ignore us."

"This is what it's about? You want to draw the Sidhe lords here?" I sucked in air, which felt unusually thick. He'd used magic again, like a toned-down version of the fear spell. I assumed he must have boosted his power while I was unconscious. Probably by torturing someone. "So what's the big deal with the drug, then? You won't have much of an army if they keep killing one another."

"I never said I wanted an army," said Calder. "An energy surge is required to open the veil."

"Where'd you learn that? Velkas? Are you mad because he ran off and left you here after you did so much to help him?" I was going out on a limb, but the dangerous expression that crossed Calder's face told me I'd guessed right. He'd been the one running around doing Velkas's dirty work, hoping he'd get to go into the Grey Vale himself. Instead, Velkas had ditched him once he had everything he needed, wanting Avakis's power for himself.

Calder slapped me across the face. I tasted blood again, but stared at him defiantly. "There are less complicated ways to open the veil than starting a war amongst the half-bloods. Just saying." Like using *my* magic, for instance. But he'd never wanted me alive. He'd never considered that my magic might be more than the living manifestation of the man who'd abandoned him.

He underestimated me. He'd never been to the Grey Vale. He didn't know his father. I'd been so wrapped up in thinking there might be some elaborate plan, I'd never stopped to consider he might have the same lack of information as most half-faeries did. Velkas had probably only told him the bare minimum.

"Talk's cheap," I said. "Let me go and I'll show you why opening the veil is a bad idea. Especially when you've clearly never read a necromancy handbook."

"Velkas told me what to do."

"He really did a number on you, didn't he?" I shook my head. "Did he feed you the whole *faerie blood equals immortality* line, too? Because it's total bollocks."

"Enough." The sharp word echoed off the walls. "Velkas was a powerful Sidhe lord. You shouldn't have been able to kill him."

I shrugged. "Avakis was more powerful, and I killed *him* without even using magic. If you get cocky, you lose. What were you doing with Velkas, then? Running around as his errand-boy?"

"He hired me to summon some changelings. He promised to take me with him to Faerie. He gave me my ash sword, like his own oak one."

Summon some changelings? "You did that?"

"He taught me a lot," said Calder. "Velkas was right when he said half-bloods are easily fooled. Mortal blood makes us weak."

Yeah. That includes you, dickhead.

"What's your point? Capturing me won't solve your problems. It's all human blood here." I wriggled my bleeding hands. "Not a drop of faerie blood in sight."

"You should never have taken his magic." He grabbed my arm roughly, yanking me to my feet. "I should have made sure you died."

"Yeah, you should." Anger seared my veins. "You're *stupid,* aren't you? You're incapable of thinking for yourself. You think Velkas had all the answers? He was just as clueless, but at least he had class."

Calder threw me against the wall. My back hit solid brick, and the thorns around my wrists dug in tighter.

"It's true," I said. "You might have fooled the other half-bloods, but you aren't powerful enough to cross the veil by yourself." My heart beat fast in my ears, and I was certain I'd overstepped the mark this time. I could hardly believe he genuinely didn't know how to get into Faerie. He'd lived *here.* In the mortal world. A changeling.

Calder's expression twisted. "You're lying."

"I'm not. By all means go ahead, but if you're gonna turn every half-blood in town against one another, I'll have to stop you."

"You're going nowhere," said Calder. "Now I've got you here, I want to see how red your human blood really runs."

Sick fear rose in my throat, but I didn't break eye contact with him. "Try me."

He reached for my arm and I lunged forward with both feet. He'd moved within range, allowing me to kick at him. My feet collided with his shins, knocking him off balance. His half-faerie reflexes stopped him from tripping over, but the distraction let me scramble to my feet. Even with my hands bound, I could do some damage.

"Don't you dare—" He grabbed for my arm and missed, and I headbutted him in the face.

Ow. I saw stars. The move probably hurt me more than it hurt him, but he stumbled back again, giving me more advantage. My head rang with pain. I ignored it and rammed a shoulder into his chest. He didn't have the full strength and agility of a pure-blooded Sidhe, and I'd taken him by surprise.

Finally, *finally,* my magic came back in a dizzying rush, pouring out of me. Calder snarled, his nose bleeding, and my attack ricocheted off an invisible shield. He whipped out his sword, pointing it at me with shaking hands. I'd spooked him somehow. Maybe he'd seen his long dead father in the magic I'd thrown at him.

"You aren't worthy," he gasped.

Jesus. He was scared of me. The creepy guy who'd confronted me in the alleyway and stabbed me to death had been an act. Now he wasn't fully in control of the situation, he'd turned into a scared kid. A blink of an eye to the Sidhe. Avakis would probably have forgotten about him. He certainly hadn't mentioned a son. Then again, our 'conversations' had mostly consisted of me begging him not to hurt me.

The fear Calder had incited in me had been from the hellhounds. Alone, he was just one lone lunatic. Albeit one who'd possibly caused a supernatural war.

I looked at him, threads of magic swirling around me. "It's not too late to call them off," I said. "I wasn't kidding when I said you're going to turn this town into a bloodbath. You can stay here and die or try to get to the Grey Vale and die anyway. The place is poison to people with human blood."

I wasn't kidding. Humans could technically survive there, and even age like normal as I had during my three-year captivity, but the air was tainted with magic. A lot of the other prisoners had got sick while we were held captive. Not to mention the fact that ninety percent of the wildlife enjoyed the taste of human flesh.

"You're lying," he said.

"I'm not. Also, the lords of the Grey Vale won't see you as one of them. They'll take your skin off and wear it as a coat." I wasn't kidding about that, either. Luckily, I hadn't met that particular faerie before Avakis had killed him.

"Stop," hissed Calder. "You won't dissuade me. The damage is already done. The half-bloods are fighting amongst themselves, the mages are overwhelmed, and the veil is on the brink of opening."

"And how would you know?" There'd be a power surge across the Ley Line, like last time, but I doubted he even knew about the Ley Line. It depended how much Velkas had told him—and it sounded like the Sidhe lord had left Calder to stumble around in the dark.

"Because I gave it my magic."

Shit. That's why he'd seemed weaker earlier. Calder had fed his own magic into the spell, and his magic had the same effect as mine. He didn't need me at all.

"So why'd you bring me here, then?"

"I want everyone to know when I open the veil," he said. "Summer and Winter, too."

Huh? "You want them to know you're throwing a tantrum because Daddy abandoned you?"

I anticipated his attack and ducked, so he hit me with magic instead. The flesh on my bones burned with cold, and I couldn't hold back my scream. I slumped down the wall, head lolling on my shoulder. Through blurred vision, I saw the other prisoner start upright, looking around. The Chief of the half-faeries had woken up.

"I've had enough," said Calder. "You've told me everything I need to know. The rumour about pure faerie blood might be a lie, but it's rooted in truth. I *can* find immortality, but only on the other side of the veil." He approached me, and I managed to tilt my head upright in time to see him holding a thorn the length of my finger.

"The hell's that for?" I shifted on the spot, wishing my legs didn't feel so numb. His magic had dampened mine. Again.

Calder's hand shot out and grabbed my arm, and he stabbed me with the thorn. Blood welled up on my wrist. He then lifted a small container seemingly out of thin air. Inside was a clear liquid.

Oh, shit. He planned to drug me.

"That only works on faeries," I said.

"Not this batch," he said. "I'll test it on you. If it works, I'll put it in the town's water supply."

"You're fucked up," I said.

Ignoring me, he continued, "I need to get as much energy into the spell as possible. It's not enough yet. The veil is close, but something's holding me back."

Yeah. The necromancers. Damn. Did he not know about them, either? I was dealing with a kid who couldn't be bothered to do his homework. Calder planned to throw everyone into chaos and feed on the misery unleashed to give himself an unlimited power boost, slicing open the veil in the process. Oh, and poison all the humans, too. Because why the hell not. And I couldn't do a thing to stop him.

I gave him an insolent stare instead.

"Stop looking at me like that," he demanded. "I'm going to drug you, and feed on your pain. His, too." He jerked his thumb at the Chief half-faerie. "How do you think the half-bloods will react when their Chief turns on them?"

"Why bring him here?"

He bared his teeth. "I wanted to leave them to do a little damage of their own, first."

"You're *just like him,*" I spat. What the hell, I was going to die anyway. Might as well piss him off and go down fighting. "Except you're stupider."

"This new drug will make you lose all sense of self," said

Calder. "As for your mage friend—" He grabbed my arm and yanked my sleeve down, exposing the mage mark on my shoulder—"I wonder what'll happen when he hears you call for help?"

No. Vance, no.

He tipped the container over my bleeding arm. My vision went fuzzy, my body jerking. A weightless sensation took hold of me, but my body continued to move even though I hadn't consciously planned to.

My body stood. I didn't. Whatever I was, I lay where my body had been, watching Ivy—or whoever controlled me—move towards Calder.

Shock rang through me, and I faded away.

CHAPTER TWENTY

The roar of a crowd brought me to my senses. I stood in the centre of the arena, where I'd left off. But there was something… disconnected about the way the world moved. Like I watched it through a sheet of distorted glass.

And facing me, my opponent was… Vance. Oh, shit.

I didn't see Calder, but he'd be amongst the crowd somewhere. Everything looked weird, like a grey film covered everything. Like… like I was outside my body.

I swore, loudly. Nobody reacted. Vance stalked closer. Holy shit. He was in full-on verge-of-shifting mode. Power crackled off him, and though I wasn't sure I even had a body, every part of me that remained froze in terror.

My body, however, moved like a puppet pulled by strings. I even had my sword, though I couldn't feel the weight of it. I watched like an observer. Damn. Had the others who'd taken the drug been in the same position? How the hell did I stop Ivy-that-wasn't-me from attacking Vance? Blood spattered the ground, suggesting more than one fight had taken place since I'd last been conscious. My heart dip-dived when I caught sight of the limp body of a contestant lying in a pool of blood. Shark. He hadn't been my favourite person, but had *I* killed him, while not in control of my body? What else had Calder made me do?

I fiercely concentrated, trying to will myself into my physical body.

"You can't."

I nearly jumped out of my skin—if I hadn't been disembodied, that is. Another figure floated alongside me, and in my shock, I'd somehow drifted a good ten metres above the scene, on a level with the balconies.

"Shit. Am I *dead?*"

No way. If I *was* dead, I'd haunt Calder until he died of fright, the bastard.

"No," said the transparent figure. "The veil is fracturing, and you disconnected from your body."

"I'm aware of that!" I said. "I want to *reconnect* before whoever the hell's controlling my body kills anyone else."

Vance. I was hard-pressed to land a hit on him in training, but the person controlling my body wasn't me. Vance wouldn't want to hurt me—right? I'd wring Calder's neck the instant I returned to my body.

A shout drew my attention back to the scene below. Vance's sword pointed at my neck. Well, my body's neck.

"Fuck," I said. "Hey! I'm here."

"It won't work," said the spirit. "You're detached from your body."

"So what the hell's possessing me, then?"

"Mindless anger. The drug was once used amongst necromancers, for easier access to the spirit world, but the side effects were too severe."

"Seriously?" I glanced at him out of the corner of my eye, unable to take my gaze off my human body. I—*she*—didn't dare move for fear of being skewered on the end of Vance's blade. Stalemate. He spoke to her, but I couldn't hear a word.

I risked another look at the spirit who spoke to me. I'd thought he sounded familiar—he was the guy who'd let me over the veil from Faerie after I'd killed Velkas. The necromancer. He was so faint, I could hardly make out his features, but the fuzzy edges of his outline suggested he wore a suit.

"For crying out loud, tell me how to get back to my body. Please," I amended. Though I didn't have a physical presence, I swore I could feel my heart beating quickly where my chest should be. Like a phantom limb. "I can't die here. I have to stop that guy."

"The drug's too powerful," said the spirit.

"I have faerie magic," I said. "You're the one who let me over the veil last time. Please—please help me. You're a necromancer."

"The veil is thinning. That foolish half-faerie is going to cause irreparable damage."

"So let me stop him."

Ivy had managed to avoid the blade and was now back on her feet, duelling Vance again. Damn. Could I really move that fast? She wasn't using magic…

Where is my magic?" I asked. "Don't tell me he's feeding on it again."

"The drug prevents magic use."

That explained why none of the murders had been committed with magic. Sure as hell didn't help me now, though.

"Please," I said, all but begging this time. "You don't want the veil to open. Right?"

"No," said the necromancer, "but nobody listens to us spirits when we offer warnings. I told Lord Evander another threat to the veil existed."

"Figures," I muttered. "Someone needs to depose him and elect a leader who gives a shit."

I winced as Vance knocked Ivy down with a sweeping kick. "I can't use magic here. What the hell *can* I do?"

"Communicate through the veil."

"With necromancers. Bit late for a warning now." If they had any sense, they'd be preparing for the second round of Faerie Armageddon.

"Anyone with spirit sight or who has contact with the veil."

Wait. "Calder. He's practically feeding his life force into the spell to break the veil." And he couldn't harm me in this form. Sure, I couldn't do much to him, either, but right now, it was my only shot. *Prepare to be thoroughly haunted, you sick bastard.*

I drifted—somehow. Calder stood apart from the crowd on the highest balcony. Well, it wasn't much of a crowd. No more than a handful of battered-looking half-faeries.

"Am I a poltergeist?" I asked the other spirit. "Can I affect the physical world at all?"

"No."

Dammit. I'd have to improvise.

I floated until I stood beside Calder. Then I shoved my

hand through his chest.

Calder stumbled back with a startled gasp. His mouth moved, but I didn't hear the words.

"You killed me," I said, inspired. "Call off the fight or I'll take you over the veil with me. *Without* your physical body."

I punched him in the chest again. My fist sailed through thin air, but his expression distorted with fear so acute he looked almost human. Behind, the fight had stopped. Vance held Ivy pinned down, and I hoped she'd stay that way until I was back in my own body.

"Break the wards on this place," I told Calder. They must be keeping Vance from teleporting out. I was running out of ideas by this point, and not having a real body was a pain in the—not literal—ass. But Calder seemed thoroughly spooked. He'd definitely never dealt with the necromancers, or seen a ghost.

To freak him out even more. I stood on top of his body so our feet were in line with one another, and moved my arm when he moved his. Then I turned, my head coming out of his neck, and grinned at him.

I didn't need to hear him yell in shock. Laughing, I pretended to shake his hand. Anger contorted his face, but he was still scared shitless. I wished I could punch him for real.

I turned to the arena to find Vance and Ivy had disappeared—Vance must have taken the opportunity to get out. *Damn.* Calder was right here, but I couldn't kill him, or stop him from influencing the other half-faeries.

I hope Isabel's cure works.

With one last kick at Calder, I floated to join the other spirit.

"What now?" I asked the necromancer. "Can I stop him?"

"If you can, the knowledge is out of my hands," he said. "The veil is fracturing already."

"And you're going to just stand there and watch?"

"I'm not standing anywhere. Technically speaking."

I groaned. "Where the hell is my body?"

"You should be able to find it, if you concentrate hard enough."

Great. I had nothing to lose by this point. I closed my eyes, and the world faded out.

***

Spirits surrounded me on all sides, appearing in the thick grey fog.

"No," I said, loudly. "I'm not dead. I'm here—I shouldn't *be* here, but…" I trailed off as the other spirits faded away until it was me and the necromancer.

"Did you do that?" I asked him.

"Necromancers on this side of the veil retain some control over spirits," he said. "But not nearly enough."

"I'm a spirit, then."

"You aren't dead," he said. "You'll remain in limbo until your earthly body regains control of its senses."

"Good." I sighed in relief. "I never got your name."

"I was Lord Sydney. I rarely bother with the title these days. You can call me Frank."

Another lord. Right. "I'm Ivy. You already know more about me than I've told most people." I shifted, trying to see beyond the smoke, but nothing remained but the pair of us. "Do you know what's happening in the mortal realm?"

"A half-Sidhe is attempting to open a way to the Grey Vale by amassing energy. He appears to be harnessing it from half-faeries and humans."

"Where? He's not absorbing it. There must be a summoning circle somewhere."

"The town is the summoning circle," said Frank. "He's warded the edges. Because the town lies so close to the Ley Line, he managed to hide this until it was too late."

"What?" Shock jolted through me. "You're telling me this

now? Can you see everything? Couldn't you have warned someone?"

He took my accusing questions with an expression of calmness. "My job is to police the dead, not the living. By the time I became aware of what he was doing, the circle had closed. If I send living necromancers to the boundaries to break the circle, they'll die. The energy's unstable."

"Because he's using his own magic," I said. "He's feeding on people's misery, and I guess that's fuelling the circle, too... because we're standing in the middle of it. Well. I *was,* before I got disembodied. Shit." Shock turned to panic. If I had a heart, it'd be racing at a million miles an hour. "We have to stop him. You at least need to warn people—the ones who haven't been affected by the drug. He said he'd use it on every human." With that much panic and misery, I could only imagine the havoc it'd wreak on the circle.

Let alone the amount of power he'd gain. More than a Sidhe. More than a Mage Lord.

"In order to stop the veil from opening, the half-faerie's magic must be sealed," said Frank.

"How am I supposed to do that?"

"You can't. Only a powerful spell can seal magic away."

"Great." Damn. Surely Vance would know. He was the

leader of the magical community, after all. "Are you sure that's the only way? People are killing each other right now. Would sealing his magic stop the drug, too?"

"No, but the magical surge is making the effects worse, particularly for the half-faeries. Under the drug's influence, they can't use magic, but it fuels their anger."

"Fan-bloody-tastic," I said. "All this because he couldn't be bothered to recruit the help of a necromancer."

"No necromancer can open a path to Faerie," Frank said.

"Right." Damn, I was tired. As a ghost, that didn't even make sense. "Of course not. Is using a magic surge and opening the veil the only way to get to Summer or Winter?"

"For anyone other than Sidhe lords, yes. I confess I don't know too much about their system. I died before the invasion."

I stared at his transparent form. "How long have you been here?"

"Long enough."

"I can imagine," I muttered, really glad I wasn't a necromancer. "So Summer and Winter... they're the same realm?"

"Summer and Winter lie on a single separate plane," said the necromancer. "They occupy the same... I suppose you might say, layer of existence. Below is the Grey Vale, a piece of their world torn away by the magic of the ancient Sidhe when they exiled their gods."

Whoa. "I didn't know *that*."

"Few humans do."

"I'm not a regular human," I said. "I've *been* to the Grey Vale. I lived there for three years, and I never heard anything about exiled gods."

"That's because they're dead," said the necromancer. "The Grey Vale is… tied to Death, in a way. That's why it's possible to reach the Grey Vale by passing through the first layer of Death—an unintentional side effect of binding the two worlds."

I shook my head. This was way too surreal for me. "So you're saying there are *four* realms… but the Grey Vale is halfway between Faerie and Death?"

"In a way. Death itself forms the buffer between the Grey Vale and the human realm. The Sidhe lords know more than I do. I only know the information passed down to master necromancers when we're allowed free passage between this realm and the human world."

"And you stay here after death?"

"If we're selected as Guardians, yes," he said. "I've helped many, many souls pass through the veil, and I've *never* met one like yours."

"My magic isn't with me, though, is it?"

"No, but I assume the presence of faerie magic altered your physical body. That's why you were able to open a way between the realms."

"Damn." Could ghosts feel dizziness? I needed to lie down. "So can I stop Calder? Because he's trying to out-crazy the last guy who opened the realms."

"You can stop him when you return to your physical body. Your friends are restraining you."

"I want to see."

"There's nothing stopping you," he said.

The grey fog turned transparent, and I choked on a gasp. We floated above my living room, where Vance and Isabel stood over my writhing body on the sofa. Isabel hovered, holding what I assumed was the cure in her hands, while the not-me did her best to avoid it. Vance held not-me pinned down in a way that made me absurdly angry at the force possessing me. Like hell would I die before he touched the *real* me again.

Vance managed to get Ivy's mouth open long enough for Isabel to tip a bright green potion into it. *Hope it's the right one.*

Ivy's body jerked, then went still.

The spirit beside me disappeared, as did everything else.

***

Colour came back into focus, and my vision resolved itself piece by piece. My head rested against a cushion. Vance was holding my legs down. I lay there for a moment, out of breath like I'd run for miles.

"Ivy?" He let go.

"This is really fucking weird." I closed my eyes. "Sorry. I was a ghost for the last twenty minutes."

"Is she still drugged?" Isabel asked uncertainly. "I thought the dosage was enough."

"No, I just died," I said. "Well. Hopped over the veil for a bit." I decided against going into detail, because both of them were gaping at me. "Hi." I waved at Vance, then passed out.

I woke again seconds later, feeling slightly less dizzy. "Sorry." I shifted on my back. "I—thanks for saving me. Vance, I didn't hurt you, did I?"

"No," he said. "Wait a moment before you move."

The world became clearer. Lights flared up around me— Isabel had put a healing spell over the sofa, surrounding me. I hadn't realised how badly I ached all over until every pain disappeared in a jolt of energy. I lay there for a second, riding the high of not being in pain. And not being dead, either.

Isabel watched me with a look of concern, while Vance deactivated his own healing spell.

"Wait, I did hurt you." Blood stained one of his hands.

"That wasn't you," said Vance. "I felt the mage mark respond, and immediately landed in the arena. A number of half-faeries waited to attack me. I put them down."

"Shark? The guy with the freaky teeth?"

"He was responsible for this." Vance held up his sleeve, which had torn open.

Oh. It hadn't been me who killed the guy, then. Sure, he'd probably deserved it anyway, but I'd rather have had the choice in the matter.

"Sorry," I said. "I wanted to—I wanted to stop her attacking you. I mean, me." Awareness of Isabel watching me like she thought I'd pass out again stopped me from saying more.

"Believe it or not, I have experience dealing with out-of-control mages," he said. "You're hardly different."

"Ha." I rubbed the back of my neck. "Good job with the healing spell, Isabel. Does the cure work on humans, then?"

"I improvised," she said, with a look at Vance. "I managed

to figure out an antidote to the drug affecting the half-faeries, but humans—they react differently. Luckily, the drug he used has a well-documented cure. The coven leader gave me the ingredients list."

"A well-documented cure," I repeated. "That'd be because it had the same effect on necromancers…" I trailed off before I ended up admitting I'd just spoken to a dead person. I didn't have time to recount that now. "I need to go and kill Calder."

Isabel gasped. "You nearly died. You aren't seriously—"

To my surprise, it was Vance who interrupted. "We need to shut down the drug's effects on the others."

"I—" Isabel looked at the mess of potions on the table. "There's not enough for everyone. I can make up the difference, but there just isn't time."

"There isn't," said Vance. "But someone knows a way to stop Calder first. Unfortunately, he's unlikely to be going anywhere soon."

"Huh?" I said blankly.

"The Chief of the half-faeries escaped the same time as we did," said Vance. "He was in the arena, but he's still drugged. I had to leave him at headquarters. We'll need to give him the cure."

"You brought him out?"

"Of course I did," said Vance. "The others would have taken him to pieces. The half-faeries need leadership when this is over."

"But why do you need him now?"

"Because the Chief knows of magic none of the other half-faeries do," said Vance, "including how to stop the magic Calder unleashed before it rips the veil apart."

CHAPTER TWENTY-ONE

My heart missed a beat. "He knows how to stop Calder?" Er. So did I. Telling them I'd been talking to a ghost would be a good way to get myself left behind, so I decided to leave that part of the explanation until after this was all over.

"Yes. We'll need to administer the cure first. He's unconscious, so he won't be harming anyone."

I nodded. "Isabel—the cure for the half-faeries. Can we take some?"

"Sure, but… you just woke up from a near-death experience."

Near death. She didn't know the half of it.

"I'm fine," I said. "You need to get on with the cure. We'll need it."

"The rest of the coven are helping," she said. "Between all of us, we *might* be able to make enough, but with everyone attacking one another…"

"I'll deal with it," I said, a lot more confidently than I felt.

"What happened back at the arena, anyway?"

"Chaos," said Vance tightly. "I don't think the entire audience was drugged, but they will be now. That, or Calder will have taken out his wrath on them."

"Shit," I said. "Guys, this is going to sound crazy, but I spoke to someone who told me the whole town's converted into a giant summoning circle. Calder's harnessing all the energy from the drug, using it to fuel his own magic, and it's out of control."

"The whole town?" Vance's tone was sharp as a razor.

"I don't know when he did it," I said. "Maybe he's been planning it the whole time—but it's true, and the necromancers can't stop it. We have to seal his magic away."

Vance's gaze pierced me, and he nodded. "Yes. That's why we need to speak to the Chief of the half-faeries. He knows how to seal another Sidhe's magic."

"He's out *there*." I indicated the world in general. "How bad is it? The half-faeries... so many of them were underground."

"My mages are dealing with the half-faeries in their own territory," he said. "We warded the human houses nearby, but if the summoning circle covers the whole town, everyone this side of the Ley Line is in danger."

I knew he was thinking of his cousin, Anabel, who lived right on the edge of shifter territory. Hell, *everyone* I knew lived inside the town. Nowhere was safe.

"All right." I turned to Isabel. "It's on you. If there's anything you and the coven can do—"

"We're ready." She hugged me briefly, passing me my sword. "Calder must have taken the spells you had in your pockets, but here—"

"Thanks," I said, gratefully taking the defence spells she offered me, ending with Irene. "You're the unsung hero of this, you know that, right?"

She smiled at me, then Vance took my arm. The room disappeared in an instant.

We landed outside the mages' headquarters. Scorch marks marked the site of the earlier battle, but nobody else remained.

"The building's sealed," Vance said. "The people inside are the ones who are injured or can't fight. Every other mage is either on half-blood territory, reassuring the public or dealing with other situations."

"Tell them not to go near the edges of the circle around town," I said. "I don't know whereabouts the boundaries are, but it'll probably kill them."

A chill wind whipped up in response to my words, a sure sign Vance was pissed off. He reached and pulled a key from nowhere. Then he walked around the fence. I followed, wondering where he was going.

Shouts and bangs drifted over the rooftops, and an explosion of fiery light flared across the sky.

Nope. No fireworks display. Just mad half-faeries throwing magic around. Presumably, the magic came from those unaffected by the drug, or maybe the mages.

"Where—"

"Here." Vance pushed open a side gate, which led to a fenced off area outside the manor. "I had to lock him away. Do you have the cure?"

I handed it to him, then stood to the side while he unlocked a small wooden shed. A flurry of movement, and someone slammed into Vance. The Mage Lord barely moved an inch, grabbing his attacker by the arm. Seconds later, he'd forced the half-faerie's mouth open and tipped the cure into it. The Chief slumped to the ground.

I blinked. "Wait. Did you test the cure on another half-faerie first?"

"On a piskie," said Vance, stepping back from the shed.

"What if it doesn't—?"

Another burst of movement, and the half-faerie launched to his feet, grappling at Vance.

"Let *go* of me," snarled the man. His face was stained with dirt and blood, his shoulder-length dark hair tangled, but his pale green eyes were as arresting as any Sidhe's. "I'm the Chief of the fey-kind, and you locked me up like a criminal—"

"You were unconscious," said Vance. "Our headquarters is warded in iron, and I considered you'd rather not get trampled in the riot currently occurring on your territory."

The Chief jerked his arm out of Vance's grasp. "You're the Mage Lord. What in the name of the Sidhe did you do with my weapons?"

"Calder took them," I interjected. "Vance saved your life, dickhead. Anyway, we need your help."

"Let me pass," he snarled.

"You'll get eaten alive," I said. "The whole town's trapped in a circle of energy generated by a drug Calder used."

"I'm aware," said the Chief, magic flaring around him in green tendrils. Summer magic. "He told me about it in detail."

"Like I said, I saved your neck," said Vance. "Calder's magic is out of control. He's generating too much power, and even killing him won't dispel it. We need to seal his magic away."

The Chief's mouth half-fell open. "You want me to use an Invocation."

Huh? I looked at Vance, uncomprehending.

"Temporarily," said Vance. "You know the terms of the contract: they still stand."

The Chief's jaw tightened. "Fine."

"I'm missing something here," I said.

Vance turned to me. "To seal a Sidhe's magic, we need to use an Invocation of power. Speaking the words temporarily resets all magic in the surrounding area. For us, that means all magic inside the circle—or the town."

"Really?" Damn. How had I never heard of it before? Sure would have come in handy last time shit hit the fan.

"Unfortunately," the Chief interjected, "the Invocation was sealed, along with all the others. It's too dangerous a spell to allow, especially to half-Sidhe who don't know its full potential. The Mage Lords—" He shot an angry look at Vance—"took away the Invocations when they gave us our territory. Only those of us aware of our half-Sidhe heritage knew."

"What? Vance, is that true?"

"The world was in a state of devastation," said Vance. "We granted mercy to the half-faeries caught up in the struggle, as they didn't instigate the invasion. As one of our terms for peace, we sealed all the Invocations so the offspring of Sidhe lords would no longer be able to potentially spark another war between our races."

"So most of the half-faeries don't know?"

"Most do not have the ability to command an Invocation," said the Chief. "I, however, do. My father is Lord Daival, assistant to the Queen of Seelie Territory."

"Uh… okay." I wrapped my head around this new information. "If the Invocation's sealed, how are we meant to undo *that* seal?"

"I'll do it myself," said Vance. "Only a Mage Lord can undo it. The Invocation is inside our magical depository. Not the manor—that has too many wards to keep faeries out."

"So basically… you hid it in a place faeries can easily get into? And we have to go there now, with this guy—" I jerked my thumb at the Chief—"who has no weapons, so you can unlock a potentially devastating spell. That can't go wrong at all."

The Chief narrowed his eyes at me. "Do not presume to know our ways, human. I want a weapon."

"Feel free to pick one of mine," said Vance. "I should warn you, they're all forged in iron."

Whoa. These two did *not* like one another. Then again, the Chief had refused to listen to reason, and was at least partly responsible for this shitstorm. If he'd tried to stop Calder or at least paid attention when Vance had told him about the Trials, we might not be in such a dire situation.

"Enough," I cut in. "You have magic, isn't that enough?"

The Chief gave me a furious look. "Who in the Sidhes' name are you?"

"Ivy Lane," I said. "You might recognise the name. I saved all your people from the Grey Vale, and they repaid me by trying to kill me. Several times. We'll go and get your Invocation, and when Calder's magic is sealed, I'm going to kill him myself."

The Chief stared at me until Vance cleared his throat. "The streets are dangerous. We'll travel my way."

I knew what was coming. The Chief didn't. Vance transported both of us at once, landing at the side of another road. The Chief spun to face Vance, his face twisted in a snarl. "You—don't you touch me."

"Save it for later," I said. "Where's this magical depository?"

"Here." Vance indicated a squat abandoned-looking building at the roadside.

"You keep important spells hidden in here? Without wards?"

"Without iron," said Vance. "The place *is* warded against evil intent."

"Good."

A snarl sounded from the shadows, and an arm reached out and pulled me into the air. I left the ground with a startled yell as the shadows came to life, a sea of glittering eyes blinking at me. From my upside-down vantage point, I saw monsters crawling out of the gaps between the run-down buildings, all of which looked equally abandoned. We were on the boundary with half-blood territory, right at the town's far side, and every faerie loose in the area had come out to play.

"Hey!" I grabbed for my sword, fingers slipping on the handle. Vance and the Chief were boxed in by shadowy faeries. None of the creatures appeared to have a distinct form—they were tangles of limbs with claws and sharp teeth. The Grey Vale's death stealers. I'd met them before. They'd *love* it if Calder succeeded in opening the veil.

My sword bit into shadowy flesh and I flipped, landing on

my feet. Vance made a snarling noise, his blade flashing, but kept missing. *Dammit. He doesn't have the Sight.*

The Chief, however, did. Green threads of magic wrapped around his hands, glyphs appeared, and with a shout of an unpronounceable word, he sent the shadow-faeries scurrying out of sight.

"Neat trick," I said.

"What the devil was that?" said Vance.

"Abominations," spat the Chief. "Vile creatures that were exiled from Faerie, and with good reason."

I stood behind Vance as he unlocked the wards on the building's door.

"You're positive it's warded on the inside, right?" I asked.

A sharp nod, then the door opened.

We walked into a dingy hallway. Vance waved a hand and torches ignited on the walls. The building was laid out like an underground passageway with stone walls and doors branching off, all covered in shimmering wards.

A horrible smell pervaded—rot, combined with decaying magic. Bile rose in my throat. I wanted to ask if faeries had died in here, but no normal human would be able to smell dead magic, and the Chief half-faerie stood right beside me. I wasn't in the mood to explain my Sight *or* my faerie magic.

Vance stopped outside a heavy-looking wooden door and held up his hands. A shimmering curtain appeared, then parted. He pressed his palms to the wood and the door creaked inwards.

Gold light spilled out onto the corridor. Inside the room lay several glass cases, side by side. Vance made for the one opposite the door, which contained three very ancient-looking pieces of yellowing parchment. I watched him undo the wards around it, my heart thumping. This room vibrated with power, thick tension layering the air. Coldness seemed to radiate from the walls, driving every vestige of warmth from my body. A faint humming noise pervaded, and seemed to be coming from both underneath our feet and within the very air. Like the room itself had a heartbeat.

Vance lifted the front of the cabinet, and a fresh blast of power lifted every hair on my body. I shook all over, every muscle locking like I'd been hit by a fear spell. My hands trembled, and a primal part of me wanted to turn my back and run like hell. Even more so when Vance turned to face me. I practically expected lightning to crackle over his head and a storm to unleash its fury on all of us.

"We can't cast the spell in here," said Vance. Even his voice seemed louder, amplified in the small room. "There are too many bindings. You'll need to go outside."

I glanced sideways at the Chief, who actually looked frightened of the Mage Lord. Vance didn't seem to notice, and replaced the wards on the cabinet like he picked up dangerous artefacts every day. The parchment appeared so old, it was a wonder it didn't fall apart in his hands.

Outside the room, the raging power calmed somewhat. I shivered as the chill receded from my skin.

The Chief of the half-faeries muttered under his breath about "blasted mage magic." Hmm. So he was affected by the power surge, too.

"Something's wrong here," said Vance, pausing beside the door.

"Huh?" I faced him, watching the wards ripple back into place. "Nobody else has been here, have they?" *Not Calder.*

"Few people know this place exists," said Vance. "Aside from the mages…" He trailed off, a blade appearing in his hands.

As the hum of power died down, I heard the faint shuffling noises behind one of the other doors. I grabbed my sword, wishing my hands would stop shaking.

The door burst open, and three men burst through. At least they *were* men… a while ago. As opposed to decaying

319

bodies in smart suits, advancing on us with their rotting arms outstretched.

Fantastic. Undead.

CHAPTER TWENTY-TWO

Vance swore, sending the undead reeling with a blast of cold air. His blade flashed, decapitating one of them, and the door to our right burst open in a flurry of dust. Six more undead appeared. Great—a party.

Pale grey hands swiped at me, hanging off their wrists and held together by skin and sinew. I swung my blade, cutting through several arms, but they kept shuffling forwards. An arm locked around my neck. The undead's grip was surprisingly strong, immediately cutting off my oxygen supply. I stabbed wildly, eyes watering at the stench, and stomped backwards onto the undead's foot. The move had no effect. Undead couldn't feel pain.

Instead, I kicked at its leg with my other foot. Bone gave way, and its collapse forced its grip to loosen. I forced its arm away, more or less tearing it off with my hands. Fighting not to gag, I threw the stringy remains to the side.

"How can higher undead be here?" I gasped, massaging

my neck.

In answer, Vance displaced the undead's discarded arm before it locked around my ankle. The twitching remains of several others lay on the carpeted floor. The Chief hovered behind the Mage Lord, visibly trembling.

Wait. He was scared—really scared of the undead. Being half-blood, he was probably as terrified of death as all the others I'd met. Admittedly, the half-decaying corpses didn't give the best impression of what awaited mortals after death.

"Who brought them back? A necromancer?"

Vance shook his head. His jaw was tense with anger. "They rose of their own accord. The veil is thinning."

Shit. We needed to get out of here. Kicking bits of zombie aside, I ran down the hall, Vance close behind.

The door already lay open, and undead surrounded the house.

I took one step back. "Please tell me there's another door."

Like my words were a signal, they swarmed us. I grabbed a container of salt from my pocket with my free hand—for all the good it'd do against this many dead. One reached out with grasping fingers and I threw a handful of salt in his face, stabbing him in the eye with my blade.

Vance moved in, sending such a wave of power through the air that my step faltered along with the undead. The air rippled, knocking some of them falling into others. Vance moved down from the doorstep, continuing to direct the flow of air to clear a path across the overgrown garden. *Damn.* I'd have stared if not for the undead baring their rotting teeth at me. The level of control he had over his ability was intense.

Didn't stop the undead, though. I cut the heads off two of them, throwing salt at the others until they tripped out of the way, hissing as their decaying skin burned. These were in even worse shape than the others, clothes rotted to rags, rib cages gaping open. There must be at least twenty, but Vance calmly sent them toppling like skittles. The Chief remained on the doorstep, hiding. Coward. This was the guy who was meant to save us all from Calder?

Kicking another undead aside, I joined Vance, who'd cleared a path to the gate. Without a necromancer to bind the undead, all we could do was take them apart. Vance seemed more hesitant to attack them than he had the last time we'd fought the undead, but when a disembodied arm tried to rip out my throat, he waved a hand and made half a dozen body parts disappear at once.

"Where in hell did they even come from?" I asked. "How

many people died here?"

Vance looked at me, oddly pale. "This territory once belonged to the mages. Before the invasion."

Mages. Oh shit. Did he know some of these people? They were hardly recognisable as human now.

"This territory was lost first," he said. "The Mage Lords at the time never found all the bodies."

I faltered, my blade buried in an undead's skull.

"Their spirits aren't here," he added tightly, making several other body parts vanish. We stood in a circle of flopping limbs. "The necromancers, however, need to seal off their territory."

"Before town becomes Zombie Central." I groaned. "Drugged half-faeries *and* dead people. Now all we need is—"

A strangled yell came from behind us. My heart dropped, and I turned around.

The half-faerie Chief struggled in the grip of one of those shadowy faeries who'd attacked us earlier. Death stealers— they'd doubtlessly been feeding on the rotting corpses. Its grasping tentacle-like appendages reached out, lifting the Chief into the air. Fury surged, and I called the faerie magic.

Blue light flared from my non-weapon hand. I threw a

handful at the creature's tentacle but missed and hit another. The beast seemed completely unaffected, its grip tightening on the Chief's throat.

"Let him go, you bastard." God*dammit.* The half-faerie Chief was fighting hard, blasts of Summer magic flaring from his palms, but only seemed to enrage the shadows more. With a lashing motion, the tentacle flung the Chief against the nearest wall. He didn't get up.

Shit.

I marched towards the beast, my own magic responding. If the veil really was thinning, I ought to get a power boost, too. And it'd be bloody welcome right now. I didn't *like* the Chief, but he was the only person who could say the Invocation and stop Calder's magic from ripping open the veil.

My sword swiped, severing a tentacle before it grabbed my foot. The mass of shadows resembled a giant octopus with a few hundred extra appendages. Behind me, Vance cut the end of one tentacle off, but another took its place. We needed to stab it in the heart to kill it.

Swiping and stabbing, I advanced on the shadowy creature. I let go of the sword with one hand and used the other to throw a handful of magic at its face. Blue light flared, engulfing the creature's huge, shadowy body. The light dimmed, and the shadow-octopus pulled itself up to its full height and spat at me.

I jumped, but the slimy substance landed in front of me, and *moved*. Another tentacle lashed at my foot, forcing me to step back, and the slime latched onto my ankles.

Immediately, the slime expanded to cover my legs, locking them together, and swiftly climbed higher. A tentacle went for my throat, latching around me and squeezing until my vision turned blue around the edges. *Vance, where are you?* Maybe he was tied up, too. Literally.

I nearly died once already. It won't happen again.

Rage flooded me, and my magic responded even as the sword clattered from my hand. My body had turned numb where the slime touched it. My hands, however, were still free.

Magic flared out from my palms, this time forming a weapon. I sliced upwards, severing the tentacle, then pulled the magic back into myself, pushing it at the slimy cage holding my legs.

The slime exploded outwards, freeing my legs. I stumbled forward but caught myself immediately, propelled by the quick speed my magic gave me. Grabbing my sword again, I sent another wave of magic at the creature. An icy breeze cut through the air, driving the death stealer into the wall at the house's side. *Vance.* He'd managed to free himself, slashing and cutting at every tentacle that came near him.

As for me, I launched myself at the injured death stealer. I moved too fast for the tentacles to catch me, letting every particle of pain and rage flow through the blue light spilling from my palms.

I landed, tackling the creature around the middle. The combination of speed, magic and momentum sent it flailing, shrinking until it was hardly bigger than a human. Pain radiated from the death stealer in the form of blue waves, flowing to—me.

Like Calder.

Blue light burst across my vision, and I swiftly jumped out of range.

The tentacles vanished as the faerie shrank back into its true form, small and withered. Dead.

"It didn't have much life left in it," I said to Vance. "That's what feeding on death does… crap."

Vance had moved to the Chief. The buzz of using magic swiftly faded. He was either dead or unconscious. Whichever it was, we were fucked.

"Shit." I walked over to him. "He's not…"

"He has a pulse," said Vance, his tone frighteningly calm. "But from the way he hit his head, he won't be waking up."

I swore again, yelling my most inventive curses to the sky. "Well. That's it." I stepped back, breathless and shaking. "We're done."

No, a voice whispered in my ear. *We're not.*

The parchment remained in the half-faerie Chief's hand, gleaming with unreadable runes. The only way to stop Calder's magic. We were all trapped in the town, behind the summoning circle he'd created. If we didn't find a way out…

"The Invocation," I said slowly. "What's the condition? Does the person who speaks it need to have a Sidhe lord's blood… or magic?"

I picked up the yellowed, gleaming paper. The other half-Sidhe were no doubt under the control of the drug, and besides, I wouldn't put a spell like this into the hands of anyone else. That left one option.

Faerie magic or not, using a spell meant for the Sidhe might kill me. But I *had* a Sidhe lord's magic. Surely that meant I could speak the words.

"I don't know," said Vance. "I've never heard of a human with Sidhe magic before. The other Sidhe lords' children, if they exist, are trapped in half-blood territory."

"And they'll be under the influence of the drug. Like everyone else." My voice sounded distant, and almost as calm as Vance's. "I'll do it."

"Are you sure?" His gaze was steady, though the tempest still brewed in his eyes.

"I have the magic of a Sidhe lord," I said. "Magic should matter more than blood. Right?"

The words on the page flared up at my touch. I stared, my vision blurring. I could *read* the text, and I if I opened my mouth, I'd be able to pronounce the words. The magic— Avakis's magic—would take over.

Power thrummed through my hands, which shook on the paper. No human had ever spoken an Invocation. Vance wouldn't be so calm if he realised it might kill me. But he'd never seen my magic in action before—not to its full extent.

God. I'm sorry, Vance.

"The Invocation needs to take place on the Ley Line," said Vance. "Ideally, at a point where the line and the summoning circle cross."

"It'll seal his magic," I said. "I'll need to kill him first."

"If his magic is gone, anybody will be able to kill him," said Vance. "But I'll leave the honour to you."

My throat clogged with emotion. I threw my shaking arms around him, clutching the Invocation that might mean my death. His grip tightened on me, a breeze kicking up. The salty taste of my own tears lingered on my tongue when I kissed him, wishing I could tell him how sorry I was. Wishing I could take back the time we'd wasted.

There was never going to be enough time.

I wiped my eyes one-handedly and forced a smile. "I'll kill the bastard. Let's go."

Vance nodded, and we disappeared, leaving the old building and the dead faeries behind.

CHAPTER TWENTY-THREE

We landed outside a row of terraced houses, all of which looked empty.

"Not here," said Vance.

I barely had chance to recover before he'd swept us off again. This time, we landed in a field.

"What're you looking for?" I asked.

"He'll be using a key point as the summoning circle's edge," said Vance. "That's where the Invocation will need to be spoken."

A fresh wave of emotion rose in my throat—*if this works, it might kill me*—and yet I couldn't form it into words. I just nodded, and took his hand again, squeezing it hard.

The third time we landed—on a hill—I knew we'd got the right place. Magic responded to my presence by lighting me up like a torch, bathing everything in blinding blue light. I blinked, and my vision adjusted sharply like all my senses were thrown into focus. I felt lighter on my feet, less tired, more acutely tuned into movements around me.

Like last time I'd been in Faerie, when I'd been buzzing all over with victory. *We're not too late. We can't be too late.* For our world to feel like this meant the veil must be splitting at the seams, and Faerie was spilling over into our world. The air hissed with magical energy—beyond Summer and Winter, but something dark and primal.

Vance hissed in a breath, his sword in hand. "This magic—it's not of our world. This is where we need to be."

"You can see it. Guess it means this is the place." Where was Calder? I needed to kill him, or Vance did, if I didn't make it. I held up the parchment, hands shaking so hard I could hardly hold it steady. The words were written in the faeries' rune language. Unfamiliar to me... at least at first.

Magic swirled down my arms to my hands, transferring over to the parchment. Shimmering lines darted across the page, and a surge of power rattled through my bones.

A yell came from Vance, and the world tipped over sideways.

Icy energy blasted the parchment from my hands. I flew into the air, mouth open in a silent scream. I caught myself as I fell, feet skidding on the grass. Vance ran to me, catching the parchment, but a blast of magic sent him flying back.

Calder stalked towards us, murder in his eyes and a handful of icy magic in his palm. I raised my sword, putting myself between him and Vance.

Not a moment too soon. Calder hurled the magic at me, which glanced off my shield. It took hardly any effort to turn the shield into a weapon and retaliate. The blood in my veins sung with pleasure, reacting to the magic around us.

An angry snarl drew my attention. Vance lay pinned to the ground by a shimmering wave of blue light. He fought against it, beating at the spell with his now clawed hands, but even his partially shifted form couldn't break the spell. At once, the buzzing sensation in my veins dulled to shock and anger. *It's not right. None of this is right.*

Another surge of magic went through the air, and the sound of clashing swords filled my ears. Just downhill, half-faeries clashed with humans—mages?—in a frenzy. Damn. Looked like Vance's patrolling mages had run into an ambush.

"You'll pay for making a fool out of me," shouted Calder. "Both of you."

Either he didn't see the parchment in Vance's hand or he didn't know what it was. *I have to stall him.* At least until Vance broke free of his spell.

"Not if I kill you first," I said, and sprang at him.

I struck solid air and fell back, wincing. The air shimmered in front of Calder. A magic shield—one that repelled *me*, as well as magic. Damn.

I raised my hands and called my own magic into me, ready to shape it into a weapon, but it faded as soon as it appeared, flooding over to Calder. He bared his teeth, hands held high, pulling my magic into him.

I pulled back, riding the tide of fury. *That's mine.*

The Grey Vale itself fuelled my power.

Calder's face twisted in anger and he threw another blast of magic at me. I ducked easily, my veins humming. *Nice try.* I countered with an attack of my own, but it rippled off his shield.

"You're too late," he yelled over the melee—the ongoing battle between the half-faeries and the mages had moved closer while we fought. They didn't even seem to be aware of us. Only the magical forcefield surrounding Calder kept them from intruding on our fight. "The veil is opening, and the transition is almost complete."

"Congratulations on destroying the world," I shot at him. I risked a look at Vance, who'd managed to get to his feet. Calder's magic held him pinned in position, right next to the warring half-faeries. Blasts of magic shot in all directions, bouncing off Calder's shield. The mages were outnumbered, though, and no amount of blood would satiate the half-faeries.

"They're completely out of control, aren't they?" I said, slightly incredulous. "Are they drugged, or just buying into your deluded lies?"

Instead of answering, Calder attacked. His attack ricocheted upwards off my shield, rebounding back into him. He was like a lightning rod, drawing on all the power coursing through the air. Faerie itself fed his strength. *It must be the same with me. We have the same power source.*

Somewhere here was the key point, the edge of the circle. Vance held the Invocation. I needed to get close to him, past the fighting mages and half-bloods—but how to do that without Calder catching on?

I waved a hand. "If you haven't noticed, we've just walked into the middle of a battle."

Calder blinked and looked to the side, apparently becoming aware we were surrounded. A mage fired a blast of fire at him, but the shield blocked his attack. Calder himself responded with a blast of fear-spell that made my teeth rattle in my head. Several mages fell, and I took my chance to run.

Horror expanded to fill my chest—he hadn't knocked the mages over, he'd killed them. My feet skidded in blood, churned up in mud and wet grass.

Vance. I looked around for him and my stomach dropped. He remained trapped by Calder's spell, battering at the shield with an animalistic expression twisting his face.

Hands latched onto the back of my coat. I swung my sword around and collided with a half-faerie. His hands clawed at me, his pupils dilated by the drug and the power building around us. I buried my sword in his chest. Two more steps towards Vance—who'd disappeared beneath fighting, grappling half-faerie warriors. One blocked my path, and I blasted him off his feet with magic. *Get away from him.*

Screw it all. I reached beneath the surface for the pain of the fighting, dying warriors, and let the magic flood through me. I ran towards Vance, the buzzing magic propelling my steps until I swore my feet left the ground.

Vance's magic exploded through the barrier with the force of a battering ram. The half-faeries didn't stand a chance. Two were immediately sent flying, while Vance's claws made quick work of another two. His eyes were dark with fury, his hands stained crimson.

He'll be okay. I needed to get to Calder. He'd moved further downhill, towards where a shimmering barrier bordered on the field. The key point. He intended to focus the power there and open the realms. Dammit.

Elbowing a half-faerie in the face, I moved closer to Vance. "The spell," I shouted at him—the half-faeries wouldn't understand my words anyway. My sword sank to the hilt in the half-faerie's neck, blood spraying everywhere. When the enemy's body fell, Vance appeared in a blur of metal and blood. The parchment pressed into my hands.

"Thanks," I gasped. "Try—try to stay back. I don't know what effects it'll have. Those guys'll probably go mad."

"They already are." Vance stabbed another of them, sheathing his claws in its chest. He looked me in the eyes. "Kill him."

I managed to nod. Another half-faerie warrior grabbed at me. I swung my blade and decapitated him, which was considerably messier than I'd anticipated. Blood slicked my sword hand—infected blood. They were all drugged.

My other hand clutching the parchment, I ran downhill after Calder. Adrenaline fuelled my movements, and the dizzying high of the power almost made me forget I was running to my death.

I raised the parchment, ready to speak, and transparent

hands grabbed mine.

"What the hell—?"

Ghosts. Half-faerie ghosts, transparent but solid, appeared all around me. I quickly conjured up a shield, but it had no effect on the dead. Their hands grabbed at the parchment, tugging it from my hands. Even if they didn't know what it was, they'd figured I intended to send them over the veil.

Calder spun around and threw a handful of magic at me. With an army of ghosts blocking my path, I was too slow to avoid the spell. Fear stopped my breath, knocked me flat like a heavy object lay on top of me, choking the air from my lungs. *Fear is a tool,* I told myself. *I can take their power away. Like I did before.*

I let the anger and pain of the half-faeries flood me again, giving me strength. I sat upright, pushing the dead away from me with the strength of the magic flowing from my shield.

"Get away."

The parchment had drifted a few feet across the grass. Calder didn't appear to have noticed, though—his eyes were on the rapidly appearing ghosts. He blasted the nearest aside with a wave of magic, fear and anger warring in his expression.

He's scared of dying. That's why he was so petrified when he saw my ghost. It's his worst nightmare. I should have guessed. Most half-faeries feared the same, as did any faerie in this realm. They didn't have any concept of an afterlife, because pure faeries didn't have souls. These mad, screaming spirits did, though. They'd targeted Calder as well as me—maybe because they'd worked out he gained strength from their misery.

So did I. Power humming through me, I conjured another shield, willing it to repel the dead. I was living, they weren't. I must have power far beyond whatever lingered on the other side of the veil, even without the Invocation.

Magic pulsed from my body, sending the spirits back. Wait—some of that was Vance, who appeared in my peripheral vision, fighting against two half-faerie ghosts. As for the living half-faeries, the ones who weren't fighting had spotted the power flooding from the edge of the circle, and figured out the way back to Faerie was on the brink of opening.

No. Oh, shit, no. Behind Calder, a gap rapidly spread across the place where the summoning circle ended. A gap... like a door.

To Faerie. No—the Grey Vale. Anyone who passed through wouldn't be coming back. Worse, it'd grow to consume the whole circle, and us along with it. I needed to close the damned thing, *now.*

Calder managed to push the spirits out of his path. Magic radiated from him, and in his eyes, too—lightning blue, raging, *scared.* He didn't seem to have noticed the gap opening behind him—his gaze was fixed on me, and the ghosts I'd shoved out of range.

I wouldn't let him run away into Faerie. I needed to incapacitate him somehow. My magic might have gained strength, but he'd taken so much into himself, he buzzed all over. If I touched him, I'd probably burn up with it. His skin glowed, rage distorting his expression as he fought against the spirits with single-minded intensity.

He saw me, and fired the magical equivalent of a lightning bolt. I rolled out of the way, the aftershock rippling through the air. My hands shook on my sword's hilt. I couldn't count on magic to bring him down, not with this much power flooding this realm. The very ground shifted underneath our feet, and the air split as ghost after ghost appeared. Damn. He'd even stirred up Death itself.

My sword felt weak in comparison, but my grip tightened. Crimson blood stained it—from the other half-faeries—and even that glowed blue in the light suffusing the air.

Wait a minute.

Before I lost my nerve, I ran at him, brandishing my sword, magic cloaking me. My sword struck Calder's weapon hand, breaking his grip on the sword. He let go and hit me with magic instead. The blow clashed against *my* magic. I'd turned it into both sword and shield, boosted by the closeness of Faerie.

He glared at me. No trace of fear remained in his expression this time. Maybe he'd realised he could use fear as a tool, like I did. But he wouldn't draw on *my* power this time. He wouldn't crush me.

Ah…

My vision turned white, a suffocating fog pressing down on me. He grinned, hands glowing with magic. Magic he'd taken from *me*.

Not again.

My sword slipped in my hands, reminding me of its presence. Even Calder's magic couldn't hold back iron, but it could hold *me* back. If we moved another few metres, we'd be on the edge of the circle. In Faerie.

Not gonna happen.

I took aim, a wild impulse grabbing me, and threw my sword at him. His eyes widened, his shield too late. Even faerie magic acted weirdly around iron, and my blade carved a path to him, sinking between a gap in his armoured arm. His hesitation gave me the chance to hit him with a blast of magic, knocking him off his feet. My blade clattered to the floor and I launched myself forward, grabbing the sword and pointing it at his heart.

"You can't kill me," he hissed. Blood soaked one of his arms and I'd knocked the armour plate loose, but the gash had already begun to heal.

He was right. Being half-Sidhe, he wouldn't normally have their unnatural healing abilities—but with the amount of power he'd taken in, he'd gained strength equal to a regular Sidhe, if not stronger.

Too bad it relied on him staying in control.

He pushed upright, readying another attack. "Your magic is mine."

"No, it isn't." I waved a hand, and blasted him in the chest. "You're weakening."

He blinked, uncomprehendingly.

"I cut you," I said, holding up my blade. "Several of those drugged-up half-faeries bled all over my sword. The drug's in your bloodstream now, unless you have some kind of immunity you never mentioned."

His eyes bulged.

"Gotcha," I said.

Calder roared with anger, launching himself to his feet, but I let the shield surrounding us drop. Ghosts swarmed him instantly. Calder's earthly body wasn't under his own control. His frenzied movements were a far cry from the controlled swordsman I'd battled last time.

Half-faeries surrounded him, some I recognised. The boy whose body had been torn apart by hellhounds. Others, killed in the fighting. Calder screamed, high and loud, as the dead held him locked in place.

And his magic was gone, disappearing by the second into the swirling torrent around the circle's edge. It wouldn't be dispelled for good, not until I read the Invocation.

I found a gap in the fighting, and I ran. *The parchment...* it had blown clear of our fight and lay on the hillside. I lunged, snatching it up, and glyphs immediately flared to life on my arms.

My eyes locked onto the words, my mouth forming sounds I'd never normally be able to pronounce. They rolled from my tongue, and the magic moved along with me, stirring in my blood and bones.

Your magic is sealed.

I fractured. Pain ripped through my body, which I was dimly aware had floated above the ground. All the power concentrated in the circle rushed towards this point. The line of the circle moved back, knocking half-faeries aside—I'd have screamed Vance's name, but I couldn't speak, and only hoped he'd moved out of the way.

As for the door to Faerie, it was already closing, sealing itself, the lights at the circle's edge winking out. Chaos erupted, but I floated, disconnected from it. I'd left my body behind, again.

Maybe this time, forever.

I won't leave until he dies.

I willed my disembodied spirit to land beside him. Calder floated above his earthly body. Like me.

"Your magic is sealed," I said. Well, more croaked. I was dying. Hell, I knew it. I'd used up my last chance. Greyness crept into the corners of my vision. "The veil is closing."

And it'll take me with it. But like hell would I leave without dragging him along with me.

I turned to the ghosts. "Take him."

Transparent hands latched onto Calder's. He yelled and fought, thrashing wildly, but he was far outnumbered. His earthly body remained, fighting half-faeries in a desperate frenzy. They'd all turned on one another, trampling each other flat in a desperate effort to find the door to Faerie again. The mages easily overwhelmed them.

So many dead, though... My vision blurred with the strangeness of seeing unmoving bodies accompanied by faintly outlined spirits, looking around with expressions of confusion and shock. The newly dead. Most of the half-faeries joined the frenzy swarming Calder's ghost, while the mages' ghosts just—watched.

Vance. He walked downhill, past the bodies of the fallen, towards where my own body lay stiff and cold at the hillside. I floated to land beside it. The emotions warring in his eyes punched me in the chest. A dead person shouldn't be able to hurt this much, not when I didn't have an earthly heart to break.

"Vance," I croaked. The veil was closing, but I knew he'd be able to see me, amongst the other ghosts. "Finish him."

He nodded, stiffly. I could tell what it cost him to retain control. His hands locked around my sword, and he strode forward, driving the blade into Calder's heart.

The final threads of magic disappeared, sealed in the parchment my body held in its hands.

As for me... I drifted.

345

CHAPTER TWENTY-FOUR

Firstly, I floated above the hillside, above the battleground. Bodies littered the hill, more half-faeries than mages, though some had run for the opening to the Grey Vale when they'd had the chance to. Someone would have to deal with the consequences. But not me. I was done, finished with this world, and it wasn't fucking *fair*. I tried to move closer to Vance, but grey smoke thickened around me, obscuring my vision.

"Don't tell me," I said, sensing the necromancer's presence behind me. "I don't get a second chance this time. I'm dead."

A pause. My heart twisted, tears burning eyes that shouldn't be able to cry. *Vance.* He held my limp body in his arms, surrounded by countless other dead. My spirit was invisible to him now. I'd gone, along with the others.

Frank floated to land beside me. "You aren't, yet."

"Yet?"

"You took an unbelievable amount of power into yourself," said Frank. "Luckily for you, most of it was absorbed into its source."

The parchment. "So I'm hanging around here… why?"

"Because I want to make you an offer," he said. "It's clear the living necromancers aren't as competent as they should be. I want to be your liaison between the dead and the living."

"My own personal necromancer? They'll never buy it."

"It's not Lord Evander's decision," said Frank. "He knows nothing of the Grey Vale and cares for little outside of his guild. I suspect he won't remain leader for much longer."

"But I'm not a necromancer," I pointed out. "If I'm alive, I need to get back to my body before everyone thinks I'm dead."

"Someone wants to speak to you."

I looked around. The other spirits had faded into the fog, including Calder. If *he* was here, I'd be spending as little time in Death as humanly possible.

One spirit remained. The half-faerie Chief, wearing an expression of fury and disbelief. He looked me up and down. "Your magic… you're human."

"And you're dead." I couldn't summon up any sympathy.

The dead people lying on that battlefield… I couldn't get the image out of my head. This man had blood on his hands. Even more than I did.

"Technically, he isn't dead," said the necromancer. "His blood contains a slow-acting healing ability as a result of him being part Sidhe."

I shot him an alarmed look. "Calder doesn't, does he?"

"Even a Sidhe can't heal from an iron blade in the heart," said the Chief, in a condescending manner. "He's dead. You and the mage killed him."

"You're welcome." I narrowed my eyes. I wouldn't be particularly thrilled to meet this guy in the waking world again. "Any reason you wanted to speak to me? Because I'm pretty sure everyone knows I can do faerie magic now."

"You said the Invocation," he said. "That's not a power most faeries can handle. Humans… never. What *are* you? You can't be pure human."

"I am," I said. "It's a long story, but I killed a Sidhe lord, not knowing I'd take his magic in the process."

The Chief blanched. "You killed a *Sidhe?* What manner of human are you?"

"Lucky," I said. "Really lucky. So are you. The guy who opened the veil is the son of a Sidhe lord, too."

"Which lord? I know them all, and I've never seen him before."

Of course you haven't. "I told you, there's a place between the realms where they send exiles. It's called the Grey Vale, and during the invasion, Sidhe lords from there came here. One of them took me, and left that lunatic behind. He's a changeling."

"Changelings." He spat out the word. "We're all changelings. Neither mortal nor infinite." He looked into the distance, like he could see the dead half-faeries through the fog.

"Being mortal isn't all bad," I told him. To Frank, I said, "You ought to send him back. There's a crap-load of drugged half-faeries in dire need of leadership."

The Chief started to speak, but was already fading away. So did the necromancer, leaving me alone in the fog.

I didn't know how long I drifted. Spirits passed me by, some of whom I vaguely recognised. Humans and half-faeries whose lives had been taken in the fighting. I tried to speak to them, apologise, even, but none paid me any attention. We might have avoided a second invasion, but at no small cost.

I found myself drifting over the place where the veil had

opened. At first I couldn't tell what drew me there. Then I heard the screaming. Calder.

"I'm *not* dead. I'm Sidhe!"

Calder's ghostly form floated above his body, clawing at it like he could force his spirit to rejoin his earthly form.

"Not gonna work," I said.

He turned on me with a twisted glare, and punched me through the chest.

I kept still. "You can't kill me." He didn't scare me anymore. Not half-faded, subdued, powerless.

"I will." Hate distorted his feature. "I promise you, Ivy Lane, I'll haunt you until I can take your life and regain mine. I swear it."

His words seemed to ripple through me, through the veil.

"But before I kill you—" His eyes met mine, icy, depthless—"I'll kill your mage first."

Ice shot down my spine. "What mage?" I asked, feigning ignorance.

"The one who killed me. He's your lover?"

"No." *Please believe me.* As long as the veil held, he wouldn't be coming back. It wasn't like he could read my mind… but he'd just made a vow. He might not be pure Sidhe, but a promise was the most powerful magic of all.

Maybe even enough to conquer death.

"You can take all the cheap shots you like, but you're dead," I said. "This realm is none of your business. You're dead. Move the hell on."

I turned my back on him, hoping he couldn't see me shaking.

Everything faded away, again. I floated some more, positive that if I had a heart, it'd be pounding. *Vance.* Ghosts couldn't harm people, in theory, but if anyone was angry enough to find a way, Calder could. If anyone had enough hate to claw his way back into life, it was the son of Avakis.

"Ivy!"

Isabel's voice sounded like it came from far away. I closed my eyes, willing my floating form to return to my physical body. *Come on. Please.*

With a surge of air, I gasped awake, struggling for breath. My whole body felt like I'd been put through a cement mixer and my head rang with pain. Voices exclaimed around me, but the noise was too much to handle. I curled in a ball, shaking all over.

"I'll kill you, Ivy," a voice whispered in my ear. *"But I'll kill your mage first."*

***

I heard him every night. Of course I knew he didn't actually come to talk to me, but his voice sounded too real. Too close. I barely spoke, even to Isabel. She told me whenever Vance came over to the flat, wanting to see me. I declined, feigning sleep. I couldn't speak to him. Couldn't tell him the truth. Because what was the point? He'd take no notice of my warnings. It wasn't in his nature to hide, especially from a dead person.

Isabel told me *I'd* been so close to death, I'd nearly passed over the veil. It took every ounce of self-control I possessed not to blurt out the truth. It'd sound too ridiculous, and I'd have to mention Calder. I'd have to listen to excuses, and reassurances that of course I'd have bad dreams after what I'd been through. Calder might be haunting my dreams, but his ghostly form would be locked away with the other spirits. The necromancers had been forced to make a statement after the battle, because the first layer of the veil had been swamped with furious half-faerie ghosts. None of them would be coming back.

Didn't stop Calder's furious icy blue eyes from appearing in my mind's eye every time I tried to forget.

Mostly, I was fucking *tired*. I'd been through hell, dying twice in as many days. I wanted to be left alone, for a long time.

I lasted a week.

One morning, I jerked awake to the smell of cinnamon cookies and coffee.

"This is my last day playing nursemaid," said Isabel, passing me a breakfast tray. "Seriously. It's been a week."

I grunted. "Thanks for the cookies."

"Ivy." She put her hands on her hips. "You're healed. Quit with the moping."

"I'm not moping."

Isabel sighed. "I know you had a shitty experience, but I can't help you if you don't talk to me about it. You're just... lying in bed all the time. It isn't like you."

"No," I said, setting the tray on the side. "You're right. I'm hiding. I never thanked you enough times for saving our necks."

Isabel and the coven had managed to brew up an antidote for most of the half-faeries afflicted by the drugs. Not all of them—some had fled the town, while others had disappeared into Faerie. Half-blood territory would be in turmoil for a while, but the Chief had survived, and the mages had helped with keeping order.

"You saved us," said Isabel. "Vance said you drew all the

353

magic to you—through you, into that spell."

"Kind of," I said. "Since when were you two on first-name terms?"

"Since you've refused to speak to him for the four days you've been awake," she said.

Touché.

I drew in a breath. "I'll tell you, but you'll think I'm imagining things from stress."

"Imagining what?"

"Ghosts."

Isabel blinked at me. "You have the spirit sight?"

"No. I... kinda died for a moment. Well, two."

I quickly summed up my experiences the other side of the veil, ending with my confrontation with Calder.

"He won't come back, Ivy," she said.

"If anyone can, it's him." I shuddered. "His magic was stronger than mine, in the end. Vance killed him. He made a promise... he'll keep trying. Forever. Until he succeeds."

"The veil's closed," said Isabel. "The necromancers will keep him out."

I gave her a look. "They're not reliable. Apart from the dead guy, he's not too bad. He said his living counterpart's a lazy idiot." I shook my head. "The necros need a full leadership overhaul, if you ask me. But that's not the point. When I died the second time… I saw *him*. Calder. He's—he was mortal, so he has a soul. It's there, over the veil."

"He's still a ghost," said Isabel. "The necromancer Guardians will send him beyond the gate with everyone else."

"He said he'd find a way."

"Cheap talk, coming from a dead guy." She nudged me. "Look, Ivy, what happened must have been awful, but don't shut me out. I'm here."

I nodded, a lump in my throat. When I could speak, I said, "He's been here."

"Yes. He helped me reset our wards. This place is as secure as the mages' place now."

"Good."

"Er, except them," she amended, pointing over her shoulder. "Look who showed up this morning."

I picked up the breakfast tray and followed her. No fewer than five piskies flew around the ceiling.

"They were hiding upstairs," said Isabel. "They freaked out when magic went all crazy."

"At this rate, we can set up a colony," I said. "Hey, Erwin."

The piskie flew towards me with a delighted yell. "Ivy.

You're back."

That's promising. "Er... do I look any different?" The piskie ought to be able to tell if my brush with death had changed me in any way.

"No disguises. Not a bad faerie."

"Good." I took a bite of the cookie, suddenly starving, and walked back to my room to get dressed. Time to rejoin the land of the living.

The doorbell rang while I was tugging a brush through my hair. I left my room to find Isabel stashing her phone in her pocket, not-so-subtly.

"You messaged, him, didn't you?"

Isabel threw up her hands. "Talk to him, for crying out loud. I don't know what the deal is, but Vance didn't move from your side the night you nearly died until we were sure you were going to live. He put someone else in charge in his place."

Oh. Shit. Maybe I needed to lie down.

The doorbell rang again.

I blew out a breath. "Okay. I meant it when I said I didn't need any more drama."

Isabel walked right behind me to the door and stood there until I'd unlatched the bolts. "I'll be in the flat," she said over her shoulder. Her retreating footsteps bounced through my head.

"I—hey, Vance." He looked tired. Really tired. The past week had hit us all, hard. "Is Drake okay?" Isabel had told me he and Wanda had survived the fight. Not everyone else had.

"Yes. He was lucky."

The implied meaning was clear. I'd reminded him of everyone else who'd died. Great one, Ivy. "So… I guess you're busy cleaning up."

"Fairly so, yes." His tone didn't give anything away. "You've recovered? Isabel said you had."

"For the most part." I fidgeted. "Sorry I didn't call."

"It's understandable." He took a breath. "Warn me the next time you decide to risk your life like that. You should have told me there was a strong chance it'd kill you."

It did kill me. The words hovered on my tongue, but I knew what he'd say if I told him Calder had threatened his life. My feelings about Vance were tumultuous enough without adding a promise from a half-Sidhe ghost.

"I'm sorry, Vance," I said. "There was no time to bring anyone else in to say the Invocation. It had to be me, even if I died in the process."

He gave me a brief nod. "I thought so."

Silence stretched between us again, almost unbearable. I inhaled his scent without meaning to, a warm familiarity settling in my bones. Dammit. Who was I kidding, thinking I could walk away from him like it wouldn't tear out my own heart? I couldn't shut my emotions down so the faeries wouldn't be able to use them against me. Nothing was ever that simple.

"Did—did you take the Invocation back?" I asked.

"It's sealed where it belongs. We've purged the faerie scum who infested the area."

"And the half-faeries? The ones under the drug's influence?"

His jaw clenched. "The ones who fought on Calder's side—the survivors—are imprisoned on half-blood territory. We rounded up the others, but the Chief is still determining which were acting under their own power or not. I suspect Calder's allies were given the same false promises."

"What about the necromancers?" I hadn't seen Frank since I'd woken up. Probably for the best. He'd be busy guiding the new ghosts beyond the veil, anyway.

"They're fairly busy," he said, distaste in his expression. "The veil stirred up a number of undead."

"At least they're taking some responsibility." Though from the look of him, Vance appeared to be shouldering most of the supernatural community's problems himself. Yet he'd come here.

I owed him the truth.

"Vance..." I swallowed. "I didn't want to tell you, in case you stopped me going after Calder, but this wasn't the first time I died."

Quickly, I summed up my experience in Death. My conversations with the necromancer, my antics against Calder as a ghost, and lastly, our confrontation in Death, after Vance had killed him.

Vance looked at me a moment, lost in thought. He seemed abnormally calm considering I'd told him a ghost had threatened to kill him. "Faerie magic doesn't survive beyond death," he finally said.

"Normal faerie magic doesn't," I said. "But promises... they work in strange ways. You know that's how I got *my* magic?"

He blinked. "I thought you took it from Avakis."

"I did, but it's because we made a vow before we fought." I'd never told anyone this much detail, not even Isabel. "It's one of their stupid rules of combat. I said if I won, I'd get to go home. I won, I killed him, and… I guess the only way home was to use his magic, because it passed on to me instead. I used it to open the veil."

He watched me for a long moment.

"If you want proof, ask the necromancers." I paused. "Or check the names of their former lords. Lord Frank Sydney. He's a Guardian now. Anyway… I guess *he'll* tell me if Calder decides to try anything. But a promise, with that much hate… I can see it enduring beyond death."

"Then it's your choice."

Huh? "My choice to what?"

"To live in fear or not."

Ouch. Guess I deserved that one.

"I have a target painted on my head." I looked him in the eyes. "So do you, thanks to me."

"I don't care." His hands rested on either side of the door frame. "It's in the nature of the job."

"I'm marked by Faerie," I said. "Permanently. This isn't one guy with a grudge, the entire Grey Vale wants my blood."

"It's never stopped you before."

"It's stopped me doing a lot of things." Damn. I didn't want to drag up any more of my history, especially as I'd had a shitty enough week already. I didn't have the emotional energy to deal with this. "I like you, Vance, but I'm not the kind of girl who sleeps with her employer. If you want a meaningless fling, go and find someone else."

A spark grew in his eyes. "I think it's obvious by now that isn't what I want. I've made my intentions clear, and I'd be more than willing to meet you on your own terms, if you'd let me know what they are."

"My terms." I licked my lips. "I'll think about it."

He leaned closer, his scent wrapping around me. The stubble on his cheek brushed the side of my face. His grip was warm, strong, and I fell into him like a drowning person onto land.

Vance's forehead rested against mine. My breaths came out quickly, heart hammering as though it had just realised I was very much alive.

"I take it to mean you won't object to me taking you out to dinner tonight," said Vance.

"That sounds—" Awesome. Overwhelming. Part of me was still tired as hell, though the pleasant humming in my limbs was the most alert I'd felt since my brush with death.

A tugging sensation grabbed hold of my body and jerked me backwards. "What the hell?"

My body moved by itself, like an invisible magnet latched

onto me, dragging me out of the house. *What the—?*

"What's happening?" asked Vance.

"I have no idea. Some kind of spell—" I yelped as the sensation pulled me off the doorstep, past Vance onto the path. "The place is warded against anything hostile." And I definitely didn't have any of the blasted drug left in my system. What the hell was going on?

Erwin the piskie flew past. "You've been Summoned, Ivy!"

"What? By who?"

"The Lady of the Tree, wisest of Summer faeries."

Shit.

"You owe her a favour," said Vance. "The promise. Right?"

"Dammit!" I yelled, half-running towards the gate. "I can't fight this. A promise to a faerie is—"

"The most powerful of spells," Vance finished.

"With awful timing." I stumbled past the wards, onto the street. Vance followed me. "You don't have to—" I closed my mouth. His jaw was set stubbornly, and I knew he wouldn't let me go anywhere, even Death, without a fight.

Maybe even Faerie itself.

I faced the path, Vance at my side, my steps already

carrying me towards the vow I'd made. Promise or none, Faerie wouldn't take me again. This time, I was ready.

Thank you for reading!

I hope you enjoyed *Faerie Magic*. If you have a minute to spare, then I'd really appreciate a short review. For independent authors, reviews help more readers discover our books. I'd love to know what you thought!

About the Author

Emma spent her childhood creating imaginary worlds to compensate for a disappointingly average reality, so it was probably inevitable that she ended up writing urban fantasy and young adult novels. When she's not immersed in her own fictional universes, Emma can be found with her head in a book or wandering around the world in search of adventure.

Visit http://www.emmaladams.com/ to find out more about Emma's books, or subscribe to her newsletter (smarturl.it/ELAnewsletter) for new release alerts and a free short story.

17797659R00217

Printed in Poland
by Amazon Fulfillment
Poland Sp. z o.o., Wrocław